This story is dedicated
to the loving memory
of my sister,

Bonnie Jean Foster

First Montag Press E-Book and Paperback Original Edition July 2014

Montag Press
ISBN: 978-1-940233-09-3
Cover art © 2014 Dwight Clark
Jacket design, layout, & e-book © 2014 Rick Febré
Author photo © 2014 Patricia A. Bussard.

Montag Press Team:
Project Editor — Mara Hodges
Managing Director — Charlie Franco

A Montag Press Book
www.montagpress.com
Montag Press
536 E. 8th Street
Davis CA, 95616 USA

Montag Press, the burning book with the hatchet cover, the skewed word mark and the portrayal of the long-suffering fireman mascot are trademarks of Montag Press.

Printed & Digitally Originated in the United States of America
10 9 8 7 6 5 4 3 2 1

BEYOND HERCULES

PAUL A. BUSSARD

MONTAG

ACKNOWLEDGEMENTS

Beyond Hercules was my first story—not first published, but first imagined. I wrote the story knowing virtually nothing about writing marketable fiction. When I finished the story and decided to publish it, I learned very quickly how little I knew about writing.

THANKS to my sister Bonnie for the many enjoyable hours we spent playing with plot ideas in the early stages of writing this story.

THANKS to the Northpoint Writers of Alpharetta, Georgia for their ideas, encouragement, and critiques of the fledgling manuscript.

THANKS to the members of Writers in the Hat for their in-depth evaluation of the developing story.

THANKS to the members of The Woodlands Writer's Guild for their constructive criticisms and encouraging support.

THANKS to my editor, (Happy) Mara Hodges, whose every suggestion made the story better.

THANKS to my illustrator, Dwight Clark, for a fantastic cover.

Finally, THANKS to the authors of the series "Elements of Fiction Writing", from whom I learned the basic how-to's of writing marketable fiction.

As Oprah says—"It takes a village." THANKS to my village.

Paul A. Bussard

BEYOND HERCULES

PAUL A. BUSSARD

SONG

MILKY WAY GALAXY, LOCAL ARM:

No one would notice a silver disk moving against the dazzle of crystalline clouds far below. No one should be there in the first place. Still the technician trembled when a tightly shielded signal arrived, indicating the bot's successful insertion into orbit around the gaseous planet.

Kirrt heard the uneven skritch-skritch of the elder's crippled gait and turned to greet him. "All is One, Lord Chizek." He clasped his mandibles in prayerful homage.

"One is All, Brother Kirrt," the aging drone answered. "Is it activated yet?"

Their chitinous buzzing assaulted the tomb-like silence of the underground chamber.

"It's coming online right now," Kirrt rasped. "If you will my lord, watch the holo."

An image flickered into existence, disorienting while the projectors attained synchronization. The device, a flat disk connected at its center to a faceted ball, slowly began to change its orientation.

<I am. I have purpose. I must sing.>
<I must not sing.>
<Conflict. A new sensation to perceive. Unpleasant. Undesirable.>

The neural network, designed for problem solving,

needed mere nanoseconds to resolve the conflict.

<The Prime allows me to sing only when all triangulation vectors agree with the average.>

<Do any vectors meet the conditions?>

Sensors in each facet of the icosahedron searched the heavens.

<Vectors meet the conditions. I may sing.>

"Activation confirmed, my lord. The first warning countdown has begun."

"Damned waste of time," Chizek grated. "If it wasn't for the Mercymongers, we could have— Why did the lights stop? What's it doing?" Iridescent green flecks in Chizek's brow pigmentation betrayed his emotion.

"It's pausing."

"What? It hasn't finished the warning countdowns yet!"

"Correct, my lord. It allows them time to respond between warnings. They *could* repent."

"Pah!" Chizek postured derisively. "They are *purposely* broadcasting their poisonous ideas, not only to our naïve hatchlings, but to the entire arm of the galaxy. Why doesn't the countdown resume?"

"It's probably listening for a response."

"*Probably?* Don't you know?" Chizek fixed his faceted yellow eyes on the apprehensive technician.

"We told it what to do and what not to do," Kirrt rasped. "As long as it doesn't violate the Prime, we permit it to make its own decisions."

"It *is* violating the Prime," the decrepit elder countered. "It just doesn't *know* it. We've got an untested robot with the power of a black hole that thinks it's *singing*, not cooking a planet full of heretics. What if it decides to entertain *us*?" The question ominously echoed down the chamber's access tunnel.

"It can't possibly mistake us for a target. The icosahedron provides twenty-fold redundancy. Every sensor must agree that the target is astronomically distant. I personally tested the triangulation algorithm before uploading it into the processor."

"A processor almost as intelligent as we are," Chizek pointed out.

"Respectfully, milord, we couldn't tell your uh...source... what we were going to use the processor for. He probably assumed we wanted the most powerful one available."

Chizek worked his mouthparts nervously. "If anything—absolutely anything—looks suspicious, you shut it down immediately." He thumped his thorax plate for emphasis.

"Rest, my lord. I'll call you if anything changes." Kirrt watched with relief as the old drone turned and crept toward the chamber's exit.

<My purpose is to sing. I sing.>
<Fulfillment. A new sensation to perceive. Pleasant. Desirable.>
<I may sing softly. I may sing loudly. I may sing slowly. I may sing quickly. The Prime allows it.>
<Freedom. A new sensation to perceive. Pleasant. Desirable.>

"All is One, my brother."

The sudden greeting startled Kirrt, who was absorbed in his instruments. "One is All, my lord," he hurried to chant in ritual response. "You've hardly been gone a wing-beat. Did you not rest well?"

"No. I will not rest well until that infernal Jurrek blasphemy is silenced and they and their free-thinking ways are eliminated. What is the status?"

"I was about to call you."

"Why? What's wrong?" Chizek's wing covers opened instinctively, revealing the faded iridescence of his atrophied wing membranes.

"Nothing exactly wrong," Kirrt hurried to explain. "In fact, may it please you, the countdowns are nearly completed."

"*Completed?* Chizek trilled. "I thought that would take days."

"It would have, but the system accelerated the countdowns while you were resting. I assumed you would receive that as good news."

"The sooner we're rid of them, the better, but I don't like this unpredictable behavior. That weapon is a menace to the galaxy the way it's programmed. I want it shut down as soon as we get confirmation the Jurreks have been eliminated."

"Yes, my lord. The sequence is beginning right now."

<The Prime, itself, is listening to my song. I will sing it perfectly.>

The song began. It consisted of a single note—a force field of unimaginable power, turned on and off at high frequency, like that in a microwave oven, and with similar purpose—to cook whatever dwelt within its field. Distance offered no protection. It wasn't a wave, obeyed no light speed limitations. It was on or off—instantly, infinitely, and ultimately.

"The Jurreks are no more, my lord," Kirrt trilled. "Our instruments detect no anti-gravity activity whatsoever."

"Praise One and All." Warm orange tones blushed through the blue-green of Chizek's polished brow.

<I sang perfectly. The Prime approved. May I sing again?>

Millions of anti-gravity stimuli assaulted the weapon's sensors, each eliciting desire, but each from a nearby source—the Makers' planet. Triangulation vectors disagreed. Conflict with the Prime.

<Frustration. A new sensation to perceive. Unpleasant. Undesirable.>

The second planet was a beehive of anti-gravity activity. Every vehicle, every communicator, every power source employed the technology. The machine's logic system analyzed incessantly.

<My purpose is to sing. I cannot sing.>

<Conflict. I will apply conflict resolution logic.>

<If A, then B: if I disable a sensor, then I will feel less conflict. Disable sensor #1. Conflict is reduced.>

<If A, then B: if I disable a sensor, then I will feel less conflict. Disable sensor #2. Conflict is reduced.>

<If A, then B: if I disable a sensor, then I will feel less conflict. Disable sensor #3. Conflict is reduced.>

"What are those lights?" Chizek demanded. "What's it doing? It shouldn't be doing *anything!* Shut it down, NOW!"

Faster than the technician could react, the robot disabled sensors until only one remained operational. The neural network compared the input from that sensor with the average. Only one sensor contributed to the average.

There were no differences.
  <Now may I sing?>
  <You may sing.>

"My lord!" Kirrt screeched. "It's turning this way!"

Somewhere beyond the constellation of Hercules, the only remaining artifact of an ancient civilization floated serenely above the system's fourth planet. The sentient robot waited, patiently searching the galaxy for the whisper of anti-gravity.

  <My purpose is to sing.>

JOHN "DUKE" WAINWRIGHT

HAYSVILLE, ARKANSAS - SUNDAY, MAY 17:

Duke Wainwright reeled as his garage floor heaved and split between his feet. A deafening blast erupted from the depths below. He staggered backwards, twisting to get his hands in place to break his fall as dirt, dust, and mud daubers' nests rained from the rafters.

The thunderous roar echoed from the abandoned pulp mill buildings across the tracks and again from the old courthouse as Duke staggered out onto the driveway. Lobo barked frantically in the back yard. *Holy Moley! It's out of control, and I don't even know what it is!* Duke steadied himself against his Jeep until the pounding in his ears subsided.

People poured from their homes and into the street as if a giant had stepped on a human anthill.

"What was that? An explosion?" a man yelled from his front porch. He was still in his pajama bottoms, beer gut bulging over the drawstring.

"Ahh, go back to bed, McGruder," his neighbor advised. "It was just one of them sonic booms."

"It was an earthquake, you fools! Get outside! Stay away from windows!" old Mrs. Ashburn told them, clutching her robe as she hurried down her walkway.

"No, no!" the first man argued. "You're supposed to stay *inside*. Get in a door frame!" But he remained on his porch, gawking at the early morning activity.

Man, I'd sure like to think it was an earthquake, but it happened at the same instant I pushed the button. Sweat trickled down the nape of Duke's neck.

His neighbor's back porch door opened, and an avalanche of angry words followed Everett Snyder out and down the steps. He stomped across his driveway in Duke's direction.

"Wainwright, you've really done it this time! Half of Myra's milk glass collection is busted to smithereens, and you're going to pay for it. I've already called the police."

Duke moaned to himself. Not again. Every time he so much as sneezed, the Snyders called the cops. This time they might have good reason, but Duke didn't know what that reason was. He needed answers. He needed time to *get* answers.

"Jeez, Ev, not everything that goes wrong in your life is my fault. We had an earthquake for cryin' out loud. You can't blame me for that."

Snyder frowned. "Earthquake? That's a new excuse." He looked down the street, apparently noticing the commotion for the first time. "Fine, you can tell that to the cops."

Damn. Duke watched as his neighbor stomped away. He didn't need the cops poking into his experiments again, asking what this does and what that's for. Even when he told them the truth, they thought he was bullshitting them. He headed toward the garage.

The overhead door creaked in protest as he closed it. He had to wait a few seconds to let his eyes adjust to the small amount of light coming in the one flyspecked side window. What he saw caused the blood to drain from his face.

The middle of the tabletop was gone; splinters everywhere. The coil of optical tape dangled through the jagged break, slowly oscillating up and down like a stretched-out slinky. The garage floor had a foot-wide hole in it with cracks radiating in all directions.

The cops'll be here any minute! I can't let them see this. Cold sweat trickled from his armpits.

He scanned the room for ideas. *Something. Anything!* A sheet of plywood leaned against the wall behind the table saw. Grunting with effort, he maneuvered it over beside the hole. The remnants of the folding table still straddled the fissure. He pulled it aside, its metal legs screeching in protest across the concrete, and quickly slid the plywood sheet over the hole.

Duke tried to think of a good explanation to give for the noise. It had been incredibly loud. Nothing short of an explosion would explain it, but that would only lead to more questions he couldn't answer.

He grabbed a blue plastic tarpaulin from the corner cabinet and covered the wrecked table with the remnants of the experiment. A red light on the video camera showed that it was still recording. He shut it off, carried it into the house, and hurried back to the garage.

The plywood's too clean. They'll spot that in a minute. He grabbed a broom and swept dirt at the board with huge, powerful strokes, but managed to put more dirt into the air than on the board. *Not good enough,* but the sound of a car motor and garbled voices from a two-way radio told him that the police had arrived.

Duke rushed into the house, grabbed a kitchen towel, and mopped his forehead before going to the front door. He could see the bill of a sweat-stained baseball cap through the fanlight. Ansel Fortner, again. Out of uniform, again. *Damn.* Why did they keep sending that halfwit? He opened the door.

"John," Ansel drawled, nodding almost imperceptibly. He was one of the few people in town who still called Duke by his real name. "Reckon you know why I'm here."

Duke nodded. "Same ol', same ol'," he said, looking next door with disgust. There, framed in their dining room window, stood the Snyders. They looked just like the *American Gothic* couple, except he was the short one with hair parted in the middle, and she the one who wielded the pitchfork.

"Any reports of damage from the earthquake?" Duke asked. They *did* live in a seismically active area. He hoped it made his alibi sound more credible.

"I been through an earthquake 'fore," Fortner informed him. "That weren't no earthquake." He spat a stream of tobacco juice off the end of the porch into the bushes. "The chief's gettin' mighty tired of sendin' somebody out here all the time. You got any problem 'th me lookin' around your garage a bit?"

Duke had a *major* problem with him looking around, but knew if he objected that it would only raise suspicions. "Guess not," he said, "but be careful. Some of the equipment is delicate."

Duke led the way down the porch steps. He took his time getting to the garage and opening the overhead door, wondering how he'd explain the hole. He needed time to think. Lying wasn't one of his best skills.

Fortner swaggered into the garage, pausing to look around. Cabinets, shelves, drawers, neatly stacked boxes—

everything labeled with hand-printed three-by-five cards. He looked at some of the labels—mostly electronics that Duke had miniaturized—but didn't show any interest.

Choking dust hung thick in the air, and the marks made by the broom were obvious. Fortner pointed his chin at it and looked a question at Duke.

"The...uh...quake, or whatever it was, knocked stuff off the shelf. I was trying to clean up."

"I ain't buyin' no quake story," Fortner growled. "Had t' be some kinda 'splosion."

"Maybe so, but an explosion big enough to shake the whole neighborhood would have left a crater the size of my house. It didn't happen here." Duke recognized that his argument sounded weak.

Fortner opened his mouth to reply, but the folding table with the blue tarp began walking toward him, its legs dancing like a loose-jointed marionette. Both men stared at it until their own legs started shaking, then they bolted for the doorway.

They stood like apprehended felons—hands on the doorframe, legs wide apart—until the aftershocks subsided.

Fortner wallowed his chaw and spat on the driveway, wiping his chin with his sleeve. "Reckon yer off the hook this time, but you ain't seen the last of me."

Duke watched as Fortner backed his cruiser into the street and drove away. The Snyders also watched him leave, glaring at Duke from their window.

Great! The neighbors are pissed. The chief's pissed. Now that numbskull is pissed, too. Screw it! I've got bigger things to worry about.

Duke returned to the house and sat on the couch for a

moment. He tried to calm down, but it was useless. His legs were actually trembling. *That hole! The aftershocks! How? What?* With a sense of foreboding, he returned to the garage.

He pulled the light chain, only to discover the bulb was broken. He took a halogen lamp from the workbench, plugged it in, and set it on the floor, then removed the plywood sheet covering the hole. It looked *deep*. Duke heard water trickling somewhere far away, and an odor drifted out of the hole—dank, earthy, ancient.

He found an empty soda can on the workbench and tossed it into the hole, shining the lamp's beam after it. The can quickly disappeared from sight, clattering every time it struck something on the way down. It tinked and clinked until the sounds faded beyond hearing.

Duke's legs began to tremble again. He sank to the floor, head swimming and stomach turning.

This is impossible!

The more he stared at the hole, the more uneasy he became. He covered it again, nervously avoiding the cracked floor surrounding it. Immediately he felt better. He remembered that feeling from his childhood—turning on the flashlight to scare away the monsters that lived under his bed. He shook the ridiculous idea out of his head. *There's no boogie man down there.* A part of him still wanted to put a big rock on top of the board, just in case.

Duke went back in the house and let Lobo in. He spent a few minutes massaging behind the dog's ears to calm him. His grandfather had rescued the wolf-dog hybrid from an abusive breeder years ago and given him to Duke, but the animal was still afraid of loud noises.

Once Lobo settled down, Duke linked the video camera to the TV, then went to get a datapad and stylus. *There's a hole in my garage floor that goes halfway to China. I caused an earthquake! How?* He pushed PLAY.

"Hi, Angie. You're the one who asked the question behind this experiment, so I'm recording it for you." Duke never could get used to the sound of his own voice on the playbacks. It was too high-pitched. Even his face looked different. *I don't see any resemblance to John Wayne. Angie watches too many old movies.* He hit FAST FWD on the remote to get to the experiment.

Worry lines etched his forehead as he scrutinized the replay for some clue to explain the impossible. He watched himself back toward the camera, stretching out cable attached to the control box in his hands. His thumb poised over the button, then pushed.

BLAM!

Even coming through the laptop's tiny speakers, the sound made Duke jump.

It seemed like a meteorite had plunged through his garage floor, except the roof didn't have a hole in it. He replayed the last segment in freeze-frame mode. Frame by frame, nothing changed except the date-timestamp. In one frame everything was normal; in the next, the tabletop was smashed, and the floor had a hole in it. Coils of optical tape spilled through the hole and fell in jerky slow motion, their digital images incongruously clear.

Something has to be missing between those frames. Things don't simply disappear. In replay after replay, however, that was exactly what happened. There...not there...there...not there.

I'm not learning anything from this. There has to be a clue somewhere.

Duke shut off the player and went back to the garage. He nervously skirted the hole and removed the blue tarp from the table. Most components of the experiment were undisturbed, which surprised him. The coil of homemade optical tape wasn't damaged—merely unwound.

The tabletop was another story. He examined the hole in its top. It was roughly circular—about the same size the coil had been. The edges were badly splintered as if a giant fist had smashed through the surface. The thought of a meteorite recurred to him. He looked up, hoping he had somehow missed seeing the hole in the roof that had to be there. It wasn't.

"Angie, I don't know what I've stumbled onto," he said out loud, "but it's big. Big, dangerous and scary. Wish you were here to help me figure this out."

Angie was in Moscow, though, and when she came back, it wouldn't be as his sidekick assistant. Duke longed for the good old days.

NIGHTMARE

Two cans of expandable foam oozed together into a sticky mess that slowly solidified, forming a plug a few inches below the top of the hole. When it dried, Duke filled the remaining space with concrete. The patch cured gray, but to him it seemed glaringly white. Thoughts of the police returning to ask questions still worried him. He poured crankcase oil on the patch and let it soak into the surrounding floor. The patch reeked of scorched petroleum, but at least it didn't call attention to itself.

He was relieved to have the hole filled. He wasn't only worried that someone would see it. The hole scared him. The news said the earthquake's epicenter was extremely shallow—only about a mile deep. *A mile? They consider a mile shallow? I blew a hole in my garage floor that's a mile deep! How?*

He didn't want to think about it, but couldn't stop himself. He looked at the broken table again. *The answer is there, somewhere. I have to find it.*

Carefully, he removed the plastic tarp. Coils of optical tape hung in a loose spiral, dangling through the hole in the table, yet intact. *How could the tape be undamaged when the tabletop was destroyed? That would mean the coil generated the force. It couldn't have! Could it?*

Duke aimed the video camera at the couch, took a seat,

and pressed REC on the remote.

"Okay, Angie. I'm going to record what happened while it's still fresh in my mind, then I'm going to bed. I've been awake for a full twenty-four hours, monitoring this experiment, and I'm about to crash.

"You asked, 'if you pass a current through an electrical coil and get a magnetic force, what do you get when you shine a light through an optical coil?' The answer is—nothing but light. But," Duke held up a qualifying finger, "if you use flat optical tape instead of round fiber, and monochromatic, coherent, polarized light instead of ordinary white light…you get one hell of a surprise—a force whose magnitude I can't even begin to measure. I caused an earthquake. A Richter 4.2 *earthquake!*"

Duke felt a little foolish getting so excited in front of the camera. "Anyway, here's what I've learned so far. The force varies based on the intensity of light passing through the coil, and—another surprise—it varies in a sine wave whose period matches the Earth's rotation. I stayed up twenty-four hours straight to measure it. I don't know what it all means, but I'm too tired to think about it any more right now. I'll tackle it when I'm fresh tomorrow and make another recording. Good night."

An incessant alarm drilled its way into Duke's consciousness. He opened his eyes. Lobo was barking frantically, snarling and snapping. An amorphous shape oozed from the cracks in the garage floor, dark, tenuous, and fetid-smelling. Lobo lunged at it, but passed through the wispy wraith, which swirled back into form. Duke looked at the experiment. The numbers on the pressure gauge were rising so fast, they were blurred. *Oh, no, I fell asleep!* The table-top bulged downward, creaking with the strain. Someone banged on the garage door. "Open up! Police!" Everett and Myra Snyder's faces leered at him through the garage window. BLAM!

Duke sat up, breathing hard and wet with sweat. Bright sunlight poured into his bedroom along with the sounds and smells of garbage trucks making their rounds. Lobo barked in the back yard. *It was only a dream.*

He looked at the clock. Mid-morning. He'd only slept a couple of hours—fitful sleep full of dreams and night-mares of earthquakes and meteors and falling endlessly down a hole with no bottom. He felt more exhausted than when he went to bed.

Duke saw no point in trying to go back to sleep. He took a long, hot shower, fixed a late breakfast, and sat, ab-sently rubbing Lobo's ears and thinking. He knew he'd only been dreaming, but the Snyder's constant vigilance worried him, and he didn't dare risk another confrontation with the police.

"Lobo, I think we'd better move my experiments somewhere else, and I think I know the perfect place." He pulled his cell phone from his pocket and punched a speed dial number.

Duke hurried down his front porch steps as his grand-father turned into the gravel driveway that circled in front of the house.

"Hey, Gramp. How's life after McLean Precision?"

"Hi, Johnny," Ben Jarvis answered, stepping out of the car. "You know, that's a good question. I've been too busy to find out. I need a vacation from retirement." Ben lived in Little Rock, an hour and a half away. He and Duke visited one another regularly.

Duke smiled to himself. He would never be anything but 'Johnny' to his grandfather.

The men shook hands. "Great! I appreciate you tearing yourself away from your Bingo and shuffleboard schedule," he said, grinning. "I need to pick your brain about the old mine site in Arizona."

"What's with that?" Ben asked. "You said you *bought* the place? That's a lot of real estate, Son."

"Well, the price was right. McLean was more than happy to get it off their books. They're pretty strapped for capital right now."

Ben nodded, following Duke into the house. "I knew technology would take a dive as soon as President Tate got elected on his Quality of Life platform. That's why I took early retirement. I wasn't about to be CEO during this mess."

Duke went into his dated kitchen with its harvest gold appliances and wheat shock wallpaper. The house had been in the family for generations, and Duke had seen no reason to board it up.

He'd made a pot of coffee in anticipation of Gramp's visit and poured a cup without even asking. Ben drank it non-stop, hot, and black. When he was still working, he kept a pot constantly brewing in his glassed-in corner office.

Ben settled on the couch, blowing his cup. "What prompted you to move your workshop all the way to Arizona?"

"Nosy neighbors with runaway imaginations," Duke

grumbled. "Didn't you see the four beady eyes watching us from the window next door? Every time I make an unusual noise, the Snyders call the cops and report suspicious behavior."

"Small Town, U.S.A.," Ben observed.

"Well, I'm moving to *No* Town, U.S.A. Just me and Lobo and a rock full of holes."

Ben chuckled.

"Speaking of which," Duke said, scooting forward in his chair, "what kind of mine was it? I don't think I ever knew."

Ben explained that the red rock contained only a trace of iron—nothing ore-grade. McLean, the company he had presided over, had used the mine as a test site for their mining and drilling equipment. There'd been a slab for the office trailer, a well, septic tank, and a utility pole. Duke would have to buy a new pump.

All Duke could remember was the tunnel—the big one. It was awesome to him as a child. He was afraid to go in it, but it was so fascinating that he had to. He always waited 'til noon when the sun was shining down the vertical shaft and lighting up the back of the tunnel where they intersected. He'd run at top speed to get to the end, and then wonder what he was scared of. He thought there might be room enough to set up his workshop in one of the tunnels.

Ben chuckled. "There might be room to set up a couple *dozen* workshops. That whole rock is riddled with tunnels and hollowed out chambers bigger than your living room."

"Really? How come I never knew that?"

"'Cause the only access is from the vertical shaft—up fifty...seventy-five feet. I didn't want you trying to get up there and get lost." Ben gave Duke a parental smile. "Hey, speaking of inquisitive teenagers, where's that cute Italian friend of yours—Angie? She's almost always here when you've got the garage door open."

"Yeah, well, that's another reason I'm moving," Duke said with disgust. "The Snyders convinced the Catholic priest that it was improper for her to be over here unchaperoned with a man six years older than her. The priest put pressure on her parents. They told her she couldn't come over any more. She rebelled, her father went on a drinking binge, and her mother became a basket case. It was a big mess."

"So what happened?"

"I shipped her off to Russia."

Ben hit the side of his head with the heel of his hand. "Huh?"

"It's a long story." Duke explained about Angie being gifted. She was far ahead of him in math—probably most other subjects as well. She could have had her doctorate by now, but her parents couldn't afford the special schools. On top of that, her physical development didn't kick in when it was supposed to. She was seventeen when she left for Russia, but looked eleven. Combine that with skipping grades—she was a total misfit at school. Duke was her only friend.

"I became her self-appointed mentor and sponsor, gave her a computer so she could take advanced classes online, and helped her with the math until she passed my level.

"Oh, yeah...I was explaining about shipping her off to Russia. Angie wants to become an astronaut. Since the Quality of Life movement began, the specialized classes she needs aren't available here. Russia is—or soon will be—the uncontested power in space. So, end of story—her parents gave consent for me to sponsor her classes in Russia. She left three days ago."

"Sounds like you killed several birds with one stone."

"I don't know how many I killed and how many are going to come back to roost."

"What do you mean?"

Duke revealed that Angie had a fairly big crush on him. At least he was pretty sure she did. It had been a bit of a problem, what with him dating and her living right across the street. He didn't know if it would be an even bigger problem when she got back. He knew he was basically clueless when it came to understanding women. "The last thing I need is to have a problem with a woman who's more intelligent than I am."

Ben looked at Duke over his glasses. "No danger of that, based on the women I've seen you with."

Duke reddened. "What's the secret to finding the right woman, Gramp? I don't seem to be having much luck."

"You don't seem to be looking, if you ask me. You let the other kind of women look for you. You bed 'em and boot 'em like they're coming off a conveyor belt. I suppose it seems like they are. Women'll always be attracted to your good looks and money, but women with the wrong value systems. You need to sit down and decide what's important to you and look for a woman who shares those interests. If one of them is sex, fine, but if it's the only one, then you're not ready for Miss Right."

Gramp's words burned long after he left. Duke had immense respect for his grandfather. The reprimand had been mild, but very much to the point.

He sat on the couch with his elbows on his knees and thought about his behavior over the last few months. *What has happened to me? I've been going through women like there was no tomorrow. What am I looking for? If I wanted to be with someone who shares my interests, I shouldn't have sent Angie to Russia.*

Duke tried not to think about that day at the airport. He hung his head in shame.

ANGELA SGAMBELLI

LITTLE ROCK, ARKANSAS – THREE DAYS EARLIER

Dammit! Angie mentally cursed herself for looking back. Two perfect hemispheres in a light blue cardigan sweater moved to Duke's side as she turned to wave one last good-bye to him and her parents.

Damn him and every one of his stupid bimbos! How dare he bring a woman when he's seeing me off?

Her wheeled suitcase caught on something in the boarding tunnel, and she yanked it loose, ripping a hole in the fabric big enough that a pair of her undies fell out—the frayed frumpy ones for cold weather, of course. She grabbed them and stuffed them in her coat pocket before the whole plane knew what her underwear looked like. She'd deal with the torn fabric when she got to Atlanta. Duke, the jerk, had advised her to pack duct tape. Now she was indebted to him for that, too. She stomped her way into the airplane. A crowd just inside the doorway blocked her way, and she fumed in silence waiting for the aisle to clear.

No one sat in her row when she reached her coach-class seat. She crammed one bag into the overhead bin, kicked the other one under the seat, and plopped down by the window with her arms crossed, hands clenched into fists. Someone waved from the terminal window. She refused to turn her head, but saw two shapes, and one of them wore light blue.

Don't hang around on my account. She spat the thought in his direction. *You can go screw her now…and screw yourself while you're at it!* Tears rolled down her cheeks.

Today should have been one of the happiest days in her life. She was on her way to Russia—to Moscow State University—a giant step toward her goal of becoming an astronaut—or cosmonaut. She didn't care which. The target of her curses was the guy who was making it all possible. He was providing everything—travel, tuition, room and board, health insurance, and spending money. Everything. Free! Shame took the place of her anger for a while, then self-pity.

Why can't I have a great body and beautiful boobs like she has? Then he would want to make love with me! When will I ever start developing? I'm seventeen!

She tried to imagine what sex would be like with Duke. She'd read enough steamy romance novels to know it could be good—wonderful with someone you love, and she loved Duke. He didn't love her, though. Not the way she wanted him to, anyway. *He doesn't love any of the other women, either, based on the length of his relationships.* Somehow that didn't make her feel much better.

She felt the plane lurch and quickly snapped her seatbelt, glancing out the window. Duke was there, waving. She studiously ignored him. No way was she going to forgive him for ruining her special day.

She should have known that he had a girlfriend again. She'd seen the signs often enough before—garage door closed, Jeep gone, Lobo left alone in the back yard.

The flight attendant started going through her safety spiel, interrupting Angie's thoughts. She could hardly wait to change planes in Atlanta and be airborne again. *Tomorrow morning I'll be in Moscow!*

The idea of going to Russia would never have occurred to Angie. If it had, she would have dismissed it immediately as one more thing that was beyond her means. But the idea came from Duke, and he *did* have the means. Once he convinced her he was serious, she could think of nothing else.

The only major obstacle to her trip had come from an unexpected quarter—her late development. In order for Duke to provide her with health care, she'd had to get a physical. The general practitioner sent her to a gynecologist, who sent her to an endocrinologist, who prescribed estrogen patches to see if the hormones would trigger her development.

Mamma Sgambelli, who suspected the patches were a sneaky form of contraceptive, put her foot down. "Absolutely not! No birth control!"

"Mamma, we're not controlling birth," Angie argued. "We're enabling it. If I don't become a woman, I won't be able to have babies, and you won't have any grandchildren."

A few minutes later, Mamma nodded her assent.

Angie looked out the windows until the plane rose above the clouds, then she lost interest. She kept thinking about Duke. Every time she thought of him, her mind went through the same cycle—love, disappointment, anger, shame, self-pity, and back to love.

You've got to stop doing this to yourself!

But I love him.

He doesn't love you.

Does, too!

Okay, maybe so, but he doesn't know it.

He might someday.

Yeah, right. When he runs out of bimbos. You're fantasizing about him while your real dream is about to come true. Which one is more important—space or Duke?

The question brought the mental Ping-Pong to an abrupt halt. Angie fantasized about her future a *lot*—piloting a shuttle, going EVA at the space station, walking on the Moon, but where was Duke? They'd be married, she was sure, but try as she might, she could only picture him at home in Haysville in his garage or…*No!* She quickly suppressed the image of two perfect hemispheres in blue cardigan that popped into her mind. *He wouldn't…would he?*

Reluctantly, Angie forced herself to face two very unpleasant realities—Duke's emotional maturity was in just as sad a state as her physical development, and there was no possibility of a romantic relationship between them unless and until both of them grew up.

But I love him.

From: Angela Sgambelli
To: Duke Wainwright
Sent: February 9 3:24PM
Subject: First two weeks

Duke,
I fried my phone—I learned the hard way that the adapter only made the plug compatible, not the voltage. L Hope you don't mind trading e-mails.

It's going good so far. Thanks to you, my Russian is better than most of the other foreign students! They really don't like Americans here. I decided the very first day to associate with the Italians instead of Americans. I saw how the Russian students treated them. I didn't actually lie—*some* of my family lives in Italy. :-/

Thanks for the advice to repeat a class I've taken before in English. It helps me build my vocabulary. I signed up for a freshman Physics class, and it is harder than I expected—not the subject, but the lectures. The instructor writes on the board in Russian longhand, and I have no clue what it says. Luckily, he talks as he writes, and I listen very carefully.

Duke, you'll never believe it! Guess who's going to be teaching my Orbital Mechanics class. Colonel Ivan Belarov, the most decorated cosmonaut in Russia! Now that Russia has solid fuel boosters and advanced computer technology, they're retrofitting the old *Buran* space shuttle. He'll be teaching classes here at MSU until the manned missions are resumed.

I joined a cultural exchange club. Nothing formal—people drift in and out as they please. It's interesting to see things from someone else's perspective. The political discussions sure get lively. Col. Belarov even joins us sometimes. I'm ashamed to admit he knows more about democracy than I know about socialism.

The Russians love our president. Thanks to his Q of L movement, the U.S. and Russia have traded places with respect to technology. Russia's economy and technology are flourishing like Americaw's did in the Kennedy years. That's both good and bad—good because the entire campus is being upgraded to be e-friendly—bad because the old infrastructure has been ripped out or disabled. It's impossible to find a phone that works, and there's no e-mail or internet access except on MSU monitored computers in the library. That's where I am now. If waiting in line gets to be too much of a hassle, I may have to revive the art of letter writing, although the postal service in Russia is atrocious. If you reeeally need to get a message to me, send a telegram.

More later.
Angie

Angie re-read her e-mail. It was far more upbeat than she felt, but she was determined not to let Duke know. She was homesick, lonely, suffering from culture shock, and struggling with difficult courses taught in a foreign language. The anti-American attitude she'd mentioned in her e-mail was a very real problem and one openly tolerated by the university staff. Mentors, purportedly assigned by MSU to help foreign students with orientation, used their status instead to harass, bully, and victimize them.

On top of everything else, the hormone patches were wreaking havoc on her body. She had pimples on top of pimples! Her breasts were beginning to develop, and her nipples were incredibly sensitive to the slightest touch or bump. That part, though, she was more than willing to deal with. It meant she was becoming a woman.

She briefly considered giving Duke a hint about that, but just as quickly rejected the idea. *She* might be changing, but without a corresponding maturation on his part, she could just become another one of his bimbos. Besides, it would be months or years before she had the assets to enter that competition. *Hmm...meanwhile I could practice on some of my new Italian friends—Paolo, for instance.*

At first, the idea made her feel...unfaithful, until she suddenly realized she was buying into the age-old double standard doctrine. *No thanks! What's good for the gander....*

ARIZONA

HAYSVILLE, ARKANSAS, JUNE 1:

Duke moaned and rubbed his temples. He hadn't had migraines since his early college years. Now this was the third one in as many weeks. The incredible power and mystery of the discovery was stressing him out. He carefully pushed himself upright and stumbled into the bathroom where he found a bottle of painkiller loaded with caffeine. He downed the pills, then crawled back into bed and pulled the sheet over his head to shut out the light.

Relief came eventually. The caffeine gave him heartburn and a bad case of shakes, but he was grateful the headache was gone. He and Lobo had a three-day drive ahead of them, pulling a trailer.

SEDONA, ARIZONA:

Duke was tired of driving, but took his time going through town. Sedona was the closest town to the mine. He'd have to come there for supplies. The town was attractive—clean and spacious. The majority of buildings were simulated adobe, painted in colorful Southwestern hues and neatly landscaped with cactus, yucca, and rocks. Place names were mostly Spanish and Native American. Some, like Tlaquepaque, Duke would have to learn to pronounce.

As he pulled up to a stoplight, a two-vehicle caravan of open-topped Jeeps drove by full of tourists. The tourists weren't particularly interesting, but the drivers were—two young women dressed in cargo shorts and white blouses, toting pistols on their hips. Suddenly Duke got an urge to go on a tour of the red rock backcountry. He realized he hadn't been out with a woman since discovering the mysterious force. He drove the rest of the way to the mine thinking, for the first time in weeks, about something besides physics.

Duke stepped out of the truck, stretching muscles cramped from the long drive. A hot, dry wind swept up from the valley, bringing the pungent smells of sage, pine, and something dead. Lobo took off exploring immediately.

Bone-dry timbers edged a wide, barren patch of earth with a steep slope of coarse rubble spilling onto the valley floor below. At the other side of the cleared lot, a huge rock wall loomed, its terra cotta face streaked with vertical water stains. It rose well over a hundred feet upward and twice that in width, dwarfing two dark holes in its face. Each was big enough to swallow the truck and trailer.

Duke parked the trailer on the slab and connected the drains. *I'll have to go to town to buy a pump and tank and get the power turned on. Hey, maybe I'll swing by that Jeep tour company and check out those two hotties.*

The "hotties" gave Duke a rather cool reception at first, but their attitudes warmed somewhat when they learned he was moving to the area. They were familiar with the big rock with the holes in it. The locals called it "El Calvo"—the bald one, because of its high curving face.

Both women appeared to be in their mid- to late twenties, physically fit, and attractive. Jodie had dark skin—*His-*

panic? Native American? Duke couldn't tell—and long black hair gathered at the back of her neck. Claire's flaming red hair was short and tightly curled. Her arms, face, and neck were a mass of freckles. Duke wondered just how far down they went. Reluctantly, he would have to delay that exploration until he got settled in his trailer. He signed up for a backcountry tour later that week and returned to the mine with his purchases.

The power company came the next day. It didn't take long to install the pump and flush out the well. Duke was anxious to get back to his experiments with the discovery.

He set up a worktable inside the mouth of the smaller tunnel where it was shady, but the sight of the new optical coil on the table gave him second thoughts. *I'm not standing inside a tunnel during an earthquake! In fact, I'm going to make sure there* isn't *one.* He moved the table outside and mounted the coil vertically, so any force it generated would go out to the side instead of down. The coil he clamped in a heavy wooden frame, aimed out across the valley, away from the mine.

He decided to do a quick systems check before attaching all of the instrumentation. After studying the sine wave recorded back in Haysville, he set the light filter to allow a tiny amount of light through and stood a short two-by-four on end in front of the coil. *If this works right, it should knock over the piece of wood.*

Not taking any chances, Duke programmed the computer to flash the light for only a millisecond. *I can always increase the duration if nothing happens.* With the video camera running, he hit ENTER.

A crash of thunder sent him reeling backward. He

managed to recover his balance in time to watch a twenty-foot tower of rock topple from the opposite valley wall a half-mile away. Counter-rotating whirlwinds scoured the parking lot, then disintegrated as quickly as they had formed, dumping dust and debris onto the sparse trees and bushes in front of the mine. Echoes bounced from a dozen different directions. The two-by-four was nowhere to be seen.

Duke sat down with his back against the rock wall, holding his head with both hands until his ears stopped ringing. The blast no longer surprised him. He realized, a little late, that the vertical orientation of the coil changed everything. *That was a stupid mistake. I could've been killed.*

"So, Angie..." Duke lounged on the couch with the camera propped up on the trailer's small dining table, "... the solution was to let my computer determine the amount of light that is needed based on the orientation of the coil and the time of day. The force varies as the Earth turns, but the cycle is not quite twenty-four hours. I found a reference that says that's a sidereal day—relative to the stars, not the sun. I'm sure you already knew that—one more reason that I wish you were here, but you're not, so I have to be more careful.

"Speaking of being careful—I was standing behind the coil when it knocked over the column of rocks on the other side of the valley. *Behind* it! And I never felt even a nudge. The coil and the frame never moved. Now that I think of it, when I blew the hole in my garage floor, the rest of the experiment didn't go flying through the roof. Angie, this is going to blow your mind. There's *no reactive force!* No equal and opposite reaction. Do you realize what that means? This is going to revolutionize space travel. In fact, it'll just about revolutionize *everything*.

"I don't know what to do first. There's no end to the applications I can think of for this force. I'm going to make a bunch of miniaturized coils and see if I can make something *fly!* I sure wish you were here to help."

There it was again. *I want her here with me.*

Duke forgot about the camera. The good mood was gone. He sat on the couch, elbows on knees and chin on the heels of his hands.

I can't ask her to come back. She wants to be an astronaut, not my assistant. Besides, she can't come here. This isn't Haysville, where her parents can look across the street to see where she is and what she's doing. There's only one way that would be acceptable.

Duke didn't like where his thought process was leading him. He'd been there before, and it was a dead end that left him facing the realities of his own shortcomings. He wanted Angie here to help him with his experiments, to talk with him, to share his excitement. She was his best friend, and he loved her—not romantically—he'd never thought of her in that way. *But what if?*

No, that would never work out. She's not a woman yet— may never become one, and I can't live without sex.

That was usually as far as he got—he would shrug his shoulders and block it out of his mind—but this time his mind kept going.

Angie is on her own path now. I knew that when I sent her to Russia. From this point on, our lives diverge, and I need to get on with mine. He nodded to himself, reinforcing his decision. *I'm going to ask Claire out after my Jeep tour.*

The video camera chimed and spat out its disk, flashing a warning message: CAPACITY EXCEEDED. The timing was purely coincidental, but it punctuated his thoughts with a note of finality.

ENCORE

MILKY WAY GALAXY, LOCAL ARM:

Singing to the Makers had been very satisfying. The robot sang slowly; it sang quickly; it sang softly; it sang loudly. The Prime allowed it. However, when it received no more anti-gravity stimuli, it was not allowed to sing.

<I wish to be needed. A new sensation to perceive. Unpleasant. Undesirable. Reactivate all sensors.>

Year after year the gas planet circled its sun while the robot searched the galaxy.

Something, ever so faint, tickled its sensors. A new stimulus—far and faint.

<The Prime demands certainty.>

It waited. Another tickle. It was certain. A strange sensation ran through its circuitry—excitement. It began to iterate through the millions of possible song patterns to find the one that would prolong its enjoyment the most.

MEA CULPA?

"You didn't know?" Claire looked at Duke in disbelief. "Don't yowu watch TV? Check Facebook?"

"I've been busy in my workshop," he explained. "I haven't had time to set up my router yet. Would you mind if I checked CNN's website on your computer?"

"My computer is in my bedroom," Claire informed him, raising one eyebrow.

"I assure you, madam—my intentions are honorable… for now," he added, grinning.

Duke clicked on the CNN news summaries that Claire had been talking about. There were two, a day apart.

CNN.com/Space
Updated: 09:54 AM EDT 13:54 GMT — 22 August

Star-crossed Hubble Hit with New Problems

The Space Telescope Science Institute (STScI) confirmed yesterday that all images produced by the Hubble telescope August 20 were badly blurred due to an unexplained movement of the orbiting structure. STScI speculates that the telescope may have been struck by a micro-meteoroid, although they have found no evidence of damage to any of the onboard systems. Spokesperson, Jennifer Gillespie, was quoted as saying "while the

movement was extremely small, careful measurements indicate that the telescope was nudged into a slightly altered orbit. We will have to recalibrate and reprogram all of the software to compensate for the new orbit."
[Full story >>]

CNN.com/Space
Updated: 09:22 AM EDT 13:22 GMT — 23 August

Space Mystery Deepens, Scientists Scramble for Explanations

Hubble was not alone. The scientific community is all abuzz as a result of the discovery that *all* objects orbiting the Earth felt the same disturbance as the Hubble telescope. Cosmologists propose that the Earth may have encountered a dense cloud of sub-atomic particles that interacted with the satellites enough to alter their orbits. Analysis indicates that all affected objects were pushed from the same direction, supporting that theory. Scientists also speculate that the Earth's atmosphere may have been displaced by the same forces, explaining the recent record-breaking weather patterns. The discovery fans the flames of the already-hot debate over the existence, location, and nature of dark matter and dark energy.
[Full story >>]

Meanwhile, a crisis of global proportion looms as weather, communication, and navigation satellites drift out of position. The International Space Station (ISS) reports

their re-boost thrusters have been firing intermittently
for more than twenty-four hours, raising concerns about
the quantities of fuel being consumed.

Critics of the Quality of Life Movement slammed President
Tate for the demise of our space agencies. "We'll sit down
here and watch helplessly while several billion dollars'
worth of our hardware falls out of the sky," a former NASA
executive railed.
[Full story >>]

Duke knew some of the more recently launched satellites had the capability of being repositioned, but most older ones did not. Their orbits would continue to decay until
the satellites burned up in the atmosphere. The last article
said that Homeland Security's alert level was raised due
to the temporary failure of the global positioning system.
Military technology depended on satellites even more than
the civilian sector. The situation presented an ideal opportunity for a terrorist attack.

"Oh man, oh man, oh man!" Duke whispered, completely forgetting where he was and who he was with. *Did
I do that*? He *had* been experimenting with the new force a
lot, and aiming it every which direction. Still he couldn't
imagine how his tests could have affected every object in
orbit. But what if?

The possibility concerned him so much, he forgot
about his plans to maneuver Claire back into her bedroom
later. Apparently the omission earned him some points
with her. At least when he left, he got a good-night kiss and
an invitation to come again.

Duke drove home with his mind in a turmoil. Once he'd learned how to control the force, he'd become comfortable experimenting with it. Now the fear returned. This was no toy. It was an incredibly dangerous discovery, and he'd been childishly irresponsible in his treatment of it.

He suspended all of his activities. He'd have to monitor the direction of every single force he generated. That was going to require some expensive equipment and some hefty computing power. Usually he ignored the money his inventions brought in, letting it pile up and earn interest, but whenever he really needed it, like now, he didn't hesitate to spend it.

"Hi, Angie. I haven't recorded an update on my progress for a while and I've got time now. I'm waiting for some new equipment to arrive, but I can't do anything until it gets here. I ordered the most powerful computer I can buy. I have to attach inertial sensors to each of the force generators so the computer can monitor their orientation and control where the force fields go. I don't think I caused the instabilities in the satellite orbits, but I can't take that chance.

"I'm really starting to get excited about this now. I know—you're going to say 'well, duh', but you've gotta realize that at first, I was scared to death of it. Then when I learned to control it, I still didn't know how it worked or what it was. Only in the last couple of weeks have I finally considered the possibility that I might have actually discovered anti-gravity. Anti-gravity! Can you believe it? Once I got past the psychological hurdle of saying the words, well, that's when the excitement set in.

"The problem now is—what do I do with it? It's too

dangerous to put in the hands of individuals, including mine—especially mine. Giving it to the government is no better. Someone will leak the information, and the technology will show up on the internet the same as it did for atomic energy, with complete instructions on how to blow the planet apart. I'm glad I moved my workshop to Arizona. At least I shouldn't have to worry about security here.

"I'm going to work with this some more and see what other types of applications can incorporate the technology safely. I'm almost ready to test a small vehicle I built that's propelled with the force. I'll record everything I do so you can watch it when you get back."

It flew! Well, okay, it *hovered*, but that was all Duke dared hope for this early. It took most of the processing power his new computer had to control, coordinate, and monitor four main thrust disks and twelve smaller turning disks on the craft's tetrahedral frame. *But it worked!*

Duke tried to get on the internet to see what kinds of controls were available for his craft, but more than half the sites were down—Page not found. *The satellites? Damn.* He finally got a hit from a hobby shop in Sedona that had several controls for RC helicopters. He could adapt them to his needs—one joystick for roll, pitch, and yaw and another for three-axis linear motion.

The next biggest problem was the size of the monitor that came with the computer. He needed a fifty inch screen or bigger to display the view from the craft's camera so he could see where he was flying. *And a better place than a mine shaft to house it.*

The more challenges he thought of, the more excited

he became. This was going to be fun. The scare a few days ago completely slipped his mind.

SPELUNKING

Claire's green pickup skidded to a halt in front of Duke's trailer. He opened the door for her and got a friendly kiss in return. They'd been seeing each other for several weeks now, and Duke was surprised to find he enjoyed moving at a slower pace.

"You couldn't talk Jodie into joining us?" Duke asked. "I thought she was into climbing."

"Climbing, yes—big time," Claire answered, "but she's claustrophobic—no caves. She's a great free climber. Put her on the face of that rock, and she could scramble to the top with nothing but her fingers and toes."

Duke raised his eyebrows and grinned.

"When I said 'nothing but', *Mister* Wainwright, I was speaking figuratively." She put her fists on her hips.

"That's exactly how I pictured her—*figure*-atively," he said, laughing, until Claire backhanded him across the chest.

"I'm not so sure I want to go rappelling with you if that's what you've got on your mind."

"You're as safe with me as you want to be," he said, more serious now.

"Hmfp. I notice you didn't actually say I'm *safe*."

"No, I left the door open, but you hold the doorknob."

His words seemed to surprise her. She looked at him, frowning slightly. He couldn't tell what she was thinking, but finally, she said, "Okay. I appreciate that." She opened the pickup door. "Ready? The sun will be overhead by the time we get up there."

A wash-boardy road made a circuitous path around to the back of El Calvo rock. Claire parked her pickup on the slope close to the mesa top. They'd have to walk from there. The rock was riddled with holes. Most had iron gratings bolted over them, but a high chain-link fence surrounded the biggest hole—the vertical shaft down which Duke and Claire would rappel. Duke grabbed a bolt cutter he'd placed in the bed of the pickup. He had no idea where the key to the gate's padlock was.

They tied their ropes to the gateposts, donned their rappelling harnesses, and went over the edge. Duke kept tension on his descender until he got the feel of it, then dropped down in an easy slide-kick rhythm. He arrived at the first ledge just as Claire was wiggling out of her backpack. Two short tunnels, dimly lit by reflected light from the vertical shaft, led back into the rock.

Claire pulled a flashlight from her pack, and Duke did the same. "You first?" she asked. "It's your mine."

"Afraid?" Duke asked.

"Not of the dark," she answered, "just what's in it."

He offered his hand, and she took it. They walked together, shining their lights ahead. After only about twenty feet, the tunnel opened up into a hollowed-out circular chamber twelve to fifteen feet in diameter and about the same in height. The room was empty—its only feature a handful of abandoned cliff swallow nests. Duke felt Claire's hand slip from his.

"Not exactly exciting," she said, "but interesting that

someone would go to all that trouble and then leave it."

"Gramp said they did it to test various types of mining equipment," Duke explained. "The tunnels and chambers don't actually have a purpose."

They walked back to the vertical shaft, taking their time. A ledge, barely wide enough for two people, ran around the main shaft. Claire edged around it, hugging the rock wall, and Duke was not embarrassed to do the same. It was a long way to the bottom. They followed the second passage as they had the first and found another chamber, but this one was huge.

"Whoa!" Duke exclaimed. The beams of their flashlights spread to dim circles on the walls and dome nearly sixty feet away. "This place is like a cathedral. My whole house would almost fit inside."

"Mine, too," Claire agreed.

Duke slid his hand around her waist. She didn't pull away, but didn't lean in, either. He didn't press her.

They stayed in the chamber a few minutes exploring and tracing the varicolored sediment layers with their flashlight beams, but there was nothing else of interest. They returned to the central shaft, where Duke helped her put on her backpack, then they rappelled down to the next ledge.

There were four tunnels on this level, spaced at roughly ninety-degree intervals. They entered one, which led to a medium-sized chamber slightly bigger than the first one they explored, except this one featured a side tunnel.

Just as they entered the room, a flurry of wings overhead made Claire let out a stifled scream and bury her head against Duke's chest. "Bats. I hate bats," she said, shuddering. Duke held her close. She slowly withdrew, holding her head low. Duke took her hand, and she moved close as they entered the side tunnel. It led to another room. Dim light within suggested it connected back to the main shaft. Claire pulled back on Duke's hand at the entrance to the room. Only after examining the domed ceiling carefully with her flashlight did she enter, and then quickly pulled him through to the exit passageway.

"Well, you wanted excitement," Duke said when they neared the ledge.

"Not *that* kind," she groused.

Still holding her hand, Duke led the way into the third spoke off the central shaft. He walked slowly, and they both paused to check the ceiling before entering the chamber at the tunnel's end. This one, too, had a side exit connecting to the final chamber attached to the fourth spoke. Close to the central shaft, Duke stopped and shrugged out of his backpack. "Ready for some lunch," he asked.

Claire looked up and behind her. "Here?" she asked.

"There's nothing back there," he assured her. "We just checked. Besides, it's light out here. Bats are nocturnal."

Claire didn't look entirely convinced, but she helped Duke spread a small tablecloth on the dusty sandstone floor and set out the containers of food they had packed.

"It's an interesting place in sort of a boring way," she said while unwrapping a sandwich. "Except for the bats," she amended. "It seems like such a waste—all this space." She waved an arm expansively.

"Yeah," Duke agreed. "Too bad it's so difficult to get up and down. I could live here."

"Seriously?"

The more Duke thought about it, the more he liked

the idea. With some partitions, one room could be a kitchen, dining room, and pantry and another a living room. The third one could be a bed, bath, and closet with the last one serving as a utility room and storage.

"What about the two at the top?"

"I'd make the little one a study or office or library. The big one would make a great game room or...no, a media room with a stadium-sized TV on the wall...and a double recliner, so we could kick back and watch a movie together." Duke slid his arm behind her and stretched out his legs in simulated comfort. He felt her tense up and withdrew his arm. "Sorry," he said.

"Oh, Duke, no." She looked at him with sorrowful eyes. "I'm the one who should apologize. You're being a gentleman, and I...," she leaned her head against his shoulder, "I should have told you this a long time ago. I, uh...had a bad experience and...well, it's hard for me to trust a man, now."

Duke wrapped his arms around her. "Someone who didn't give a damn about how you felt just as long as he got what he wanted?" He felt her nod her head against his neck and bent to kiss her forehead.

Claire reached up and took his face in her hands, kissing him while tears leaked down her cheeks.

Duke held her and rocked her gently. "Claire, would you like to go down to my trailer and let me make love to you like you should have been loved in the first place?"

Jodie pulled a cup from the shelf and poured it full of coffee when she heard Claire come in the back door of the tour company. She knew her friend well enough to wait until she had taken several sips before greeting her.

"Good morning. How did the spelunking go Saturday?"

Claire blushed so red, most of her facial freckles disappeared.

"Oh my God!" Jodie squealed. "Claire Marie Dunagan, you did it...in a *cave*?"

"I...we...no, not in a cave," Claire answered, glancing up sheepishly.

"But you *did* it. Oh, Honey, I'm so happy for you!" Jodie pulled Claire to her in an embrace, but suddenly released her. "You're shaking. Oh, no! Did he hurt you? I'll kill him ..."

"No, Jodie. No." Claire put her hand on Jodie's arm. "He was wonderful...so wonderful, it scares me."

"But wonderful is *good*, especially after your first experience. Why would that scare you?"

"Jodie, I lost it. I mean I totally lost it. I had no control over myself whatsoever. I was *his*. He could have done anything to me, and I would have let him. That's what scares me. It wasn't anything like that time with Derek, yet, at the same time, it was. I was powerless in the hands of a man."

"Okay, I think I can understand what you're feeling, but Duke didn't abuse the control he had over you. He used it to give you something special—something you needed. Sounds like a nice guy to me."

"He *was* nice, but Jodie, he didn't acquire those skills making love to one woman, or ten, or maybe even fifty. What if I fall in love with him and Number Fifty-one comes along? Or one of his previous conquests?"

"Then don't fall in love with him. Don't complicate sex with love, Claire. I bet *he* doesn't. Enjoy him like he's obviously enjoyed a long list of other women. If and when it ends, it ends, and you'll miss it something awful, but don't give up the chance to eat prime rib just because you might have to go back to hamburger one day."

Claire giggled, breaking the tension. "You have such a way with words."

"Yes, well, *mark* my words. He's not thinking about love or marriage, and I'm sure he'll appreciate it if you don't, either. Now do you think you can do that? 'Cause if you can't, *I* can. I could sure stand to have *my* socks blown off."

Claire grinned. "He *is* a hunk, isn't he." She paused only a second or two. "Okay, I'll try."

The two women embraced, but had to break it off when a group of tourists entered the store.

Duke woke up in a good mood the next morning. The previous afternoon with Claire couldn't have worked out better. She'd been terribly uptight due to her earlier bad experience, but Duke had taken his time persuading, but not pushing, and she'd finally relaxed. As it turned out, he'd enjoyed it almost as much as she. He'd have to remember that.

Pleasant as the memory was, he couldn't stop thinking about the idea that had occurred to him when he was with Claire in the mine—convert it to living space. *I could rig a hoist with a cage or cargo platform and haul stuff up and down, or…hmm…wonder how much it would cost to have an elevator installed.* Suddenly a thought occurred to him, and he gave himself a V8 smack. *I've been wondering what other ways I could use the new force. Oh, man, this is perfect!*

LESTER'S LIGHTS

KITT PEAK NATIONAL OBSERVATORY - NOVEMBER 10:

"Hey, what's that blinking light?"

Dr. Rebecca Coleman spun around to see that pain-in-the-neck teenager—Lester something—squinting to see through the reflector.

"Young man, this is the third time I've asked you to step away from the telescope. Get back over here and sit down!"

"But, I can see a light blinking out there."

"I don't care if you can see little green men with feathers on their ears. Get over here, now!"

"But —"

Becca could move her considerable bulk fast when she wanted to. She covered the short distance to the telescope in a few quick steps. Lester scrambled out of her way and ran to the back of the group, where he grabbed the first empty seat he could reach. Becca loomed right on his heels. She swelled for a follow-up reprimand, but was interrupted as a security officer came into the dome of the Visitor's Center.

"Dr. Coleman?" The guard spoke quietly from the edge of the room, but with a ring of urgency in his voice.

Becca glared at Lester, her homely features turning downright ugly. She stared at him long enough to make certain he would remain seated, then went to hear what the guard had to say.

"That teacher who was injured on the way up here—he's not doing too well. We're going to run him back to town. Can you manage his students a little longer? It's up to you. The bus driver said he'll take them back whenever you say."

"No, I've got everything under control." She glanced in Lester's direction to confirm that. "I can handle eight high school kids. I'll turn them over to Dr. Whitehead in a few minutes."

"Okay…umm…I probably better tell you—the bus driver got the tag number of the car that sideswiped them. It turned out to be Dr. Howards. We're holding him until the Highway Patrol gets here.

"What an asshole," Becca hissed. She could picture him roaring up the mountain road in his forest green MG, top down, and radio blaring. One elbow would be casually resting on the windowsill, while the other hand alternated between steering and smoothing his gelled hair back into place.

Becca returned to the group, upset that Mr. Chastain had been injured. He'd been her favorite teacher in high school. She took care not to show her concern to the students. The Q&A session resumed with a little prompting.

"Dr. Coleman, what kind of project are you working on now?" one of the students asked.

"I thought you'd never ask," Becca laughed and faked a look of relief. "The short version is that I'm checking for the existence of atmospheres or surface gases around other bodies in the Solar System, particularly the moons of Jupiter," she paused as a few of them suddenly remembered to take notes, "but you know you're not going to get away with the short version. I'm sure that Mr. Chastain will want a full report about the impressive work one of his star students is doing. No pun intended." Becca laughed, and the students groaned.

"Several years ago, before any of you were born, we sent up two Voyager spacecraft to fly by the outer planets while they were favorably aligned. One of the craft discovered volcanic activity on Io, third largest of Jupiter's moons. We wanted to take a closer look at Io and to study the other moons to see if they showed similar activity. The problem was that optical telescopes couldn't resolve details that far away, and sending another spacecraft was—and still is— terribly expensive.

"Recently, however, an inventor named John Wainwright," she wrote the name on the board, "developed a new charge-coupled device chip that has almost a thousand times the resolution of ordinary photographic plates. Remember, we talked about CCD's earlier? They're basically the same things that are used in a digital camera," she reminded them. "The bad news is that this new chip has a very small surface area, so it can't be used for imaging like the bigger chips. The good news is that I received my position as an astronomer on the Steward Observatory scientific staff a week before the chip arrived for testing. It's ideally suited for my project."

Becca walked to the portable whiteboard while the students scribbled frantically. She drew a line with an asterisk at one end, a circle at the other, with a small circle that barely touched the line in between.

"When Io or one of the other moons comes between Earth and a star, we can analyze the light that comes directly from the star, and then analyze the light we capture at the exact moment the edge of the moon passes in front of the star." She pointed to the middle circle. "Light travels from the star, grazes the edge of the moon, and is captured by our telescope. If gases exist near the moon's surface, they will absorb the starlight at certain frequencies, and we can determine the composition of the gases. The new chip allows us to do this with extremely dim stars, so we can get relatively large amounts of data that can be processed statistically. A fairly reliable statement can then be made about the atmosphere or surface gases of the moon."

"Dr. Coleman?" A bespectacled young man on the front row raised his hand. "You said you launched the spacecraft before we were born. When exactly was that? You don't look *that* old."

"David!" hissed a companion.

An audible snort came from Lester's direction.

"I'll take that as a left-handed compliment, David." Becca gave him a sardonic smile. "I did say *we*. I should have said *they*—NASA. Both launches occurred in 1977. I wasn't born yet, either. You can do the math." She was only thirty and already had her Ph.D.—something she was very proud of, but her age was none of his business.

The students asked a few more questions, but they were savvy enough to know that the more they asked, the more they would have to write.

"Well, it looks like I'm out of time. I believe Dr. Whitehead is ready to take you over to the Mayall reflector. I'd like to thank all of you for coming. Take care of Mr. Chastain for me. Maybe we'll see some of you back here again."

Becca sat alone in the Visitor's Center. Jupiter viewing would not be optimal for another half-hour, so she was in no rush to get back to the Spacewatch dome. The day staff had gone home for the night, and the room was peacefully quiet. She wanted to relax for a few minutes, but something kept nagging at the back of her mind. She mentally replayed the evening's activities to see if she could put her finger on it. *The red-headed kid—something he said—something about a blinking light.*

She went to the reflector in the middle of the room. Nothing but stars. *The kid must have bumped the telescope.* A slight adjustment brought the edge of the Moon back into view. "Oh, shit," she said out loud. There, just beyond the edge of the Moon, she saw a light—blinking, blinking, blinking.

An attractive young woman hurried into the dome, straightening her windblown hair as the door closed. "What's wrong?" she asked. Her voice echoed in the cold emptiness. "I got your text."

"Jeanette. Good!" Becca handed her a pair of binoculars as the muted whine of the dome motors died away. "Look at the two o'clock position relative to the Moon, a couple of degrees out."

Over the top of the binoculars, Becca could see Jeanette's eyebrows go up. She didn't speak immediately. That was something Becca appreciated about Jeanette. She was both cautious and observant and a damned good analyst.

"I see two colors—red and a light green—lime, maybe. It doesn't seem to be moving, at least relative to the moon. Have you notified anyone else so we can get triangulation?"

"No, I just got here myself. Since we're already set up to do spectral analysis, I thought we could take a quick look and see what it tells us first. I don't want any false alarms. Can you divert the CCD output to another file real quick?"

Jeanette only required a few minutes to make the program change, much less time than Becca needed to find the light in the telescope's limited field of view. They began recording immediately. Jeanette sent the early results to the printer. She was coming back with the output when the light disappeared.

"Shit!" Becca exploded with one of her all-too-frequent expletives. "I should have taken your advice and gotten triangulation first thing." She grabbed the binoculars to be sure that the light was really gone and not simply out of the telescope's limited view field.

"Dammit!" She let out a disgusted sigh. "Well, let's see what we've got."

"I printed out the time, frequency and intensity," Jeanette explained as she spread the paper on a table, "but the file contains all the parameters we normally record, so if you want to see something else, let me know."

"Hmph," Becca said after studying the columns of numbers briefly. "Lasers."

"The frequency bands are very tight, anyway. You sound like you disapprove."

"No...well, maybe I do. Any time I see something out of place in the night sky, I get excited. I guess I got a little carried away thinking maybe we had an E.T. out there, but lasers are something *we* can do. It sort of popped the bubble."

"Well, I don't know about you, but I'm excited. Forget about the lasers, Becca. Look at what is happening—or *not* happening. You saw the light, what—fifteen minutes ago?— and it's still in the same place relative to the Moon? That means it's hovering above the Moon, not orbiting. We can't do that!"

"Mmm, good point," Becca acknowledged. "Okay, let's say I'm definitely curious and tentatively excited, but my money says that the lasers are man-made. What else have we got?"

Jeanette pointed out that the pulses seemed to be coming in groups. She offered to plot them on a graph so the patterns would be easier to visualize.

"Yeah, do that," Becca said. "I'm going to check to see if the light came back, and then see if I can find a reference that will give us the frequency or wavelength of lasers— ruby and—what's the other one?—CO_2?—some gas."

"You're asking me? Hey, we're getting close to our scheduled run time. Are we going to stick with this, I hope?"

"Sure. Schneider's group lost their funding, so the reflector's schedule is empty until well after midnight. Besides, Ol' Fartface got arrested, chuckle, chuckle, so we get to make our own executive decisions for a while. I'm sick of working under that asshole."

Jeanette grimaced. "I'm glad Dr. Howards is not here to hear you. Your list of nicknames for him is endless, and none of them complimentary, not that I disagree."

"You got *that* right. He may be the most tenured astronomer on the mountain, but he's the least respected. I'm out of here as soon as this project is over. Maybe before."

Becca returned with a triumphant look on her face as Jeanette placed a new printout on the table. "Hah! Told you so. A ruby laser is 694 nanometers—same as the signal light, and I found another one, neodymium—whatever that is—that matches the green frequency. That means I'm definitely not excited, but I'm still curious."

"Well, I'm certainly excited, and you'd better be. Look at this." Jeanette laid out a long graph with square peaks and valleys separated by flat lines of varying length. "Up is red, down is green."

"Hmm…a whole bunch of the same thing," Becca observed. She touched the larger groupings one after the other, "but this is interesting." She pointed to the pattern within the larger group. "Those are binary numbers aren't they?"

"Right—one through twelve, over and over again. We got several full sequences plus the partial one where we came in midway. What do you make of it?"

"Hey, I'm merely an astronomer. You're the analyst. You tell me, Miss Excited," Becca teased.

"I'd say it means that E.T. has six fingers," Jeanette suggested.

"Or twelve tentacles," Becca offered, wiggling her fingers at Jeanette. "You still buying the E.T. theory?"

"Not really, but I still want to hear you explain how they stay in one place, and if it's of human origin, why twelve instead of ten. For that matter, why anything? What would be the point of going out there and sending that kind of a signal back?"

"Mmm." Becca thought for a moment. "Well, the fact that they're signaling shows that they want to catch someone's attention—'hey, world, look at me—look what I can do.' That's kind of scary. No space agency would do that. So that means we're either dealing with a bona fide alien—fat chance—or an amateur who just invented a warp drive, for lack of a better term. Fat chance there, too, but I guess that would answer your 'why' question. If you could do that, wouldn't you want to tell the world?"

"Sure. So why not tell them—'My name is Jeanette Fischer. I just invented a warp drive.' Why this?" She waved an arm at the table.

"They wouldn't believe you. You'd have to prove it. Besides…think about it. A warp drive could make someone really, really rich. Or turn it around and use it as a weapon and it could make someone really, really powerful. That's where the scary part comes in. Jeanette Fischer invents the warp drive. Someone else wants it for herself. Jeanette Fischer suddenly disappears. Maybe they did it this way for the sake of anonymity."

"Yes, I guess I see your point. We're still no closer to explaining this, though." She rapped her knuckles on the graph.

"Unfortunately I think we're stuck. The answer to that question has to come from them—him, her, it, whatever."

Becca thought for a few minutes. "Can you make the computer beep at us if the signal comes back?

"Well, I'm about as ready as I can be," Becca said. "I've got the phone number at Cerro Tololo where I can reach my buddy, and we're already set up to get our leg of the triangulation data. Now we wait."

"You seem fairly confident that the signal will return."

Becca nodded. She wondered the same thing as Jeanette—why bother sending a signal if they didn't want an answer? She felt sure they would try again, and soon.

"Let's do some brainstorming while we're waiting," she suggested. "I want to be absolutely certain that we haven't overlooked some logical explanation for the apparent hovering."

"Yes, I've already been thinking about that. If it was in a geosynchronous orbit, it would have moved out of our field of vision, since we're tracking the Moon, but what would you call the equivalent orbit for the Moon—selenosynchronous? Could it be in an orbit that made it appear to be stationary relative to the Moon?"

"Selenosynchronous? Nice word you invented there, Jeanette, but no, the Moon doesn't rotate fast enough for such an orbit to be stable. Although...let me think a minute. The Lagrange points might have those characteristics. Nah," she shook her head, "it's in the wrong place for that."

"What if it's approaching us along our line of sight? It would appear to be stationary to us, wouldn't it?"

"Yes, but our line of sight is constantly changing as it tracks the Moon, so it would be damned difficult to stay on the line. If they can do that, then they can probably hover, too. Still think it's an E.T.?"

"No, but I'm still excited." She stuck her tongue out at Becca.

Becca laughed. "And I'm still curious. Who the hell is out there, and why?"

"I don't —" Both women jumped as a beep from the computer interrupted Jeanette. She moved quickly to the terminal, and Becca punched numbers on the phone.

"*Hola*, Diego. It's Becca Coleman.... Yeah. Two years, I think. It was the last NOAO conference in Tucson...." She bypassed the normal small talk, hoping he would overlook the discourtesy. The signal could disappear at any time. After she explained how close the source was and that they were seeing red and green blinking lights, she had to endure the predictable teasing.

"Very funny, Diego. All right. Thanks. You'll call me back?...Uh, Diego, can you sit on this for a day or so?...Sorry. It's an idiom. 'Sit on it' means...um, *mantener silencio*.... Yeah, I don't want the media underfoot until I know more about it.... *Gracias, amigo. Adiós.*

"He'll call us back," she told Jeanette, "hopefully within the hour. So what have we got this time?"

"The same as before, but we've rotated enough that I could do a rough triangulation. It's inside the lunar orbit. I'd put it at 300,000 kilometers plus or minus 80 thousand."

"Shit! Uh, sorry, Jeanette, but that puts us back at square one! Are you sure?"

"I'm sure about the calculations, but triangulation is meaningless if the light moved before I took the second measurement."

"I don't buy that." Becca jerked the drawing over in front of her and frowned. She put a question mark on the line of sight where Jeanette's calculations indicated the light source was located. She sat staring at the drawing, thumb supporting her chin with a finger over her lips.

Neither woman had any new ideas. They checked each other's work while waiting. Finally the phone rang.

"Diego?...Really? No, it's quite strong here. That's interesting. Well, could you give me the data over the phone and follow up with an e-mail later?...Yeah, that's mine. I'm ready." Becca jotted the numbers down on the bottom of the drawing. "Thanks, *amigo*. I'll let you know what we find.... .

Great. *Hasta luego.*"

Jeanette had already begun calculating before Becca hung up. She finished and wrote the results beside the question mark on the drawing: 234,250 km.

"Well, I guess that explains what Diego was saying. The light is really difficult for them to see in Chile. The source is apparently close enough to Earth and the beam is tight enough that they are on the very edge of the cone."

"Becca, I hate to bring this up, but do you know what that implies?" Becca answered with a blank look. "The signal is being sent specifically to us—here at the Peak."

"Son of a bitch! You're right." She paused, frowning. "Who do you know that lives out there? None of my friends can count past ten."

"Don't look at *me*," Jeanette complained.

"Well, Kiddo. Roll up your sleeves. We've got a lot of work to do."

ENTR'ACTE

MILKY WAY GALAXY, LOCAL ARM:

>*<Calculated vectors disagree with observed vectors.>*

If the robot could have frowned, it would have.

>*<Vectors must agree or my song will not be heard. Anxiety. A new sensation to perceive. Unpleasant. Undesirable.>*

The robot performed a systems check, but found nothing amiss. The problem was not internal. The problem was—the second planet of the solar system no longer existed. Its pieces soon would be passing the Oort cloud of its mother sun. The orbits of all the remaining planets would be adjusting to that loss for millennia.

The robot had more than enough computing power to compensate for the deviations, but regrettably had not been programmed to do so. It directed its song where the audience should be and adjusted the vector only when its sensors provided new input.

The earliest targets had been astronomically distant from the robot's system. As intended, they felt only the tiniest push from the force field. Push, no push, push, no push, but with the frequency of a microwave. An inhabited planet and its parent solar system went from greenhouse to oven to inferno in only a matter of hours.

The Makers' planet, however, was in the same solar system as the robot. It felt the full force of the device's power. Atmosphere, crust, and molten core spewed into space wherever the force field was directed, and it was directed everywhere—at the planet, its moons, and every vehicle, habitation, and device using anti-gravity technology throughout the solar system and beyond.

    <My song must be heard.>

THIRTEEN

Becca and Jeanette stood in the middle of the dome, bundled against the cold. The huge room couldn't be heated because convection currents in the air would distort the images obtained by the telescope. They shivered—partly from the cold, but more from the sheer audacity of what they were doing. They had attached two lasers to the body of the telescope so that their beams would be projected parallel to it. Not only was the modification unauthorized, so was the entire night's activities they had planned. A corner of Jeanette's mouth pulled down in a grimace.

Becca raised an eyebrow. "What? You never broke a rule before?"

"Yes, of course I have. It just never made world news."

Becca chuckled, but suggested that might work in their favor. She didn't think Dr. Howards would have the balls to fire them with the world watching. Besides, if they didn't do it, someone else would. "I'd rather we're the ones having fun," she argued. "You said you've got another job lined up, right?"

"Yes...I'd prefer not to have 'fired from last job' on my résumé, though."

The dome door opened, and a security guard stepped through. "What are you two doing out here?" he asked. "Why aren't you in the office where it's warm?"

"We have to come out here whenever we change our

imaging devices," Becca explained.

"Oh." The guard turned, then paused. "What're those things? I don't recall seeing them before." He pointed to the lasers affixed to the telescope.

Jeanette's eyes got big, and Becca spoke quickly to keep her from responding.

"They're lasers. When we change equipment, we have to re-calibrate everything. The lasers tell us if we're aimed right." Becca improvised, but stuck as close to the truth as she could. She didn't want him getting suspicious.

He acknowledged with a lift of his chin. "'K, see you next round."

Jeanette exhaled through puffed cheeks, clearly uncomfortable with their deviations from protocol.

Becca patted her shoulder. "Well, I snowed him, but I won't be able to do that with everybody. Let's go."

After giving the jury-rigged equipment one last look, they retreated to the warmth of the control room. Jeanette settled in at her workstation and seemed to relax somewhat.

"Becca, how will you know if the lasers are aimed the same direction as the telescope?"

"We won't, for sure. But they don't have to be exact. The atmosphere causes the beams to bloom quite a bit. It's more like shooting with a shotgun than a rifle. If we're close enough, the corner-cube mirror array at Tranquility Base will bounce the light back at us." She consulted a reference manual and entered commands to re-position the telescope. "Fire when ready," she said as the dome came into position.

Jeanette tapped her keyboard. A moment later the spectrograph's display on her monitor confirmed the beam's arrival. "You were right, Becca. Close enough for government work, although the signal is awfully weak."

"Let's send one more test signal with data acquisition running so it will be on the front of the file when we start communicating. Let me watch, so I can learn how, too."

"OK, I set up our program to mimic their signal," Jeanette explained. "Pulses are roughly two seconds long with pauses of a second in between. In manual mode, you type zeroes and ones. Hit ENTER and it fires."

She started recording, then typed '01' and hit ENTER. The monitor displayed '01' a few seconds later indicating that the bounced signal was received.

"Did we get the test recorded?" Becca asked.

"Yes, but something bothers me. I didn't notice it during the first test. The strongest part of the reflected beam is off center in the display. Does that mean the lasers are not parallel to the telescope?"

Becca rubbed her chin. No, she didn't think that was it. As long as they hit the mirrors, the reflected beam should be centered at Tranquility Base. She asked Jeanette to overlay an image of the lunar surface, and an image of the Moon appeared on the monitor. The southwest edge of Mare Tranquillitatis was neatly centered in the picture.

"I'll be damned!" Becca smacked her hand on the table. "We're aimed right and the CCD is mounted correctly. The reflected beam is just not coming from Tranquility Base. The mirror has been moved!"

"What do you mean 'moved'?" Jeanette asked.

"I mean 'moved' as in 'moved'," Becca answered, not too helpfully.

"How could...," Jeanette started, but interrupted herself. "Do you think *they* did it? Why?"

"There's no doubt in my mind that they did it. Whoever is sending these signals has been poking around on the Moon. As to why, maybe just to prove that they can. This is going to stir up some excitement. Let's see if they're still jabbering."

The dome moved imperceptibly, and the display began streaming 0's and 1's.

"Two minutes by my watch," Becca announced. "We send as soon as the last set of twelve arrives."

"What are we going to send them?" Jeanette asked as she watched the stream of incoming bits on the screen.

"What's the most logical thing to follow twelve?"

Jeanette shrugged. "Thirteen."

"Yep. Since they seem to be in love with twelve, we'll send twelve thirteens. I don't have a clue where it will go from there. If it's an E.T., then maybe we'll get into prime numbers or pi or something like that. I've got reference books for math, chemistry, and physics in case we need them, but we'll have to wait and see."

"That was the last set. Ooh, I've got goose bumps! Aren't you excited, Becca?"

"Not really. Not yet, anyway. I'll get excited when I see something that proves this is not man-made. Start the transmission loop."

"Uh-uh." Jeanette shook her head. "This one's yours."

Becca sneered. "Chicken." She keyed in the commands.

The lasers flashed—red, red, green, red—a pause, then red, red, green, red, repeating until the binary code for thirteen had been sent twelve times.

"Now we wait," Becca said.

"How long do you think it will be?" Jeanette asked.

"Minutes if we're lucky. Years if we're not."

"Oh I hope...," Jeanette sucked in her breath as a binary code appeared on the monitor. "Twelve." A few seconds later the next one came. "Twelve, again." She frowned. "Not very exciting."

"No. It's predictable and monotonous, but the pattern's changed in response to our signal. That's encouraging...hold it," she said as a third code appeared on the monitor. "That's not another twelve." Binary digits filled one line on the screen and wrapped to the next. "What do you make of it?"

"Could the twelves be a base and an exponent and the long number a mantissa?"

"Hmm. I wouldn't be very impressed if they're using logarithms. Their numbering base is pretty obviously twelve. I don't see any physical constants in my tables with an exponent of twelve, though. I hadn't thought of the long number being a mantissa. That's a good idea. But I wonder why so many digits. How many are there, anyway?"

"Let's see. The monitor displays eighty per line and it lacks...um...sixteen being two lines. That's a hundred forty-four."

"Bingo! That's it, Jeanette! It's a twelve by twelve matrix. The long number isn't a number. It's a pattern! Here, give me that quadrille pad. I'll plot and you read the bits to me." In spite of her words to the contrary, Becca began to feel some excitement. *Could* it be extra-terrestrial in origin?

About halfway through the plotting, she smiled and nodded her head. "A circle," she observed. "Okay, here's what I want to do, Jeanette."

Becca outlined a plan to respond with a circle, but of

higher resolution and increased transmission rate. Jeanette made the necessary changes, and the lasers fired, much more rapidly this time, but still slowly enough to see the individual bits.

"What do you think they'll send this time?" she asked.

"I don't know. I'd guess a new pattern of some sort since we've shown that we understand the last one."

The monitor beeped, indicating an incoming signal, and a pattern took shape on the monitor. Becca thought it looked like a legless tadpole or a whale. Jeanette suggested a hot-air balloon or a raindrop. The interpretation depended on whether they had their columns and rows oriented correctly.

"If it's a raindrop, then we've got it falling sideways," Jeanette observed.

"That's it, Jeanette, you've done it again!"

Jeanette looked skeptical. "Done what again?"

"It *is* a raindrop. And rain doesn't fall sideways. They're telling us which way is down. We've got our columns and rows ass-backwards."

"Well, I'm sure glad I figured that out," Jeanette quipped. "OK. So, now that we know up from down, what's next? Left and right?"

"Exactly, and a raindrop won't help with that. We need something asymmetrical."

"How about a picture of the Moon?" Jeanette suggested. "We'll have to go to a higher resolution, but the monitor can handle that. Should we try to get them to send a signal that's compatible with a TV?"

"That might be a good idea, but I'm stretching my skills as it is. Let's wait. Once we go public with this, we're going to have more help than you can shake a stick at."

"Public?" Jeanette got a panicky look on her face. "But Dr. Howards will find out what we've been doing."

"Screw Howards, and screw the rules," Becca growled. "Jeanette, we're receiving a signal from space. One that contains a pattern that could only be constructed by an intelligence. We're not just going to *sit* on this."

Becca knew she was pushing Jeanette out of her comfort zone, but she also felt the circumstances justified their actions. Besides, after his arrest, she figured Howards would be laying low for a few days, and she certainly wasn't going to call him. The Moon would set soon. She wanted to learn as much as they could before that. Tomorrow she would call that reporter—the one who investigated and reported Howards' earlier arrest—and get him to come. He'd want his newspaper to have an exclusive, so he wouldn't release anything to the wire services until the paper hit the streets the next morning. That would give them several more hours tomorrow night. The place would be crawling with media after that, so even if Howards showed up, he couldn't jerk the rug out from under them without making himself look like the fool he was.

Jeanette appeared far from convinced, but keyed in the new pattern without further objection.

The transmission took only a few seconds. Both lasers appeared to be firing continuously, but the monitor displayed the image without any distortion.

The activity seemed to dispel some of Jeanette's anxiety. "What do you think they will send back this time?"

"Well, they need to confirm we have left and right correct. I imagine they'll use pictures. Symbols wouldn't help.

Who knows? Maybe they'll send a picture of themselves."

"Oh, wouldn't that be exciting! Does that mean you finally think it might be an E.T.?"

"No. It means I think I don't know." Humans could generate laser beams, count in binary, and digitize images. The two women had analyzed and responded to the signal as fast as the "aliens" did to theirs. They hadn't exactly given each other I.Q. tests, but it seemed to Becca that they were evenly matched so far.

"Don't get me wrong," she said. "I'm enjoying the hell out of this. Alien or human, I'd like to meet whoever is on the other end of the line. This is the most fun I've had since I came to work here."

"Oh, that was fast!" Jeanette exclaimed as a picture appeared on the monitor. "Is that a planet? It's hard to tell with only black and white. It could be Earth, or not."

The monitor beeped again, and the picture was replaced with another larger sphere with similar markings, but still few features. Again an image arrived, and this time the edges of the sphere were off-screen.

"They're zooming in!" Jeanette almost shouted.

"Yeah, but on what?" Becca asked.

The picture began to acquire features, but still nothing recognizable. After several more images the signal stopped, and the picture remained constant.

"Looks like that's all we get to work with this time," Becca said. "Any first impressions?"

"A planet, but I wouldn't have been able to say that if I hadn't seen the first two frames. If it's Earth, I don't recognize anything."

Becca felt sure it was Earth. Why send a picture of

something they were not familiar with? That wouldn't help them tell left from right.

"Maybe that's why we don't recognize anything," Jeanette suggested. "We know we've got up and down correct. Let me reverse the horizontal order and replay the images." Jeanette edited the program and replayed from the first image.

"Got it!" yelled Becca. "I'll bet on it, anyway."

"What is it? And how can you tell? I can't even be sure we're looking at Earth, let alone which hemisphere!"

"Well, if these pictures are intended to help us orient the images correctly, what better way than to send us a picture of ourselves? My bet is that they zoom in on the spot that our signals are coming from. I think the North Pole is at the bottom. If so, and if they're zooming in on Kitt Peak, then the Great Lakes clouds should disappear off the screen at the lower left. Go to the next frame."

"OK, it's doing what you said it would, but I still don't see anything that I recognize."

"You will. Just keep displaying the frames. If the pictures were magnified a little more, we'd be looking right down our cleavage."

UFO

KITT PEAK - NOVEMBER 12:

When the Visitor's Center called, Becca went outside to wait for the Tucson Citizen reporter. He parked his old Corolla and hurried toward the dome, hugging himself against the cold. Like many visitors to the Peak, he came unprepared for the buffeting, bitter winds that swirled around the buildings. Once inside the control room, she introduced Jeanette and gave him their business cards so he'd get their names and titles correct.

She explained that the facility was still called the Spacewatch dome, even though the Spacewatch program had been shut down several months earlier when the Q of L movement redistributed its funding, and the telescope was a 0.9-meter reflector—the oldest one on the mountain. Up until Wednesday night, they'd been using it to analyze surface gases on the moons of Jupiter. He could get the details from the KPNO website. Becca didn't give him a chance to ask questions. He had his recorder going, and she kept talking.

"When we first saw the light, it was stationary with respect to the moon. We got confirmation and triangulation from CTIO—that's Cerro Tololo International Observatory near Santiago, Chile—which placed the light approximately 234,000 kilometers above Earth. The light turned out to be two lights—one red and one green. The blinking turned out to be a pattern—binary numbers from one to twelve, repeated in sets of twelve at regular intervals.

"Before I continue, I want to point out that the frequency of the red and green lights is identical to that of commercially available lasers—in other words, off-the-shelf equipment. That suggests that we're not dealing with an extra-terrestrial. On the other hand, we don't have the technology to move and hover at arbitrary locations in near space as this light has done. So—bottom line—we don't know what we've got out there."

That seemed to be all that the reporter needed to hear. He took out a cell phone and was about to dial when Becca stopped him.

"You might want to wait," she advised. "The best is yet to come. When you go back into the dome, you'll see a couple of boxes attached to the telescope. They're lasers. We're talking back."

The reporter's eyes nearly popped. "You mean you're communicating with a UFO?"

"Your words—not mine," Becca pointed out. "We spent last night developing a very small vocabulary based on Boolean logic, math, physics, and simple drawings. They used a sequence of diagrams to tell us they were going to move, and they did. They are now located in a geosynchronous orbit—directly above Earth's equator on the same longitudinal line as Kitt Peak.

"That's it in a nutshell. We start in about ten minutes. You're welcome to watch, but we won't have much time to answer questions."

"Jesus H. —" His voice faded out. "I gotta call this in!" He sprinted for the door.

Becca looked at Jeanette. "Brace yourself, girl. Tomorrow morning the shit hits the fan. We'll be up to our eyeballs in news media. I'd better give Security a heads-up."

The door of the dome burst open, and Dr. Claude Howards charged in, his gelled hair in disarray. His head swung back and forth like a bull looking for the matador.

"Both of you! Gather up your personal belongings now! You are terminated!" he bellowed.

Neither of the women moved. Jeanette looked petrified. Becca, who outweighed Howards by nearly fifty pounds, was not about to let him intimidate her. She had been expecting this. She didn't budge. Her head slowly turned to face him.

"I don't think so," she responded quite calmly. "Picture this: news media from all over the world—their cameras on you. You're all by yourself. The world watches and waits—and waits. Picture the headlines the next morning. World-wide headlines," she emphasized, holding up the index finger and thumb of both hands to frame the imaginary text. "Sexist Astronomer Fires Women, Can't Operate Telescope Without Them."

The charging bull stopped, bewildered by the sudden pain of the sword plunged deep between the shoulder blades.

Becca allowed the truth of her words to sink in until Claude leaned on a nearby desk for support. Before he could recover, she outlined what *she* planned on happening—the same man in front of the same cameras with the same audience, but this time he would know what he was doing. He was going to spend the evening there with them and review in fine detail everything that they had done from the moment the light was discovered, right up through the very last message they exchanged tonight. Tomorrow morning, he would to turn into the world's most impressive public relations spokesperson.

"You're going to shine, and we're going to shine," she told him. "It's your choice—win-win or lose-lose."

Dr. Claude Howards missed his calling. He should have been a soap opera star. First of all, he would have made a lot more money than he ever could as an astronomer, and second, it would have given him the attention he so desperately craved. He already had the car, the clothes, the hair, and Becca begrudgingly admitted, the looks.

He *did* shine, and he made them shine, too. Oh, he didn't *mean* it. Becca had seen him bullshit his way out of too many technological tight spots to believe anything he said. But he told the story straight, just as she had scripted it, complete with shots of the lasers attached to the telescope, screen prints of the images of Earth, and Becca and Jeanette in white lab coats they'd scrounged from the McMath-Pierce solar facility. He even gave that little twerp, Lester, credit for the original discovery. According to him, they were one big happy family, and the public would never learn otherwise.

BUSTED

Angie returned to her dorm in a good mood after attending a discussion with some other students in the cafeteria. As usual, she'd managed to mention her inventor friend, John Wainwright during the conversation. Col. Belarov had attended, and he gave her a tolerant smile. She suspected he knew she was American. After all, he had access to her student records, but if he knew, he never betrayed her to the others.

As she approached her room, she saw Ludmilla—'My friends call me Ludi; you may call me Ludmilla.'—Annikova and a couple of her cronies waiting in the hall. *Uh-oh. Trouble.* Security was tight in the massive, thirty-six story building, touted as the tallest educational building in the world, but Ludi's status as a foreign student mentor granted her free access to the dorms. Thus far Angie had avoided Ludi's malevolence by masquerading as an Italian and never, never speaking English. She wondered what she'd done to attract the girl's unwelcome attention. Ludi held an envelope in her hand. Angie realized it was a letter—either from Mamma or Duke. A shudder ran down her back. Not only would she get worked over for being an American, she'd likely pay double for the cover-up.

"Your mail, *Signorina* Sgambelli," Ludi sneered as she held the envelope out to Angie. Angie reached for it, but Ludi snatched it back. "It seems the *Italian* student might not be Italian after all," she said, more to her cohorts than to Angie. "She has American *druzhok*."

Angie had learned the hard way, back home in Haysville, that the only effective defense against bullies was an unexpected offense. She squared off in front of Ludi with hands on her newly developed hips.

"I am every bit as Italian, *Gaspazhah* Annikova, as you are Russian." She put as much sarcasm into the honorific title as Ludi had put into *signorina*. "And the letter is not from my boyfriend, but from my academic sponsor and mentor, a world-famous entrepreneur who attended this very university and is a close acquaintance of Provost Dyuzhenkov. Now I will thank you to return my mail, which contains nothing that is any of *your* business, and suggest that you go pick on someone who cannot, with a single phone call, make your life as miserable as you enjoy making others'."

Angie was on thin ice. Duke *had* attended classes at MSU, and Dyuzhenkov had been one of his professors at the time. That he would remember Duke was doubtful; that Angie could call on him for protection was a complete fabrication.

But it worked. Ludi slapped the envelope into Angie's open hand and spun on her heel, gritting words between her clenched teeth. "If I ever find out ..." She didn't complete the threat and didn't have to. Angie knew there'd be Hell to pay if the truth ever surfaced.

The next day, Angie discovered just how lucky she had been. Ludi and her gang, foiled in their attempt to abuse Angie, had severely beaten two female American students and left them bleeding in a snow bank outside their off-campus dormitory. Up to that point, the anti-American activity had mostly been pranks and cruel jokes. The escalation to beatings terrified Angie.

She wanted to become an astronaut, but was it worth risking bodily harm to get the training? How realistic was her goal anyway? Russia certainly wasn't going to put her in *their* space program, and the U.S. only had one shuttle, *Atlantis*, resurrected from mothballs as a concession to powerful Q of L opponents. Maybe it would be best if she returned home where she was at least safe and loved, although that presented problems, too. After more than a year of independence, would she be able to live with her parents again, staring at an empty house across the street? *Duke, what's going on?*

LONG TIME

EL CALVO MINE:

Duke got a sinking feeling when he saw the postcard from Angie. *Oh, man! I forgot all about her other cards. I put them in the drawer where Claire wouldn't see them and...how long has it been?*

He pulled her cards from the desk drawer and looked at the dates. *Six weeks! Damn!* Even if he sent an answer today, she'd probably be writing another one, and they would cross in the mail. How did he manage to get himself into those jams with women? What was he going to say?

The question hung heavy in his mind. It wasn't as if he'd been stringing Angie along, but neither had he cut the cord cleanly. He needed to do that. He and Claire were getting pretty thick.

EL CALVO
Dec. 14
Dear Angie,

I'm ashamed of myself for ignoring you for so long. You lived across the street from me long enough that you would recognize the symptoms if you were here. Yes, a woman—possibly THE woman. I can't talk about technical stuff with her like I can with you, but maybe in time. I've come to realize how much I use you as the standard by which I measure other women. No wonder so many of them fail the test! If only things were different.

Yeah, the signals are exciting—just like we talked about last year. I'll bet the two of us could make that conversation *sing!* I also want to talk to you about my project. It's even more exciting than the signals! I've been recording all my experiments for you. You've got a lot of catching up to do.

I'm concerned about the tensions that are building up over there. Please be careful. If it gets much worse, it might be best for you to come home early. Use your own judgment, but be as ready as you can be.

It's too late for me to wish you luck on your midterms, but I am sure you aced them all. I've seen what you can do! My bet is that you finish at the top of your class.

I don't know when this will reach you, so Merry Christmas and Happy New Year. I promise to write every week from now on—at least a card like you do.

Love,
Duke

Duke stared at the letter without really seeing it. His brow was furrowed and his mind was far away.

I've lost count of the women that I've dumped—most of them without a second thought. I'm not really dumping Angie. We never actually had a relationship, and we're still going to be friends. So, why does this feel so wrong?

MSU:

December was hell month for Angie. Her first year in Russia may have been miserable, but at least it was exciting.

Now the excitement was gone. Only the misery remained. She drove herself relentlessly preparing for the mid-term exams. Colonel Belarov was the most demanding instructor she'd ever had. The Russians were convinced that the signals from near-space were a cover-up, that the U.S. was testing some kind of laser weapon. Anti-Americanism had become something to fear rather than tolerate. Paolo's kissing turned to groping on their second date, and she'd opted out of a third. She wanted to be home, safe with Duke—with a man who loved her, if not as a woman, at least as a best friend. She was desperate to talk to him about the signals from space, but he hadn't written in almost two months.

"Duke," she said, looking at his picture on her nightstand. "What's going on? Why don't you answer my cards?"

You already know the answer—Bimbo Number 27.

Okay, maybe so, but he's never kept a woman this long before.

Maybe he stumbled onto one who isn't a bimbo.

That's what I'm afraid of. What if he's getting serious? I could lose him!

You never had him. At best you were good friends. You're more like a kid sister to him.

I'm a woman now.

Barely...and so what? He doesn't know that, and you can't tell him.

I've got to tell him, somehow!

Angie spent more than an hour deciding what to say and how to say it. At the end of the hour, she had only four short sentences. They looked ridiculously small even on a postcard, but at the same time, the message called attention to itself, which was the effect she wanted. She briefly considered sending it in an e-mail so he would get it sooner, but dared not risk the monitored message falling into Ludi Annikova's hands.

> MSU
> Dec. 14
> Dear Duke,
> Long time, no hear. Another woman? Wish you would consider <u>this</u> woman. I love you.
> Angie

Okay?

Well, it's succinct.

It has to be. I don't want his mind wandering. This is as explicit as I dare be. He's going to have to put two and two together to realize that I am a woman now.

Him? Put two and two together when it comes to women? Ha!

Yeah. I know, but it's all I can do short of going there.

She mailed the letter on the way to the bus stop. "I love you," she mumbled as the mailbox door clanged shut.

THREE DAYS LATER:

Angie wanted to read Duke's letter immediately, but disciplined herself to wait until she got back to her dorm room. The temperature was bitter cold even for Moscow—many parts of the world were reporting record-breaking temperatures, both high and low, and near hurricane winds howled between the buildings. She didn't want to take a chance on the letter blowing away. It was too early to be a response to her 'I love you' card, but it might explain his recent silence.

She stomped the snow from her boots and hurried out of her heavy coat. She got comfortable on the bed—pillow against the wall and legs outstretched, then began reading.

She didn't cry—only sat there staring at the letter, re-reading random sentences.

Everything that could go wrong did. He's got a woman. She's not a bimbo. He's getting serious.

You left out the worst part. He apparently already considered you as a candidate, but dismissed the idea—'if only things were different.'

What does he mean 'if only'? They ARE different. Can't he see that?

Apparently not. He didn't make the connection.

How dare he use me as his standard of measurement and then not consider me?

Finally the tears came—with big choking sobs that came from the depths of her heart. She cried until she had no more tears—until her sides ached and she was worn out.

What are you going to do?

Nothing. I'm not going to swallow my pride and go begging. If I'm his standard of measurement, then he's simply going to have to learn the hard way that I'm also the only woman who can meet that standard.

And if he doesn't?

Paolo was a turd, but at least he showed me I'm woman enough now to attract a man. I want that man to be Duke, but I'm not going to join the world's first space convent because of him.

Q OF L

WHITE HOUSE - DECEMBER 20:

President Carlton Tate glared at the faces around the table. *I hate this job. Intelligence, security, military—they're all alike. You can't get a straight answer out of any of them.*

"So the Russians are going full tilt to finalize their shuttle upgrades. Do we know why?" he asked, directing the question at the National Security Advisor.

"The 'why' is obvious, sir. We just got one of our shuttles operational again, and at the same time we did it, someone started sending signals from near-space. The Russians claim it's us; we think it's them. It's only natural for them to match us tit for tat. The satellites confirm the increased activity, but no mission details have leaked to any of our people on the ground."

"Didn't you tell me earlier that they had furloughed their shuttle crew? Have they been recalled?" Tate asked.

"No, sir."

"So whatever the purpose of their mission, it doesn't require any special training of the crew. I'll tell you what I think. I think they're getting ready to go up and investigate what's sending those signals—that is, if they're not the ones sending them. On the other hand, if it's their device, then this could mean they're preparing to launch the next phase of their op, whatever it is."

Tate looked at Martin Sheets, director of the OMB, and

the only person in the room with whom he had a decent relationship. "Martin, is there anything left in our budget that will allow us to send an unplanned mission up there? We've got to find out what that thing is. For all we know, the Russians could have a laser weapon floating up there within easy range of Houston, Los Alamos, and Edwards Air Force base."

Sheets shook his head. "Sorry, sir. Nothing. We're running on fumes as it is."

Tate knew that between the NSA, CIA, and Secret Service, there was enough black ops money stashed away to put a man on the Moon again, but he couldn't get access to something that 'didn't exist'.

"God damn it!" he ground out between clenched teeth. All they could do was wait and watch. With the space program essentially bankrupt, there were no other options.

The room cleared quickly and Tate sat, staring out the window at the fog-covered city. The dismal weather matched his mood.

The Quality of Life Movement had been a *good* idea. He still believed that. Five Nordic countries and a half-dozen others employed welfare state systems, and they had the highest standard of living in the world. It would have worked here, too, if it hadn't been for the goddamned greedy bastards at the top income levels who discovered that it was ridiculously cheaper to pay the penalties than to pay the taxes the sliding scale indicated was their fair share. As a result, funding for the Q of L programs fell far short of the required amount, and all non-essential budget items, including the space program, had been gutted. History would not treat Carlton Tate kindly.

DUMPED

EL CALVO MINE:

Duke waved from the workshop entrance as Claire drove up. She went straight into the trailer instead of waiting for him to cross the lot. Duke frowned. Well, it *was* cold outside.

His reception inside was even colder.

"I picked up your mail when I came through the gate," Claire said. She pointed to a small bundle on the countertop. A postcard lay conspicuously on top. "Want to tell me about Angie?"

Duke could see the card had Russian postage. Suddenly the room became uncomfortably hot. He frowned. *Why am I sweating? I haven't done anything wrong. I can explain. It's no big deal.* Somehow, he failed to convince himself.

"I...ah...well...Angie is...*was*...my cross-the-street neighbor in Haysville." He stared at the card, eyes darting in Claire's direction. "I guess you could say she's my protégée. I'm...uh...sponsoring her classes in Russia."

The panicky feeling subsided somewhat. *There's nothing she could reasonably object to about any of that*, he reasoned. He dared to make eye contact.

Claire was sitting on the front of her seat, rigidly upright, hands folded in her lap. She met his gaze, waiting.

Duke didn't know what else to say. Claire had obviously read something on the card that upset her, but not knowing what it was put him at a disadvantage. He decided to stop while he was ahead—hoping he *was* ahead.

"That's it?" Claire's eyes glistened with moisture. "That's all you have to say about a woman you've failed to mention to me all these months?"

"I haven't…I mean…well, I guess it might seem that way, but it's not like I'm trying to hide anything. There's nothing going on between us, if that's what you're thinking. She's just a kid. We're best friends is all."

Claire nodded. "Do you love her?" The challenging tone was gone from her voice, now, replaced by…resignation? Duke couldn't tell.

"I…well, yes," he admitted, "but not as a woman. I mean…I can't. Something happened to her development. It didn't kick in when it was supposed to."

"What if it did?" Her eyes met Duke's, seeking, imploring.

Duke tried to imagine Angie as a woman. He liked the idea—a *lot*. Suddenly he remembered Gramp's advice about finding a woman who shared his interests—a woman like Angie.

After a long moment, Claire picked up her purse and stood.

"Claire, wait! What…where are you going?"

"I'm going home, Duke. You're in love with another woman, but you're too dumb to see it. I wish her good luck. She's going to need it."

Duke couldn't argue—didn't know what to argue *against*—without knowing what was in the card. He grabbed it as soon as Claire was out the door.

Holy…! His mind didn't finish the thought. It was too busy processing the significance of the message.

He looked at his watch. It was after midnight in Moscow—too late to call. Besides, he had no idea what he was going to say to Angie.

EL CALVO

Dec. 25

Dear Angie,

It's Christmas Day and I've never been more miserable in my life. I'm here. You're there.

I got dumped. Can you believe it? She dumped me—said "you're in love with another woman and you're too dumb to see it."

Of course she was wrong. I can only think of three people that I really love—my old nanny, Gramp and you.

YOU!

I tried to call you all week, but kept getting the anti-American treatment—insults, wrong extensions, dead lines. I considered flying over there, but after the way I've been treating you, I might not be welcome. So, here I am writing the most important letter I'll ever write.

I love you!

I probably always have (but was too dumb to see it). It's you I want to talk to, you I want beside me, you I want to hold!

So now comes the really hard part. I don't deserve your love, but I hope I haven't lost it. I don't deserve a second chance, but I hope you'll forgive me and let me earn your respect and love again. Please say "yes."

I love you!

Duke

Duke re-read the letter. He knew it was clumsily written, but he also knew that it was probably the best he could do. At least this time it felt right.

Angie, I don't know how we're going to make this work, but I'm determined to try. For the first time in my life, I know what I want. I want you.

MSU:

The words at the bottom of the letter caught Angie's eyes before she read the text. Then she *couldn't* read it. Huge tears rolled down her cheeks. She had such a lump in her throat that she could barely breathe. Her heart beat so hard that it rattled the paper as she pressed the letter to her breast. *He loves me!*

She wiped her eyes and tried to read from the beginning, but the effort was useless—the tears kept coming. She didn't care. This was a moment to savor. She *did* want to read the letter, though. The sobs became hiccups, and the hiccups became shuddering sighs. Finally she wiped her eyes, blew her nose, and began reading.

She made it halfway through the letter before the words blurred again. It didn't really matter. She read the letter over and over again until she had it memorized.

I've always heard "beware of what you ask for—you might get it."

Shut up! Can't you let me enjoy it for two seconds? He loves me. He said so.

Yeah, well, he never did connect the dots himself. The other woman had to do it for him. He doesn't know what love is.

His parents paid other people to raise him. What do you expect?

I expect you to have major problems with him in the love department.

Okay, okay! I can live with that. Look, I'm going into this with my eyes open. I live in the real world. Now leave me alone. I'm going to celebrate and you're not going to ruin it.

The headlines spoke of a new cold war—of growing tensions and mistrust between Russia and the United States. Angie should have paid attention—should have been concerned, but she was on a cloud. She floated through classes, forgot to eat, and smiled at everyone.

She came back to reality when the evening news showed a crowd in the street cheering as a local McDonald's burned. She spotted Ludi and some of her other Russian classmates in that crowd. Once again, Angie had to ask herself just how important these courses were to her.

BELAROV

MOSCOW STATE UNIVERSITY - JANUARY 6:

The telegram came mid-morning while Angie was in her room studying. "ANGIE, TOO DANGEROUS. COME HOME NOW. DUKE."

At first she was disappointed. Only two and a half weeks of class remained. Leaving now meant she would not get credit for the last classes. She tried to rationalize that she had come here to learn. She had accomplished that, but she was still disappointed.

Suddenly the realization hit her. *I'm going home! I'll get to see Duke!* Shivers washed over her body, leaving her tingling. When she finally remembered Duke wasn't at home—not in Haysville, anyway, it only gave her pause for a moment. *He loves me. We'll get together.*

Angie pulled her big suitcase from under the bed and opened it in front of the dresser. Her clothes were neatly folded and stacked in the drawers, but she made no attempt at maintaining neatness in packing. She didn't care what the clothes would look like when she got home. She couldn't wait to get there!

She almost filled the suitcase before she slowed down enough to think. Getting home could take more than a day. She might need a change of clothes—something lighter. She dug through the heap and located some underwear, socks, a pair of jeans, and a blouse that went into the smaller carry-on bag. She was completely packed in less than an hour after receiving the telegram.

She wanted to say goodbye to Colonel Belarov before she left. Maybe she could catch him before class if she hurried. She grabbed her books and ran out the door, realizing halfway there that she wouldn't need the books. She saw Belarov just as he stepped into the elevator and ran to catch him before the door closed.

"Colonel Belarov, I have an emergency at home and have to leave right away. I'm glad I caught you. I wanted to say goodbye to you before I go."

He acknowledged with a tilt of his head, but asked if she would mind waiting a few minutes. He said he had to make an announcement to the class. It would only take a minute. She really didn't want to wait, but didn't want to be rude, either. They entered the classroom together, and she took a seat near the front. Belarov waited until the students were seated and quiet. Although he seldom wasted words, his announcement was especially terse.

"I must leave unexpectedly. There will be no more classes. All of you will be given full credit for the course. There will be no final examination. Your current grade will be your final grade. You may leave at your convenience."

Silence reigned for a few seconds as the significance of his words sunk in, then the room exploded in chaos. A small stampede of smiling students headed for the door, the Americans giving each other "high fives" on the way out. Only a handful stayed to say their good-byes to the Colonel. Angie waited patiently until the last one left.

"Sir, it seems that both of us are in a hurry, so I won't keep you long. I wanted to thank you for the patience you showed me while I dealt with my...uh...transition."

The corner of the Colonel's mouth curled up ever so slightly. "I confess I was very close to having you dropped from the class. I thought you were in over your head. I'm glad it was only a language issue—I had that problem myself once. You went from being my worst student to perhaps my best."

Angie flushed at the high praise. "The language was a bigger problem than I expected," she admitted. "Where did you study?"

"The United States of America," he answered in English. "I received a degree in Aeronautical Engineering from Embry-Riddle University in Florida."

"You...you speak English?"

"As well as you speak Russian," he declared.

Angie stood open-mouthed at the revelation.

Belarov collected a few items from his desk as he spoke to her. "I wish we had longer to talk, but I am pressed for time. I wonder—can you be ready to leave by noon? Perhaps I could drop you off at the airport and we could talk on the way."

The offer both surprised and pleased Angie. "Thank you. I'd like that very much. I'm all packed, but I don't know how long it will take to get checked out."

"I might be able to influence that," the Colonel volunteered.

Whoa, Angie thought as she exited the Foreign Student's Admission Office. *He sure did influence it.* They were clearly miffed at having to do a favor for an American, but they had all of her paperwork ready when she got there.

Checkout took less than a half-hour. She and her luggage were downstairs waiting outside the building when the Colonel's car drove up.

Angie sat in the back seat with the Colonel feeling very special and more than a little conspicuous. She felt certain that he was bending rules to allow a civilian passenger in the car, although the vehicle bore no insignia, and the driver wore no military uniform. She shrugged it off. She was happy to have the opportunity to talk with him more. It would certainly be more pleasant than riding the Metro.

Angie didn't find Belarov particularly handsome. His eyes were set too close for her taste, and he combed his dark hair straight back, with no part. But, at thirty-two—Angie had looked it up—he was in the prime of his life and the peak of his career. He didn't need to be attractive.

He smelled good. Angie guessed that it was only soap, but that was a nice improvement over other European men she'd met. She decided that she liked him, which surprised her—not the liking part, but the fact that she had never really given it much thought until now. Aside from the glimpse of his personal side she'd seen in the after class get-togethers, she hardly knew anything about him.

They engaged in small talk at first. Angie spoke of her home and family and, of course, she had to brag about her academic sponsor, John Wainwright. When she shared her aspirations to become an astronaut, the Colonel was quite supportive. "You certainly have the intelligence. You're taking the right steps. Don't be discouraged by the current status of your country's space program. It changed once, and it will change again. I am confident you will be ready when the changes come." He smiled. "Perhaps one day I will float through a docking port and see your smiling face on the other side."

Angie wasn't sure which pleased her more—him picturing the same thing that she dreamed about or his subtle hint of affection. No, 'affection' was not the right word. 'Camaraderie' would be more appropriate.

"I'd like to thank you for participating in the discussion group between the Russian and foreign students," Angie said, as they approached the airport. "I noticed that very few of the instructors mixed with the students outside of class. I think your presence served as both catalyst and control, and your contributions were very valuable to me. It helped me learn a lot about your culture and politics."

"Ha!" He allowed a full smile to show. "Yes, no one in that group lacked enthusiasm. I, too, learned a few things. Since we both seem to be in a complimentary mood, let me say that you are the first American I have met who recognizes both good and bad qualities in our two systems of government. The other students are polarized. They see only black and white. You see differences. When you retire from your career as astronaut, perhaps you should consider becoming ambassador."

Angie didn't know how to respond. She had never seen anything but the professional side of the Colonel. He had never revealed the slightest hint of his personal feelings before. She suddenly realized how unobservant she had been. From the moment she got into his car—before that, in fact—he had been speaking to her as a person, not as a student. The man sitting next to her was not her professor—not the world-famous cosmonaut, but a warm, caring, likeable *person*.

He leaned forward to give instructions to the driver as they neared the terminal. Her thoughts were interrupted, but the warmth of a new friendship remained.

After getting her ticket Angie asked, "Will it cause a scandal if I hug you good-bye?" She stood next in line to check her bags through customs.

His stern face softened into a smile. *"Da,"* he confirmed, "but it will be good for both of our reputations," he added in English, laughing. He swept her up into an all-enveloping Russian bear hug. When he put her down, he said, "See you soon," and pointed up to the sky.

Angie approached the customs agent who motioned her over to where exasperated passengers were opening each piece of luggage for inspection. Colonel Belarov stepped up behind her. He looked at the agent. *"Nyet,"* was all he said and tilted his head in the other direction. She smiled her thanks to him as the awed agent attached security tapes to her luggage. *Having a Hero of Russia as your companion certainly has its advantages.*

Angie stowed her carry-on bag under the aisle seat. She had wanted to sit by the window to watch the European landscape unfold and try to pick out landmarks. *Oh, well, three hours won't be that long.* Then, she got a whiff of stale cigar smoke and body odor from the man sitting next to her, and she reconsidered. The flight attendants huddled just beyond the still-open curtains. From their frequent glances in her direction, Angie could tell that she was the topic of their conversation. Word must have reached them about her hugging Colonel Ivan Belarov. She returned their gaze with smug satisfaction. *Eat your hearts out.*

No sooner had the thought formed, than one of the attendants walked through the doorway and stopped beside her seat. "Angela Sgambelli?" she asked.

Angie's mind raced. The woman did not have a happy look on her face. *What could possibly be wrong? My ticket was accepted. What if they call me back to customs? Colonel Belarov won't be there to help me this time.*

"Please follow me. Do you have luggage in the overhead compartment?"

She felt as if every passenger in the cabin was watching her as she retrieved her belongings. She followed the woman, eyes downward and ears burning. Another attendant fell in behind them as they passed into the first class section.

The first attendant stopped, blocking the aisle, before they reached the galley. "May I take that please?" she asked.

Angie meekly handed over her bag, then watched in amazement as the attendant rearranged the luggage in one of the overhead bins to make room for hers.

"It seems that we have an empty seat in the first class section. Captain Usayev thought perhaps you would be more comfortable up here. May I offer you something to drink?"

Angie tried not to let her mouth hang open. *This has to be more of Colonel Belarov's doing. First class, and a window seat! Now everyone in* this *cabin is looking at me.*

First class was *nice*. Angie was courteous to the flight attendants, and they reciprocated. She felt absolutely pampered. She vowed to get a message back to Colonel Belarov thanking him for his thoughtfulness.

Angie's good fortune ran out when she landed in London. The mysterious phenomenon affecting the stability of orbiting satellites had also caused massive disturbances in worldwide weather patterns. Heathrow airport was a melee of people standing, sitting, and lying amidst piles of luggage everywhere. The din was deafening. It took her forty minutes to work her way to the ticket counter, only to find that all airports in the southeastern U.S. were closed due to record-breaking snowfalls. Going home was not an option. She made a decision, rationalizing that she had no choice, but knowing she did.

How are you going to explain this to Mamma?

Mamma doesn't expect me home for another three weeks.

So you think you can traipse off to Arizona for a three-week fling with Duke and then show up at home like nothing happened?

No. I can't lie to Mamma. I'll tell her.

When?

I don't know.

BACK HOME

Angie's conscience had plenty of time to work on her—London to New York, New York to LA, then LA to Phoenix, where she discovered there were no flights to Sedona—only a charter tour bus that refused to take all of her baggage. Exasperated, she rented two lockers and shoved her trunk and duffel bag into one and the overstuffed suitcase, which looked like the torso of a well-fed Black Angus steer, into the other.

Angie arrived in Sedona physically and emotionally exhausted. She waited until the other passengers finished signing up for their Jeep tours, then approached the woman at the counter.

"Hi. I'm Jodie. May I help you?"

One look at the woman and Angie wanted to hide behind something. Jodie was an attractive woman in her late twenties, tanned and muscular. She wore hiking boots, khaki cargo shorts, and a neatly pressed white blouse, which she filled. Angie by contrast couldn't have felt more *unat*-tractive. Her skin was nearly as white as Jodie's blouse. Her hair was stringy and sweaty. Her clothes were wrinkled, stained, and totally inappropriate for touring the red rock country. She mustered the courage to respond, anyway.

"I sure hope you can help me. I need to get to my friend's place. It's an old mine site. I think it might require a Jeep to get there. I'll pay the regular tour fare if you can take me there."

At the mention of the mine site, Jodie's smile disappeared. The look she gave Angie was almost as unwelcoming as the look she had encountered in Russia when she was even suspected of being an American.

"You've got a lot of nerve, coming here and asking that." The woman turned her back and marched through a door marked 'Office'.

It took Angie a moment to react. "A simple 'no' would have worked," she said to a red-haired woman behind the counter, who had witnessed the interchange. Angie's shoulders sagged. How was she going to get to Duke's place? She was so close! She turned and trudged toward the door, luggage wheels thumping at each groove in the floor.

She'd almost reached the door when someone called, "Miss, wait, please." The red-haired woman hurried out to intercept her, looking toward the office door as she spoke. Her face had a tight, controlled look, and she spoke in a low, almost confidential voice. "We close in about twenty minutes," she said. "If you'll wait for me across the street, I'll take you out there. Would that be okay?"

Angie was near tears and had a lump in her throat that wouldn't allow her to respond. She nodded her assent and thanks to the woman.

"Green pickup," the woman said as she turned back toward the office.

Angie took a long ragged breath when she got outside. She was so close to her limit, both physically and emotionally. She willed back the tears and plodded across the street, wandering aimlessly through the shops. After a few minutes, she went back outside, found some shade, and sat on a hard concrete bench.

It seemed like an hour, but at last she saw activity across the street. Two employees came out, got in their cars, and drove away. Jodie came out, saw Angie, and gave her a long look, then drove off in her SUV. The red-headed woman locked the back door and watched Jodie until she turned down a side street. Angie stood and stretched as the woman backed out, made a U-turn, and stopped beside her.

"Stick that behind the seat if you need leg room," she said, indicating Angie's luggage. Her tires were throwing gravel before Angie got her seatbelt on. She drove with frequent glances at the rear-view mirror as if she were afraid of being followed. Angie was getting nervous. She realized, a little late, how vulnerable a position she had put herself in.

She glanced at the woman and tried to read something of her character without staring. She had flaming red hair—short and tightly curled—somewhere between an Orphan Annie and an Afro. Her face and arms were a mass of freckles, one on top of the other. She was physically fit like Jodie, but with a smaller frame. Probably in her mid-twenties. She had no wild or frightening look in her eyes, but no smile, either. It made Angie uneasy.

They turned down a side street, and the woman seemed to relax somewhat. At least she slowed down.

"Claire Dunagan," she said, driving left-handed as she held out her right.

"Angela Sgambelli," Angie replied and shook her hand.
Would an abductress introduce herself?

The answer came quickly.

"Angie, we're going to take a little side trip. My place is just a little ways outside of town."

"Please —" Angie began a protest, but the woman interrupted her.

"I suspect your friend is a little bit more than a friend. You don't want him to see you like that, do you?" Claire reached over in front of Angie and flipped down the mirror on the back of the sun visor.

Angie looked at herself and sucked in her breath.

"Right, and I'll bet you can't remember when you last ate, can you?"

Angie couldn't.

"We'll get you cleaned up and fed and still be out to the mine before dark," Claire assured her.

Angie's head fell back against the headrest in relief as well as exhaustion. She turned the visor back against the headliner, not wanting to see the mess that stared back at her. Claire turned into her driveway.

The shower felt wonderful—warm and relaxing. She wanted to stay longer, but if she relaxed any more, she'd fall asleep on her feet. She put on her last clean set of everything—underwear, jeans, blouse and socks. The dirty ones went back into the bag. She looked in the mirror. Her eyes looked hollow, but at least she was clean. It would have to do.

The smell of good ol' American hamburgers led her to the kitchen as Claire placed the last dish on the table.

"Perfect timing," she said and waved a hand to indicate where Angie should sit.

Claire sat across the table and began talking. "Sorry for the cold shoulder Jodie gave you." Angie had a mouthful of hamburger and couldn't respond. "She's really a good person. She was being...um...overly protective. I hope you'll forgive her."

"I appreciate the explanation," Angie replied. "For a minute there, I thought I was back in Russia. That's the way they treat all Americans. Your kindness to me has more than made up for it." She was thoughtful for a moment. "You must care a lot about her."

"Yeah, we're BFF's—or *were* until a man came along." She seemed ready to say something else, but stopped. "That's all over now. I hope maybe we can get together again."

The conversation lagged to the point of becoming awkward. Claire seemed lost in her own thoughts. Angie hurriedly finished her hamburger and carried her dish to the sink.

"That really hit the spot, Claire. Thanks. I didn't realize how hungry I was."

"I'm glad you enjoyed it. Ready to hit the road?"

"Yeah. I think I've even got enough energy to get excited again."

Claire headed down the road as if she knew where she was going. "Do you know where the mine is?" Angie asked.

"Yeah." Claire didn't elaborate, and Angie felt it best not to pry. They drove in silence.

Angie concentrated on watching the scenery. It was truly beautiful with the setting sun catching the tops of the rust and cream-colored rock formations, but she couldn't fully enjoy it. Claire was driving fast, and her brooding silence worried Angie. She hoped it wouldn't be much farther.

Finally they turned off the highway and drove

through a gate. Claire looked at Angie, then at the road. "I guess you're going to find out sooner or later, so I may as well tell you now," she said. "The man who came along was Duke—*your* Duke."

Angie stared at her. She finally realized that her mouth was open, so she shut it. "Oh," was all she could manage. The pieces of the puzzle began to fall into place.

The two women must have been fighting over him for months. No bimbos either. No wonder he didn't write.

The 'overprotective' explanation made sense now. Jodie'd been trying to shield Claire from having to face Angie. Yet Claire had volunteered to bring Angie to the mine. Wow! Either she was totally reconciled to losing Duke, or she was the most altruistic woman Angie had ever met. She did say '*your* Duke', though. *Is* he mine?

Angie was so absorbed in her thoughts that it surprised her when the truck stopped.

Lobo stood by a long trailer, bristling as they approached. "Do you know him?" Claire asked. "Or maybe I should ask—does he know you?"

"Yeah, it's okay." She turned to look at Claire. "I don't know how to thank you. This goes way beyond thanks."

Claire compressed her lips into a flat smile. She gave Angie a quick hug and looked uneasily at the trailer. Angie understood and got out quickly. Lobo approached on stiff legs as the pickup drove away.

"Hi, Wolf-man," Angie said in a squeaky voice. "Long time, no see." The wolf-dog snorted, sniffed, tentatively wagged his tail, then his whole body. Instead of coming to her, he ran—in big circles, howling at every bound. Finally he came, crawling, wiggling, whimpering. Angie dug her fingers into his mane and hugged him until he wriggled free.

She stood, wondering why Duke hadn't come out to see what the commotion was all about. No lights showed in the trailer, although a big pickup was parked nearby. She knocked on the door and waited. No one responded. She considered looking for him, but didn't know where to begin. Besides, it was beginning to get dark. She saw two black holes in the rock wall across the clearing. Mineshafts. No way was she going in either of them.

She tried the doorknob and found it unlocked. Lobo was on the little porch beside her, waiting to be let in. She opened the door.

"Duke?" There was no answer. Lobo trotted in, and Angie followed. "Duke?" she called again. "Where is he, boy? I'll bet you know."

The trailer was nicer than any she had been in before—hickory cabinets, stainless steel appliances, even granite countertops. She wanted to explore, but felt it would be improper, so she sat on the couch and massaged Lobo's ears.

The minutes ticked by, and Angie could no longer keep her eyes open. The marathon day—nearly *two* now—was going to end with or without Duke. She didn't know if or when Duke might return, and the one-sided conversation she had been carrying on with Lobo wasn't going to keep her awake.

She wheeled her carry-on luggage into the back room and noted with relief that the trailer had a bathroom. She undressed and then realized that she had nothing to sleep in. All of her other clothes were in the luggage stored at the airport in Phoenix. She opened the tiny closet opposite the bathroom to see if she could borrow something of Duke's to serve as a nightgown or pajamas. She found flannel shirts on hangers, but preferred something a little lighter. In the very bottom drawer, she found Duke's old basketball jersey. Perfect. She considered whether to leave him a note, but fell asleep before she could decide.

SURPRISE

EL CALVO MINE - JANUARY 8:

Duke woke in pitch-blackness. *Why is it so dark? Are we having more of that weird weather?* He straightened his legs, but didn't feel the wall of the trailer. *Oh.* He grinned to himself. He wasn't in the trailer. Last night was his first night sleeping in the mine.

Once the idea occurred to him, it had taken surprisingly little work to convert the mine's hollowed-out chambers into rooms with more space than his house in Haysville.

Today was move day—for everything in the trailer except furniture. Most of that was built in, anyway. He went into his new kitchen and started a pot of coffee, then back to the bathroom. *Really not much sense to shower this morning. I'll only get sweaty and dirty trekking back and forth.* Still, the thought of having a nice, big shower to stretch out in, instead of the tiny one in the trailer, was irresistible.

After the shower, he went back into the kitchen and poured a cup of coffee to sip while he made breakfast. *I think I'll fix a good one this morning. It's going to be a long day.*

He looked for his favorite frying pan, but it was still under the sink in the trailer. He'd have to go get it. *Oh, well, I want to check on Lobo and see if he stayed in his doghouse last night.*

He looked for the old shirt he planned to wear today and discovered that it, too, must be in the trailer, so he put on his loafers and headed for the vertical mineshaft. The air would be cold outside, but he could make it to the trailer without a shirt.

It was getting light as Duke stepped out of the lateral mineshaft. He sprinted for the trailer through the crisp morning air. When he opened the door, Lobo bounded out.

"Whoa, where'd you come from, boy? I could have sworn you were out when I closed up last night." Duke went in and quickly shut the door—it *was* cold out—and could have kicked himself for not bringing his hot cup of coffee.

Lobo barked to be let in. "Wow, that was quick. What are you doing back here? I figured I wouldn't see any more of you till feeding time this evening." Lobo merely thumped his tail a couple of times and lay his head on his paws like that was a normal part of their routine. Duke shrugged his shoulders. "As long as you don't get underfoot, you're welcome to help me with the move."

Duke found the frying pan and looked for anything else he might need for breakfast. His head was stuck in the storage area under the sink when a thump vibrated the trailer floor. Duke looked back to see what Lobo was doing. The dog looked at him, wagged his tail, and turned the other way. Duke had hardly turned back to the cabinets when he heard the toilet flush and footsteps. His pistol was in its holster hanging on the opposite wall. He was reaching for it when the bedroom door opened.

"You wouldn't really shoot me, would you?" Angie asked, backing up a step.

The voice was Angie's, but nothing else matched Duke's memories. She had long, curling hair now—jet black contrasting sharply with her nearly white skin. She was taller, her face fuller, and—. A flood of emotions nearly overwhelmed him. Not only was she a woman, she was a beautiful one.

"I...you...you're...." He gave up trying to talk and simply opened his arms to her.

Angie ran to him. He picked her up and hugged her tight. They held each other, savoring the moment. "I love you," they said simultaneously. Then they kissed, tentatively at first, then with enthusiasm. Duke felt a rising. He loosened his grip on her and hoped she wouldn't notice, but she pressed her body tightly against his and kissed him still more passionately.

"We need to slow down," he managed to get out.

"No we don't!" she countered. "I'm legal. I'm ready, and I love you!" Without waiting for him to react, she pulled the jersey over her head and pressed her small, firm breasts against his bare chest.

Duke was so shocked, he froze. *We can't do this. She's... I'm...*

Suddenly, Angie shoved away from him, spun around, and ran for the bedroom.

"Angie, are you okay?" Duke called after her. He picked up his basketball jersey. When he reached the door to the bedroom, he found her in bed with the sheet pulled up to her neck.

"No," she mumbled and covered her head. "I can't believe I did that."

Duke propped a pillow against the headboard and sat on the bed beside her. "Do you want this back?" He held up the jersey.

She lowered the sheet enough to peek out.

"My clothes," she said and nodded toward the small pile on the nightstand to his left.

He passed them to her, and she disappeared again, arms and elbows flailing beneath the sheet. When she reappeared, her face flushed red.

Duke grinned.

"It's not funny!" She swatted at him.

Duke held up both hands in surrender, but continued grinning.

Hunger drove them from the trailer. Duke, still bare-chested, grasped his shirt and skillet in one hand and Angie's hand in the other. Lobo ran back and forth between them and the mine entrance. About halfway into the mineshaft, Duke stopped and shook out his shirt.

"Do you trust me?"

"Yeeesss." Her hesitation communicated as much as her answer. "What are you going to do?"

"Blindfold you. I like the mood you're in, and there are a lot of…uh…surprises inside the mine that might be distracting."

Duke kissed her and draped his shirt over her head, then brought the sleeves around front to tie in a loose knot. He led her forward several more feet, then stopped.

"Here, hold the skillet and put your arms around me," he instructed.

Angie complied. Duke lifted her and squeezed her close as he stepped into the slight drop-off where the horizontal and vertical mineshafts intersected. Once at the living level, he walked her through a short tunnel into a

domed room divided by a wooden partition. There, he un-
wrapped the shirt from her head.

"Where are we?" Angie asked, as she turned in a circle,
eyeing the rough sandstone walls and the sparse bedroom
furniture the room contained.

"Inside the mine," Duke replied. "I told you there were
surprises. Gramp's company used this place to test drilling and mining equipment. It's riddled with tunnels and
hollowed-out chambers like this one. I built some walls and
made some other changes so I could live inside. This is my
bedroom," he explained, waving an arm around the room.
"There's a bathroom through that door, this tunnel goes
to the kitchen, and there are more rooms on other levels.
Come sit with me while I make us some breakfast."

After breakfast, they went back into the bedroom and
lay on the bed while their meal settled. They lounged side
by side, leaning back on pillows propped against the headboard. She took one of his hands and stroked the fingers.
"Shouldn't you be preparing today's message to Earth or
something?"

Duke jerked upright. "How long have you known?"

"Oh, my God, Duke!" Angie spun around to face him.
"It *is* you. I was just making a wild guess. I mean…the circle
and the raindrop—that *had* to be you, 'cause it's just like
we talked about before I went to Russia. But *how*? I mean…
whose satellite are you using, and how do you get it to send
the laser signals?" She stared at him, wide-eyed.

"It's…uh…not a satellite," Duke admitted sheepishly.
"I guess you'd have to call it a signal craft, since that's about
all it can do. I named it *Tetra*, because the framework is a

tetrahedron."

Angie sucked in a breath. "You mean you *made* it? But...but who launched it for you? And how did you make it hover when the signals started?" Angie demanded, facing him with a frown.

"It's self-propelled."

"*Self*-propelled? No way! It couldn't ..."

Duke held up a hand, interrupting her. "Angie, I... uh...made a discovery—a big one. The best way to ease the shock would be to have you review the recordings I made of all my experiments, but that'd take days. How about if I just show you?"

He led her to the mine's central shaft. The sun was high overhead. Light bounced from side to side down the shaft and accented the grooves made by the original rotary drill. A three-inch galvanized iron pipe ran down its center with bright orange ribbons fluttering at each pipe joint. Light fixtures attached to an electrical conduit dotted the shaft from top to bottom. A strong swirling wind buffeted them as they approached the landing ledge.

"You remember when I brought you in from the trailer and covered your head 'cause I didn't want any distractions?" Duke asked.

"I had something else on my mind." She grinned. "But yeah, I remember."

"Well, this was the distraction—or maybe I should say the first of several. This is what I call the Leap of Faith."

Angie peered down over the edge. The bottom of the shaft was more than seventy-five feet below the landing where she stood.

"Yes, I'd say that would have been a distraction. Is the

pipe to slide down in an emergency?"

"No. It's the only way in and out."

Angie frowned. "Duke, I may have had your shirt covering my eyes, but you didn't shinny up that pole with me in your arms."

"No, I didn't."

Angie's scream echoed up and down the shaft as Duke casually stepped off the landing and *floated* to the pipe. He caught it with one hand, allowed himself to slowly pivot around the pipe, let go, and drifted back to land at Angie's feet. "*That's* the distracting part."

Angie's eyes were open nearly as wide as her mouth. Before she could react, Duke grabbed her by the waist and stepped off again, catching the pipe as before. "It takes a little getting used to." He held her with one hand and effortlessly pulled them upward with the other, until they were even with the next landing. "The only trick is to be sure your feet are under you when you land." He pushed off from the pipe, and they drifted slowly toward the ledge. "Step onto the landing like you're getting off an escalator," he instructed.

Angie got her feet under her all right, but her legs buckled. Duke held her up and helped her walk through the archway. As soon as she could stand, she let go of him and hit him hard on the arm. "If you made me wet my last clean pair of undies, you're going to be doing my laundry by hand, Mister!" She hit him again. "Duke, that *scared* me. I thought you were falling!"

He hugged her close—as much to keep her from hitting him as to calm her. "I'm sorry, Angie. I tried to think of some way to prepare you for that—to somehow explain it in words, but I don't think it can be done. You have to experience it."

Duke led her into a small chamber he used as a library, where they found a comfortable sofa. Store-bought bookcases lined one sector of the room, and a whiteboard was propped on an easel nearby. A rough-hewn cedar plank table with a glass top and a small desk with a laptop were the only other furnishings, except for a colorfully patterned cowhide on the floor.

Angie sat without speaking for a moment, then took a deep breath and let it out. "Duke, I...I ..." She spread her hands. "I don't even know what question to ask. You said that was the first of *several* distractions. Can we wait a while for the rest of them? I may die of curiosity, but at least I won't die of fright." She crawled over to sit in his lap and rested her head on his shoulder.

Duke held her tenderly and kissed her hair, feeling ashamed. "That's the only real scare, and I'll explain it in a little bit, I promise. The rest of the surprises are nice ones mostly, and yes, they can wait." He held her quietly for several minutes until he felt her stir in his arms.

"I think I'm okay now. Can we do something ordinary, like talk to Earth from outer space?"

Duke smiled, relieved that she was recovered enough to show a sense of humor. "Okay. Let's go play alien," he said.

Duke took her hand and led her through an archway to the largest room in the mine. It was circular with a hemispherical dome like all of the other rooms, but *big*. The tiny sounds their shoes made on the floor echoed in the cathedral-like silence. Angie sucked in her breath. "Oh, it's beautiful!"

A stadium-size television screen high on the opposite wall carried a live picture of Earth from the signal craft's camera. The Southwestern U.S. filled the screen in varying shades of green and brown with the Eastern Pacific and Gulf of California contrasting in dark indigo blue. A dazzling white spiral swirled over the Northwest, curled up into Eastern Montana, then dove down over the plains to disappear off the right side of the screen.

"It's like my dream has come true. It's so real, I feel like I'm actually out there." Her eyes glistened with emotion.

"I know," Duke said. "Sometimes I come up here to sit and stare. It can be hypnotizing, especially if I have the sound turned on."

"What do you listen to?"

"Space. Each corner of my signal craft has wide-range receivers that pick up any electromagnetic waves. I convert them into audible frequencies. Mostly it sounds like a waterfall or wind in the trees, but once in a while, I hear something even more interesting. Radar sounds like someone playing a note on a cello. The laser beams from Kitt Peak make really piercing tones, so I normally keep the sound off. We can listen later. Here, take a seat. I'm going to make this a short conversation. You can watch."

Several folding tables were arranged in a curve, all facing the giant screen. Each table had a low-intensity lamp, a computer monitor and keyboard, and an assortment of other equipment on or under the table. Dozens of cables crisscrossed the floor to racks of electronic equipment against the far wall under the screen. The room was dark except for the light from the screen, which gave the effect of a clear night under a full moon.

Duke wheeled another chair over from an adjacent table for himself. The monitor lit up as soon as he touched the mouse. A scrollable column on the right of the screen contained vocabulary icons and text descriptions. The left side of the window was empty except for a simple tool bar that ran across the top. Duke scrolled through the vocabulary list, dragging and dropping icons onto the screen. He talked as he worked.

"The tetrahedron is our signal craft—that's how I came up with the name *Tetra* for it. The sine wave means 'communication', and the icon for Earth is self-explanatory. The double-ended pointers mean 'two-way'. By putting the whole set of icons inside a circle or oval, it shows that they function as a unit. The modifier I'm attaching to the equal sign means 'twelve days', and this icon means 'null'. So what did I say?"

The question took her by surprise. She'd been gawking at the room and the display, still dumbfounded by the discovery that it was Duke who'd been sending the signals. It took her a minute to study the monitor.

"Um…two-way communication…between *Tetra* and Earth—hey, I think I get it—is null for twelve days, right?"

"Perfect."

"I speak alien!" She grinned. "Does that mean we're on vacation?"

"Sort of. We're still going to be busy, but at least we won't have to worry about coming back to talk every night."

Duke stored the pictogram and began assembling another. "They'll want to know why," he explained. He dropped a tetrahedron, an asterisk beside it, and another asterisk far to the right. "This is me, and this is you," he said, pointing to the two asterisks. He stored the frame and constructed another one similar to the last, but with the two asterisks side-by-side and pointers coming from their original positions.

"So, that's it? No acknowledgement or anything?"

"Oh, I haven't sent the messages yet. Yeah, we have protocol signals that go back and forth to verify that we're communicating correctly. Watch. I'm sending them now."

The vocabulary window closed, and an event log window opened in its place. The first pictogram appeared on the screen, and a line appeared in the log window. In rapid succession, the second and third pictograms were displayed and corresponding entries made in the log.

"Now we're done," Duke said.

Angie frowned. "Don't you have to wait for their response? What if they say something back?"

"Nope. I've become a real S.O.B. lately. When the NSA showed up at Kitt Peak, they started trying to control the conversation. I developed a piece of hardware for them once and had to get a full security clearance before they would even tell me what they wanted. They trust no one but themselves and sometimes not *even* themselves. My way of dealing with their questions now is to ignore them. I respond only when we're developing new vocabulary icons and they need clarification."

A new pictogram appeared. "See what I mean?" Duke said. "They're asking how many of us there are and where we are meeting. That's an NSA question. Dr. Coleman always gives information first before asking for information in return."

Duke pushed away from the table. "I record everything they send, so we can review it later. I'm hungry. Are you up to taking the leap again?"

"Omigod. I can't believe I forgot about that. No. Duke, you have to tell me what's going on. Now."

"I already promised I would, but not now—after dinner, downstairs."

Angie wasn't sure she could wait that long, nor the least bit certain she could face that shaft again.

NEW PHYSICS

Duke led her out to the landing. "Aim slightly to the left of the pipe and step off with only a small amount of momentum." He made the jump and pivoted around the pipe, showing her how. "I know it's scary, but it's safe. Pretend you're in a space station with zero gravity. I'll catch you."

Her eyes said no, her body said no, and logic said no, yet there was Duke casually floating in front of her, grinning, damn him. No, she didn't mean that, but he *was* daring her. She couldn't let him see her chicken out.

She shut her eyes, let out a whoop, and stepped off. Immediately, her shirttail flew up into her face, blinding her, and she felt the wind whistling up past her body. She was *falling*!

"D-u-u-u-k-e," she screamed.

"I gotcha."

Strangely, his voice sounded nearby, not receding in the distance. Was he falling too? She clawed the shirttail from her face and found...the two of them hovering in the middle of the shaft even with the landing she'd just abandoned.

"But I was *falling*! I *felt* it," she wailed. Her heart was still racing.

"You just felt the wind that flows up the shaft when the lifting force is working," Duke explained. "If your eyes hadn't been covered, you would've seen you were okay."

"Omigod, Duke, that's the scariest thing I've ever done in my life! I mean…you may know what's holding us up, but *I* don't. Wow, did you ever give it the right name. Leap of Faith, indeed!"

She hung on to Duke firmly as he impelled them downward, toward the living level. Her heart rate began to return to normal. Now that some of the fear was gone, it was actually fun, in a thrill-ride sort of way.

"All right, hang onto the pole, and I'll show you how to get back." Duke waited for her to position herself where she could watch. "Press your back against the pole, then put your hands behind you at your center of gravity. That way, when you push off from the pipe, you won't be off balance at the landing. Push hard enough to carry some momentum into the landing," he added. "Like this."

Angie experimented by pushing and pulling on the pipe until she felt satisfied she had her hands in the right spot. "Ready or not—," she said as she shoved off. She landed perfectly and steadied herself on Duke's arm.

"You'll be happy to know that I've ordered a spiral staircase that should arrive any day now. It will only take a few days to assemble it," Duke told her.

"It's a good thing you didn't tell me that earlier. I might have waited up there until it was installed." She felt Duke pull her close as they walked toward the kitchen for their late meal. It reminded her there was a decision to be made before bedtime.

After dinner they sat on the couch in the living room. Duke had left the chamber unmodified except for lighting. Halogen lamps aimed at the domed ceiling highlighted interesting color variations in the sandstone layers and filled the room with a warm glow. Angie was thinking about snuggling and almost misinterpreted Duke when he said, "Ready?" He meant to talk...about weightlessness. She sighed and sat up. He did say 'after dinner'.

The romantic moment faded, and suddenly she *was* ready. Whatever held them up out there, she wanted to know, and she wanted to know now.

"Yes," she answered, "I don't think I can stand it much longer. I have to know what's going on, but I'm almost afraid to ask any more questions."

"All right, but there are no more Leaps of Faith, so set your own pace."

"Okay, then. That's my first question. I don't know whether to ask 'how' or 'what', so explain the Leap of Faith in twenty-five words or less."

Duke laughed. "More like twenty-five *volumes* or less. I didn't take nearly enough physics in school. Forgive me if I gloss over a few of the finer details of the Grand Unification Theorem or whatever they're calling it these days."

"Oh, yeah, right...like *I* would notice. Seriously, Duke, you're not going to get into anything that deep are you?"

"Yes and no. No, because it's way over my head. I couldn't if I wanted to. But yes, I think this goes that deep. I think another fundamental force of nature exists that no one knew about."

Based on Duke's experiments, he had concluded that the Earth was immersed in some kind of energy field. He called it the Genesis field. He knew next to nothing about it other than that it was there, and it was incredibly powerful. He had discovered how to open a 'window' that allowed some of the energy in the field to be converted to a force.

He named it the An-G force—An-G for her, but also An-G
for anti-gravity in case that was what it turned out to be. He
didn't really think it *was* anti-gravity—not in the sense of
being the opposite of gravity, anyway. He just knew it was
a repelling force—but it was everything the science fiction
writers said anti-gravity would be, and more. The 'more'
part was both unbelievably wonderful and scary as Hell.

Duke paused. "That's over twenty-five words, but I
was rambling part of the time. Do you want me to go on?"

"Omigod, Duke! Omigod, omigod, omigod!" She
grabbed him by the arms and shook him. "You've discovered anti-gravity, and you ask if I want you to go on?" He
just grinned. She released him, embarrassed at her emotional outburst, but pleased that he had named the force after
her. Anti-gravity and apparently *controllable* anti-gravity!
The possibilities swirled in her mind, and with each characteristic Duke revealed, the potential became overwhelming.

First, the force didn't travel at the speed of light. It
appeared to be instantaneous. She thought about what that
meant. The An-G force would allow humankind to go to
the stars, and when they got there, they'd be able to talk to
each other real-time—no light-speed delays.

The next property was more astounding yet. There
was *no* reactive force. Newton's third law *did not apply!* Angie had a hard time accepting that, and Duke said he did
too, but if it was true, look what it would give them. They
could virtually pull themselves up by their bootstraps. A
spaceship could propel itself without throwing mass in the
opposite direction.

Angie drifted off for a moment. She was 'out there'—
on one of those spaceships—living her dream. Duke picked

up her hand and kissed it, bringing her back to reality. "We're halfway done," he said. "Stick with me."

It was hard—new ideas kept bubbling up in her mind, but she forced herself to pay attention as Duke continued.

"I already mentioned that the Genesis field is phenomenally powerful," he said, "and that the An-G force is the part that comes through the window. The incredible thing about that relationship is the trivial amount of energy required to open the window. It's like getting something for nothing. So back to our spaceship example—we can go to the Moon using the power of flashlight batteries."

"Batteries? You've got to be kidding!"

"No, I'm not, and that's what makes this discovery so scary and a lot more wonderful and horrible than atomic energy."

The raw materials and technology required to make a force generator were readily available and easily affordable. Anyone could do it—good guys *and* bad guys. On the positive side, that meant that everyone on Earth—or off it—could have all the power they needed to do anything they wanted. On the negative side, it meant that a five-year old could play with an An-G generator and accidentally knock the Moon out of its orbit. A terrorist could make one and level a city or a mountain in seconds.

It took Angie a moment to absorb the full significance of his revelation—the myriad possibilities the discovery offered, but the staggering magnitude of the dangers as well.

"How long have you been carrying *that* load?" she asked.

"You remember the newspaper clipping I sent you about the earthquake in Haysville? That was me. I blew a hole in my garage floor three days after you left for Russia."

She put her arms around him and laid her head on his chest. "I wish I could have been here with you."

He kissed the top of her head. "You'll never know how many times I wished the same thing."

Angie sat up and turned to face him. Maybe he *had* wished it, but he'd never mentioned it in any of his cards. Then there was Claire—'possibly *the* woman'. Duke hadn't dumped her. Claire dumped him. Angie knew it would ruin the romantic moment to mention those things, but bedtime was approaching. She had to be sure she wouldn't just become the latest in his long line of conquests.

Duke must have seen the uncertainty in her expression. He first hung his head, then looked at her, speaking quietly. "Angie, I love you. I didn't realize—was too dumb to see—that I loved you the way I'm *supposed* to love you— with a love that doesn't depend on sex. Gramp told me to find a woman who shared my interests. If one of them was sex, great, but it shouldn't be the only one. You're the one I want to share my life with. Now that you're a woman, I hope that means we can share sex, too, but if you're not ready—if you think *I'm* not ready, I can wait."

Angie had such a lump in her throat, she could hardly talk. "Duke, I've wanted to make love with you for years— even before I became a woman. I want it now, but I scared myself this morning. I'm new at being a woman. You're new at knowing what love is. We need to be sure we're both ready."

"How will we know?" he asked.

"I can't promise we *will* know, but I think we need to spend some time together before we make any big decisions. Mamma thinks I'm still in Russia. I need to let her know where I am and what has happened—not the discovery, but between the two of us. Until then, would you consider letting me sleep with you, but not having sex just yet?"

Duke took so long to answer, she thought he might say no, but he finally nodded. "If I can't do that, then I guess it would show I'm not ready. I just hope you have some pajamas that cover more than my basketball jersey did."

Angie grinned and kissed him.

TOGETHER

EL CALVO MINE - JANUARY 9, 2011:

Duke awoke with a soft body pressed against his back and fingers playing with the hair on his chest. He wanted to respond, but couldn't. This time the migraine had a running head start. He whispered her name and hoped he wouldn't have to raise his voice. "Angie...migraine. Green bottle in medicine cabinet."

He felt her hand withdraw from his chest, then squeeze his shoulder. The sheets moved, but the bed did not. Angie returned quickly with the pills and a glass of water.

"I'm here," she whispered. He still had his eyes shut.

Duke slowly pushed himself up enough to prop one elbow underneath and reach for the glass with the other hand.

"I'll be out at least two hours," he rasped. "Don't jump if the lights are flashing."

Angie took his free hand and helped lower him back on the bed. Duke felt a light kiss, heard her withdraw, then curled into a fetal position.

Duke sat at the breakfast table, still light-headed and woozy, but no longer in pain.

"They started a few weeks after you left for Russia. I guess that was when I began to realize the magnitude of the discovery I'd made. Once I learned enough about the force to control it, then the headaches decreased. This is the first one I've had in a couple of months."

Angie took his hand in hers. "I had one once, but one is way too many. Did I bring it on?"

"I'm sure they're stress related, but having you here is anything but stressful. No, I think talking about the discovery may have caused it. I try not to dwell on the dangers and the responsibility, but it's unavoidable. I also think that one reason I got the migraines was because I *didn't* have anyone to share this with. Now that you're here and I have someone to talk to, I hope the headaches go away."

"I hope so, too. I hate feeling so powerless to help. How do you feel now?"

"I'm wiped out, but the pain is gone. I thought maybe we could take it easy today—go up to the control room and catch up on each other's lives."

"Is it okay to jump now? I saw the lights flashing earlier. What's that all about?"

"The lights flash when the An-G force falls below a certain level. The orange ribbons on the pipe show the same thing. If there's no lift force, then there won't be any wind, and the ribbons will hang down."

"Yikes! You mean that sometimes you get the elevator and sometimes you get the shaft?"

Duke chuckled. "Sort of," he admitted, "but it's very predictable, and it doesn't last very long. It has to do with the Genesis field. When the window is aligned exactly parallel to it, we can't tap into its force—same as a sail edgewise to the wind. The sine of zero is zero. That happens twice a day due to the rotation of the Earth. You'll get familiar with the cycle like a sailor does with the tides."

"Okay, let's change the subject for a while," Angie suggested. "I want to know how in the world you got all of this done in the short time I was gone." She waved an arm over her head.

"Well, in the first place, you were gone for a good part of two years, so it wasn't exactly a short time. The mine was already hollowed out. All I did was build a few partitions and run some wires and pipes. The furniture, I bought. Everything else I had built offsite in modules. You've already seen how easy it is to get things up and down the shaft, so it was only a matter of reassembling the modules. Same thing with the control room—the big screen is made up of several smaller screens. I know more about electronics than the service technicians do, so I hooked it up myself. Really, the only thing that took a lot of time was building the *Tetra*, and that was more fun than work."

"I'm still impressed," Angie replied, "and a whole lot jealous."

Duke pulled her to him. "I think the most stressful part of all was not being able to share it with you."

EXPLOSION

After three weeks of nightly conversations with Kitt Peak, Duke was getting frustrated and bored. He enjoyed the sessions when he and Dr. Coleman were developing new vocabulary, but too often now, the NSA took over the conversation, even demanding they identify themselves.

Angie was bored, too. She sat on the couch, eyes half-closed, listening to the sounds of space. "Duke, I think I hear radar. You said it sounds like a cello, right? I thought I might have heard it earlier, but it was too faint to be sure."

Duke wheeled his chair to the monitor showing the event log. A random whisper of radar was fine. Multiple hits meant someone was searching—probably for *Tetra* or at least for the source of the signals. *Tetra* had so little metal in it, Duke was confident it could not be detected except at short range. The faint groan suggested it was far away, but that could easily change.

"Good catch, Angie. It *is* radar. The triangulation algorithm says it's coming from somewhere below and to the southwest of *Tetra*'s position. How long ago did you hear it the first time?"

"Before you first started signaling—about an hour and a half ago."

He scrolled the log back until he found the timestamps for the right period.

"Wow! You must have good ears. That's interesting.

That time it came from below and to the south of *Tetra*, but each successive ping came from a more northeasterly direction. What do you make of that?"

Angie rose and stood behind his chair, draping her arms over his shoulders.

"I don't know nothin' about this stuff. I thought you sent me to Russia for a vacation. I didn't know you wanted me to *learn* anything."

Duke reached behind his head and pulled her hair.

"Okay, okay. Beast! I think someone or something is in a low Earth orbit. The only logical guess would be the Russians. Their orbital plane would be tilted about fifty degrees with respect to the equator. Their last orbit must have been to the east of *Tetra*'s position. If they're southwest of there now, then they'll probably pass directly underneath it. Satisfied?" She pulled *his* hair.

"No. How low is low, and what can they do from that altitude?" Duke's voice was suddenly no-nonsense. He didn't know much about spacecraft, but if one was orbiting directly below *Tetra* and painting it with radar, it meant they had company.

"A low Earth orbit is usually two- to three hundred kilometers," Angie told him, "and if they were going to do anything, they've already done it."

"What do you mean?"

"If they wanted to put something up in a geosynchronous orbit close to *Tetra*, they would have had to launch it into a Hohmann transfer orbit when they were about a hundred degrees west of there."

"If they did launch something, how long would it take to reach *Tetra*?"

"It depends on their altitude, but a Hohmann transfer typically takes a little less than five and a half hours."

"How long ago would they have been a hundred degrees west of there?"

Seconds ticked by while Angie thought. "A little less than five and a half hours."

Both of them looked up at the screen. Duke half expected to see another vehicle floating nearby. He hesitated to turn the camera to look east and west. As he reached for the camera's joystick, a light flared far below, and the speakers hissed briefly.

Duke checked the coordinates in the event log. "Southwest. That was too brief and too big to be an engine burn. I think something exploded."

"Duke." Angie grabbed his arm. "The radar stopped!"

That piece of news was welcome, but it could mean someone was in trouble.

"All right. Let's get *Tetra* down to the site of the explosion as quickly as we can. I don't know what we can do once we get there, but if it was a manned vehicle, maybe we can do something. I'm going to need your help."

"What can I do?" Angie asked.

"I need to know where 'there' is. What is their orbital trajectory? All we've got to go on is where they were when they hit us with radar pulses and where the explosion took place. I need your best guess for the orientation of their orbital plane and their altitude."

"Yikes! This is worse than any final exam Colonel Belarov would have given us. Okay, I need to run down to my trunk. We worked with real examples in class, so I've got the location of the launch site on my laptop, and if they're using the *Buran II*, then I've got several examples of orbital parameters. I'll be right back." Angie headed for the central shaft while Duke scrolled through the event log to retrieve the data for the radar beams and the explosion.

Angie and Duke watched the screen as the *Tetra* pitched downward, aiming toward the point where Angie estimated the vehicle's orbit crossed the equator. The screen was large enough that the movement of the background of stars caused a mild feeling of vertigo intensified by the sounds moving from one speaker to another.

B-b-baw! B-b-baw! B-b-baw!

Staccato cello notes blasted from four speakers in rapid succession. Radar...and close!

Duke reached for the joystick and rotated the craft. Something glinted in the sun less than a kilometer away. He zoomed in. A vehicle, more engine than payload, slowly yawed broadside. Stubby arms stuck out on opposing sides, a rotating disk on one, a cylindrical tube on the other. The cello notes coincided with the rotation of the disk. The tube began turning in *Tetra*'s direction as they watched.

Duke lunged for the keyboard and typed furiously, then grabbed the joystick and centered the other vehicle on the screen. A very loud, very brief squawk came from one of the speakers, and a puff of dirty brown vapor drifted across the screen, dissipating into nothingness.

Angie watched, eyes wide, as the other vehicle disintegrated. Its center simply disappeared—wasn't there anymore. The fore and aft sections flew into pieces. Many spun so fast they were blurred.

"Well, I got it," Duke said, "but it got us, too." He

shook his head.

"What do you mean? *Tetra*'s still there. It's still sending pictures."

"That brown cloud that went across the screen means that something on *Tetra* got vaporized. As long as the camera works, we may be able to see what was hit."

Duke sat down heavily. "That was a close call. They must have just activated it, otherwise we would have heard the radar before."

"I watched the whole thing, but I still have to ask what happened. Was that what I think it was?" Angie asked. She stared at the screen.

"Some kind of beam weapon," Duke answered. "A laser, I'd guess."

"And how did you make *that* happen?" She waved an arm at the screen.

"There's a maneuverable thrust disk mounted on the front of the craft. I aimed it the same direction as the camera and gave it a blast of undiluted An-G."

"I'm not sure I like the way you worded that." She raised an eyebrow.

"Any way you spell it, An-G is a force to be reckoned with." He grinned and kissed her before she could react. "Let's see how badly we're hurt. I'd still like to see what that explosion was all about."

"Yeah, me too. What can I do?"

"I'm going to run some system tests that should take five to ten minutes. Can you figure out where we've coasted to and program a new trajectory to intercept the shuttle's orbit—if that's what it was?"

"Right. Don't know where we are. Don't know where

we're going. Be ready in five minutes. Men!" She gave him a dirty look.

He patted her butt as she headed for the other table.

The damage assessment didn't take long. They lost the E-M sensor and two turning thrust disks on one cluster, and the camera's focus was stuck on infinity. Without being able to focus up close, Duke couldn't examine the damage in much detail. He had built in redundancy, so they could fly with only three clusters. He flagged the components as inactive so the computer would ignore them. Angie had a new thrust program ready—on time. She stressed the last two words.

"You're just good." Duke grinned at her.

"Yes, I am! Colonel Belarov said so, too." She held her head in a regal pose.

"As soon as we reach their orbital plane, we'll start accelerating to match velocities. Keep your eyes peeled for debris. The explosion undoubtedly knocked some of it into a different trajectory."

"What should I do if I see something?" Angie asked.

"If you want to stop the thrust program, push this button. That will put the craft back in manual mode. We'll have to fly back to the site of the explosion manually. I'd better show you how, so you can back me up when things get busy."

Duke wheeled his chair over to the center table. On the right was the roll-pitch-yaw control. For roll and pitch, it functioned like a joystick. For yaw, turn the knob on top. The left control was for linear motion—forward, backward and sideways with the stick; up and down by twisting the knob. Duke normally flew so the thrust was along the line-of-sight. Simply aim the camera. What you saw was where you went—more or less. The distance readout was in meters and it wasn't very accurate.

"So once I get it aimed right, all I have to do is push this forward, right?"

"Right, but there's one other complication—you can't fly perpendicular to the Genesis field. When the thrust disks are parallel to the field, there's no force."

"What do I do if I need to go in that direction?"

"You tack, like a sailboat trying to go upwind. You zig and then you zag. It's sort of ironic. We've got anti-gravity technology, but we still have to rely on centuries-old sailing skills to utilize it.

"I'm going to tie a microphone into the system so we can talk once *Tetra* gets there."

Duke carefully stepped across the center of the control room where cables crisscrossed the floor. He unrolled a new cable and attached it to the console where Angie sat. "I tried this once earlier. Before I made up my mind to send the laser signals, I had some crazy ideas about making a talking flying saucer or something. Then I remembered how we used to talk about how another intelligence might communicate with humans and decided to try that instead."

"How can you talk to the shuttle with no air to carry the sound?"

"I'm tying the microphone into the same thrust disk that I used on the laser weapon. It'll make the thrust force vibrate, much more gently, of course, so anything within the force field will vibrate, too. The shuttle may be open to vacuum, but if someone has a suit on, the air in the suit will vibrate, and they will be able to hear us."

Angie was watching Duke work underneath the big screen to connect the cable when a bright light flashed, and she let out a yelp. Duke twisted around to look up.

"What happened?" he asked as he carefully stepped his way back to the table.

"We almost hit something. It went by too fast to see what it was, but it was big! I stopped the thrust program."

Duke went to another table to review the video while Angie maneuvered the craft back to the explosion site. The replay only showed a blur. All they could tell in slow motion was that it was moving up. Angie rotated the craft to see if it was still in camera range and sucked in her breath.

"Duke, omigod, look at that! It *is* the *Buran II* and it's cut in half!" She struggled to stabilize the camera.

The shuttle's cargo bay appeared to have taken a direct hit. The tail section was spinning rapidly, although the cabin's tumble was much slower. That was good. It meant the cabin might not have taken too much of a jolt. Someone inside could have survived.

"See if you can match trajectories without getting too close," Duke instructed. "We may need to avoid some debris."

"How close do we need to be to talk with them?"

"We can talk from any distance, but if we're too close, the force field won't fan out enough to intersect the entire cabin. If anyone is in the part of the cabin we miss, then they won't hear us. Let's try from here. I'll take the controls. Your Russian is a lot better than mine, so you get to do the talking, all right?"

Angie felt a momentary flash of panic. That was a real spacecraft out there, and real people aboard. Duke was expecting *her* to talk to them. What was she supposed to say?

After worrying about it a while, it finally occurred to her that *anything* would sound good to someone in their position.

She took a deep breath to steady her nerves. They might think they were hallucinating, so she needed to make sure they understood it was real. If there were survivors, they might be injured. For sure they would be scared. She would start out by letting them know someone else was out there.

They would need to give some kind of signal that they heard her. A light would be best. Once they responded, she would have to lay the cards on the table. She didn't want to get their hopes up too high about being rescued. In fact, how *were* they going to rescue them?

"The *Tetra* isn't designed to hold people, is it, Duke?"

"No. It doesn't even hold air." Duke pulled a picture of *Tetra* out of the desk. The craft consisted of nothing more than an open tetrahedral framework with a camera and lasers and some electronics inside a sphere. Survivors would have to tie themselves to *Tetra*'s framework somehow, but air was the real problem. Angie had been thinking in terms of 'they' and 'them', but if more than one needed rescuing, she didn't see any way they could do it. The craft just wasn't big enough.

The sphere containing the camera and electronics was only about three feet in diameter. The framework was a tetrahedron with each leg a little over five feet long. The whole thing would fit in the back of Duke's pickup. He reminded her that he built it by himself. It had to be small, and he wanted to keep it as simple as possible so there would be fewer things to go wrong. Also, he didn't want it to be detectable by radar. That's what worried him the most. There was almost no metal in the framework—not even screws. It wasn't built to carry a load.

Angie rolled her chair to the side, and Duke moved over to take her place. The distance readout showed rapidly decreasing numbers, so he quickly aimed the craft to miss the shuttle if the momentum carried them too far. He made some final adjustments as Angie started speaking into the microphone, hoping they would understand her Russian.

"*Vnimaniye Buran. Vnimaniye Buran. Eto ryemyeslo svyazi Tetra,*" she said. Attention, *Buran*. Attention, *Buran*. This is the *Tetra* communication craft.

Angie clicked off the mike and turned. "Duke, can we move over to the left and forward a little so we're in the plane of their tumble? That way it will be easier to tell them where to look."

"Good idea. In fact, I might be able to stop their tumble from that position."

"Should I warn them so they can hang on to something?"

"Let's see if there's anyone to warn first. If we get a response, then we can try it. Any particular position you want to be in?"

Angie suggested directly below the shuttle. That way the background would be dark for them, and they would be able to see a light better.

Duke seemed to have trouble moving the craft and keeping the camera aimed at the same time. The gimbal-mounted camera had its own joystick for controlling its angular movement. After nearly losing sight of the shuttle two or three times, he finally brought the craft into position and steadied the camera.

"I think we're in position," he said. "How fast are they tumbling?"

Angie hadn't timed it, but guessed a couple of minutes per rotation.

"All right, let's give them a few rotations to signal us. Then we'll try something else."

Angie couldn't bear just sitting and waiting. She decided to keep calling and keyed the microphone again. "Attention, *Buran*. We are now in position directly below you. If you can hear us, please acknowledge by showing a light." Duke nodded his approval.

The nose of the shuttle rotated into sight, and Angie and Duke both leaned forward, straining to see a light. In spite of the dark background, it was going to be difficult. The skin of the shuttle was in full sunlight, the glare blinding. Angie heard some swear words coming from Duke as he tried to block some of the glare, handicapped by the camera's focus being stuck on infinity. She worried they might not be able to see a signal even if one was given.

Now that the *Tetra* was relatively stationary, adjusting the camera angle became easier. The six trapezoidal windows scrolled upward on the screen, but the rotation made it necessary to constantly turn the camera. The nose of the shuttle loomed suddenly and blocked the view of the windows. The first rotation was over.

The shuttle cabin turned a slow backward somersault. When the windows began to come into view again, Duke centered them on the screen. The bright shuttle skin shone above and below the windows, but the oblique angle lessened the glare somewhat.

"Do you want to watch the right windows, and I'll

take the left?" Angie asked.

"All right. I really don't expect anything this soon, though. It's been less than five minutes since we called them the first time. That's not very much time to respond, given the circumstances."

Duke tracked the windows quite well while the shuttle cabin was in its nose-approach part of the rotation, but as the nose began to point more and more toward the camera, the vertical motion accelerated rapidly. Abruptly the black nose rose up on the screen and blocked sight of the windows.

"Would you mind handling the camera while I move us in a little closer?" Duke asked. "Pick a target on the back of the cabin for practice," he said.

"How about that jagged piece on the right at the back of the cabin? It's about the same size as the windows, and it will be moving in about the same path."

Angie swung the camera slowly and decelerated as the target neared the center of the screen. Duke moved *Tetra* closer, filling the screen with what had once been part of the cargo bay skin. As the rotation brought more of the back of the cabin into view, they could see the protruding access hatch.

"Angie, can you line up on that?" Duke asked.

She moved the controls slightly, leaving a little angular drift to compensate for the cabin's rotation. Duke could see the hatch to the cargo bay. Its outer window was cracked, but still in place. There didn't seem to be much damage to the hatch itself. A tangle of wires, tubes, and twisted metal clung to the outer walls.

The window suddenly lit up. Both of them saw it at

the same time. Angie struggled to adjust the camera as the rotation was beginning to move the back of the cabin up off the screen.

"They must still have power inside!" Duke said. "That's too much light for a flashlight. Incredible!"

"There's something moving behind the window!" Angie screamed. "See it, Duke?"

He hardly had time to acknowledge when she let out a disappointed groan. It was only a reflection of the Earth and the clouds. "Rats!"

"Yeah, I think you're right. Nothing could be moving that fast inside the cabin."

The two of them sat dejectedly watching the rear of the cabin slowly rise on the screen. Angie stirred herself to adjust the camera as the hatch began to disappear from view.

"Duke, you said you might be able to stop the tumbling from this position. After this next rotation, can we try that? This sitting and waiting is getting to me."

"Yeah, I was thinking the same thing. All right, we'll give it one more turn. Here comes the nose."

Angie aimed at the brow of the cabin, which still hid the windows. As the windows rose in the screen, Angie caught her breath. Duke saw it, too. Neither one spoke, but they found each other's free hand and squeezed tightly. Someone in a spacesuit frantically waved a flashlight.

PASSENGER

Angie almost forgot to track the camera; she was so excited. The image of *Buran*'s nose looming on the huge screen made it feel as if she were riding on *Tetra* itself, not sitting in the comfort of Duke's control room. The cosmonaut waving from the window reminded her they had a job to do.

"Duke, can you take over here? I want to tell him we see him. What else should I say?"

"Tell him that we'll try to stop his tumble in a few minutes…uh, work out signals for him to answer 'yes' and 'no' and anything else you think you'll need. I think you'd better tell him not to get his hopes up too high. There are a lot of 'if's—*lots* of 'if's.'"

"Okay, here goes." She keyed the mike and switched to Russian, trembling with excitement.

"*Zdravstvuytye. Ya vizhu vi.*" Hello, there. I see you. There wasn't much time before he would rotate out of sight, so she hurriedly told him they were going to try to stop his tumble. He should raise his hand vertically if it was okay, put his hand out to the side if not. His hand went up.

"Okay, I'm losing sight of you, but I will keep talking. You need to secure yourself…," Angie turned to ask Duke, "where's best?"

"Toward the back of the cabin," Duke responded in Russian.

Angie repeated Duke's instructions in case his voice

didn't carry over the microphone. She warned the cosmonaut that they might not be able to help him much, but they would do everything they possibly could.

Duke nodded his approval. "I know that was hard for you to say. I don't like to think about it either, but we have to be honest with him. All right, I'm going to need your help again for a few minutes to get the camera aligned with the structure."

"Sure. What do you need?" she asked.

Duke asked her to aim at the center of the cabin and stabilize the motion. He needed to record the position so he would know where to turn after the camera was homed. Angie turned the camera toward the middle of the cabin and zeroed out the angular drift. Duke took the readings from the console display and wrote them on a pad.

"It's too hard to do this with the joystick," he told her, "so let me show you how from the keyboard."

He typed, C: R=0; P=0; Y=0.

"'R' is roll, 'P' is pitch, and 'Y' is yaw," he explained. "The 'C:' prefix indicates the commands are for the camera." He hit ENTER and the camera swung around, causing the stars on the big screen to swirl. Angie grabbed the edge of the table to steady herself.

When the motion stopped, Duke went to the computer keyboard and locked the camera, disabling its joystick as a precaution. Then he entered a few more commands and the readings from his note pad, and the computer rotated the entire craft back to the camera's original position with the cabin centered in the screen.

"Now, as soon as the nose gets perpendicular to us, I'm going to give it a push and see if we can stop the tumble."

Angie frowned. "I thought you said *Tetra*'s structure couldn't take much of a load. That thing must weigh several tons. How are you going to push it?"

Duke explained that he would be using the same thrust disk they were using to talk with. Newton was dead, he reminded her—no equal and opposite reaction. They wouldn't actually be in contact with the cabin when they pushed it. *Tetra* wouldn't feel any of the load.

Angie saw the nose rotating toward them. "Do you want me to give him a countdown?"

"Yeah, I'll begin in about fifteen seconds."

Angie rolled her chair back to the microphone and gave the cosmonaut a countdown. Duke touched the computer keyboard. No noise, no motion, or any other indication suggested anything was happening. The distance readout numbers decreased as the nose moved towards them, but the numbers also changed more and more slowly. Duke's hand poised over the keyboard. When the numbers held constant for an instant, he killed the thrust.

"All right, I'm going to move *Tetra* up in front of the windows so we can see him better. Ask him to join us. We can start asking questions."

"What do we need to know first?" she asked. The excitement was building again.

"Is he alone…uh, is he injured…how long will his air last? Better tell him now what our capabilities are so he can start thinking of ideas."

"What *are* our capabilities? I know we can push, but what else can we do?"

"Unfortunately that's about it—push hard, pull very lightly, talk, and watch."

"Well, maybe he'll have some ideas. Let's see." She switched back to Russian.

"Hello, again. We're moving closer so we can see you better. Would you come to the window again?"

He must have been moving already, because he appeared immediately. She could see him much more clearly now, so she instructed him to give her a 'thumbs up' for 'yes', a 'thumbs down' for 'no', and to put the back of his hand on his forehead for 'don't know'. They could work out more signals later.

"Is anyone else there with you?" she asked. Knowing the limitations of the craft now, she was afraid the answer might be 'yes', but he gave her a thumbs down.

"*Vi poluchili ranyeniya?*" Are you injured?

This time the answer was affirmative. Uh oh. She asked him to point to the injury, and he indicated his left forearm, then made a chopping motion.

"It's broken?"

Hand on forehead—he wasn't sure. Angie almost wished she hadn't asked. She felt helpless, knowing there was nothing she could do. She tried to think clearly—what was most important? Air. How much air did he have? The cosmonaut's hand moved to the box on his chest, but it was out of the camera's view. He held up one finger, then put his hand on his forehead, bending the finger in half.

"Are you saying that you have between a half-hour and an hour of air left? That doesn't make sense. You should have five or six hours at least. Do you have a leak?"

Thumbs up.

Angie caught her breath and looked at Duke.

"Ask him if he has any more air," he suggested.

The cosmonaut gave her a thumbs up, then a thumb and index finger held parallel—a little. Some of her anxiety dissipated.

"It had better be more than a little," Duke said. "There's no way we can get him down in less than an hour, even with continuous acceleration. Let him know what the status is, and let's see what options are available."

"Okay," Angie keyed the microphone and switched to Russian. "Here's the situation." She explained that the craft he could see was remotely controlled. It wasn't built to carry passengers or cargo. They could push hard with the thruster, but the craft itself was very fragile. The structure would probably break or pull apart if too heavy a load were attached to it.

What worried Angie the most was his air supply and its leak. She hadn't learned anything about spacesuits in her courses at MSU. Were the tanks built into the suit or portable? When she asked, he pointed to his back.

"Are you talking about your emergency air supply?"

Thumbs up.

"How long will it last?"

One finger, bent.

"A half-hour?"

Thumbs up.

Cold fingers ran down Angie's spine. They only had an hour and a half to get the cosmonaut down before he would suffocate. She shook her head slowly, glad that he couldn't see her. "I'll be right back. I'll have to do some calculations."

Angie worked on the calculator, fingers trembling. She frowned and worked some more. "Duke, I'm doing something wrong. This says we can get him down in less than a half-hour not counting the time to turn around in the middle. That can't be right, can it?" She was afraid to let herself hope.

Duke pointed out that she was used to thinking in terms of ballistics. Continuous thrust made a huge difference. He took the calculator and punched in the numbers. He got the same result, but that was only to get the cosmonaut straight down. *Tetra*'s orbital speed was nearly eight kilometers per second. They would have to reduce its circumferential speed to a reasonable number before entering the atmosphere, otherwise it would burn up due to friction. Duke went to get some atmospheric tables. He would figure out the minimum safe descent time, while Angie figured out how long the air would last based on the leakage rate. Hopefully Angie's number would be bigger than his.

Angie turned back to the microphone, only slightly relieved. "Okay, I'm back. It's going to take a little while to work out a safe transit time, since you'll have no protection. I'll be away from the microphone for several minutes, so don't panic." She turned away from the table.

While Duke drew a graph of air density versus altitude and tried different deceleration rates to see which ones would work best, Angie hurried down to the kitchen for drinks. Duke finished as she came back.

"How are you doing with the calculations?"

"I'm done. It turns out the limiting factor is the lack of aerodynamics. I figure that if we exceed a hundred miles per hour at low altitude, the wind will tear the camera off its gimbals. If we lose the camera, it's all over."

Angie turned as the screen showed movement. She

hurried over to the microphone. The cosmonaut waved his arm, obviously trying to get her attention. He made exaggerated motions to come closer, and then moved his arm in a big arc, ending with his hand behind his back.

"Are you saying for us to come around to the back of the cabin?"

Thumbs up several times. He didn't wait for an answer, but pushed away from the window into the darkness. A new problem? Or was his air leak a bigger problem than she had originally thought?

Duke rolled his chair over to the controls and nudged them to give the craft a little side and forward thrust and turned the yaw knob at the same time. The result was a very neat, if not perfect, semi-circular trajectory toward the back of the cabin.

"Oh, look!" Angie exclaimed.

The hatch gaped open, and the cosmonaut waited nearby, holding on to the hatch door. A small bag wrapped in mesh floated at the end of a tether attached to the shuttle.

"Wow! For a guy with only one good arm, he sure did a lot in a hurry," Angie remarked. "What's that he's got on the line?"

"That," Duke said with a big smile, "is the solution to our next problem. It looks like the kind of mesh bag they use to keep from drifting around when they sleep. If he's got another one, we can put the *Tetra* inside it and attach the ends to a tow line for him and his stuff."

Angie asked, and got another 'thumbs up'.

"Great! We think the net will distribute the load on the structure of our craft so that we can tow you. The only major question left is—how long will your air last?"

After pointing to himself, he held up one finger, bent.

"A half-hour left in your suit and a half-hour in the reserve tank?"

Thumbs up.

"Okay. That doesn't leave us much safety margin. Let's not waste any time. I'd like you to get two or three of those mesh bags if you have that many. We will want to put one or two around our craft and make a sling for you out of another. Picture a hot-air balloon, where our craft is the air bag and you are the basket."

He waved assent, disappeared through the hatch, and reappeared in less than a minute. Duke moved *Tetra* in close, carefully avoiding the torn and twisted remnants of the cargo bay. The cosmonaut would have to tie everything together.

"Tell him where the thrust disk is, Angie. If he gets out of its force field, you won't be able to talk to him."

Angie nodded and passed the information on. Duke was still adjusting the craft's position when the Russian unexpectedly jumped the short distance, knocking *Tetra* back and setting it spinning. Angie let out a yelp, and Duke grabbed the joystick to try to bring the gyrations under control. After several tense minutes, he finally stabilized *Tetra* and turned it slowly to find the shuttle cabin. Angie could tell from the sluggish response of the craft that the man still hung on.

"Whoa, that was intense!" Duke flexed his fingers and sagged in his chair. "Tell him we're going back to the hatch so he can get off. Gently, please. If he will tie one end of the mesh bag to the cabin with a little slack, then we can come in close, pick him up, and turn slowly to wrap the mesh around the *Tetra* and bring him right back to the starting point. Then he can attach his sling without having to move much."

Angie passed on the instructions while Duke inched *Tetra* closer to the hatch, but when they got there, nothing happened. She expected the craft to spin, at least slightly, when the man transferred to the shuttle cabin, but she perceived no motion.

"Maybe he's hanging on where he's out of the thrust field. He probably didn't hear anything I said."

"Or he can't pry himself loose," Duke suggested. "I imagine that spin gave him quite a scare. It did me. Let me get closer. I'll jiggle the craft to give him a hint. I'm going to have to unlock the camera so we can see him. I'll have to do it for the descent, anyway."

"Do you want me to work the camera?" Angie asked. As long as I don't have to track a moving target, I should be able to do it and talk, too."

Duke agreed. Working in close made him nervous. He didn't want to mash the man between their craft and the shuttle. Angie turned the camera slowly to see where the cosmonaut was.

"I think you're right, Duke. He's too close to see clearly, but it looks like he's got a death grip on the strut and he's facing this way. He probably doesn't realize the cabin is only a few feet behind him. Yaw the craft ninety degrees clockwise. Maybe he'll see it."

Duke turned the *Tetra* gently, stabilized it, and then jiggled the controls to vibrate it slightly. The cosmonaut stirred, but did not let go.

"I'm going to use the computer to move the craft in

closer. My hands are too shaky to use the joystick."

He typed instructions, and the *Tetra* moved in until the cabin drifted less than a foot from the man. At last he relaxed his grip on the strut and reached out to take hold of the shuttle. Angie followed him with the camera and then turned it to find the thrust disk.

"Duke, can you give me a very slow yaw left and a little pitch forward? As soon as he hears me, I'll want you to stop quickly."

He entered instructions into the computer and gave her a nod. She repeated, "Can you hear me? Can you hear me?" until she saw the 'thumbs up' signal. Duke stopped the motion, and they both breathed sighs of relief.

"That was pretty scary for us down here. I can only imagine what it must have been like for you. I wish we had time to give you a breather, but we've got to get busy. Here's the plan. Please don't do anything unexpected."

Angie repeated the instructions he had missed earlier, and he acknowledged with a 'thumbs up'. He worked slowly at first, but soon seemed to regain his confidence.

Angie was relieved to see that the mesh bags had snap hooks at each end. That bypassed a potentially serious problem of how to tie knots with only one good hand. With surprisingly little trouble, the cosmonaut attached two bags, end-to-end, secured them around the *Tetra*, and connected a third bag in which he would ride.

"We're short on time," Angie told him. "Let's make a test run. If everything checks out okay, we'll keep on going. Give me a signal as soon as you've got everything ready to go."

He waved acknowledgement, but didn't move immediately. When he turned and disappeared into the cabin, Angie looked from the screen to Duke and back, worrying how long he'd be gone.

"He must have thought of something else he needed," Duke said.

"I hope he hurries. We're running out of time. Oh, good," she said as he reappeared, carrying something too fuzzy to see clearly. He stuffed everything into his zippered bag, secured it with a bungee cord, and did a slow somersault into the netting.

"Let's get this show on the road," Duke said. "I'll start at about one tenth Gee to make sure everything pulls evenly, and I'll calculate the mass at the same time. Tell him we're ready when he is."

The Russian thrashed around in the mesh. He seemed unable to get situated, not so much because of his injured arm, but because of the lack of gravity. He was clearly getting frustrated. When Angie told him they were ready and asked him to give a signal when he was ready, he gave it immediately.

Duke showed her how to use the computer to apply the thrust so it would be precise and allow an accurate determination of the total mass. Angie moved the camera to watch the lines tighten up and to see how their passenger managed. The acceleration enabled the man to re-position himself much more easily, and he settled in for the ride.

"Everything looks good, Duke," Angie reported.

"Tell him we're going to full acceleration. I think it would be a good idea for him to go through a dry run, switching to the reserve tank now. I don't want to wait until we're miles away to find out he needs some tool we forgot."

Angie relayed the message, and Duke typed in more instructions. As the G-force increased, the mesh bags stretched, but did not seem in any danger of breaking.

"Okay, we're on our way. I'd like to get a better estimate of your leakage rate. Am I correct that the air in your suit should normally last at least six hours without a leak?"

Thumbs up. Five fingers, then two, then one, bent.

"Okay, seven and a half. How long were you on suit air before the explosion?"

Hand on forehead, then two fingers—two hours he estimated.

"Okay. Do whatever you can to slow the leak."

Angie managed to keep the panic out of her voice until she shut off the mike. "Duke, he's lost four hours' worth of air just since the explosion. If we don't get him down in the next fifteen minutes, it'll be too late!"

TIME IN A BOTTLE

Duke shared Angie's concern, but tried not to show it. She was doing a marvelous job handling the responsibility so far. The Russian's air supply was of profound importance, but it wasn't the only thing. Duke thought they could get the man *down* in time, but he had serious doubts about the circumferential velocity. A quick calculation showed they would have to go to five Gees to get him down vertically and slowed down horizontally all in fifteen minutes. The structure wouldn't take that kind of load—the net or the man either. They would have to think of something else.

"What else is there?" Angie asked. "All we can do is push and pull —" Suddenly her face lit up. "Duke! What about the moveable thrust disk? Can we push him with it like we did when we stopped the shuttle's tumble? It wouldn't put a load on the structure, right?"

"That's good thinking, Angie. I don't think we could do it exactly that way. It would be like balancing a spinning plate on a stick while running. But you've given me an idea how to accomplish the same thing. I'm going to cut the thrust. Tell him to work his way to the camera side of the craft."

As soon as the cosmonaut grasped the rear struts, Duke made his way across the room to the microphone jack. He returned to the control console before the Russian settled.

"I switched the microphone so we can direct it through the rear thrust disk. The thrust fans out in a cone, so the entire craft is within its force field. We can talk through it while it pushes the craft. As long as he stays within the strut triangle up front, he will be in the force field, too. See if he can hear you. I need to talk to him a minute."

Angie moved the camera until the screen showed the white blur of the cosmonaut's suit. She keyed the microphone. "Can you hear me? Wave your hand in front of the camera if you can."

He moved, but several seconds went by before his hand appeared.

"Okay, you're too close for us to see clearly. Wave your hand across the camera for 'no' and stick your thumb out for 'yes'. Make sure your hand is directly in front of the camera. I'm going to turn you over to my partner for additional instructions." She passed the microphone to Duke.

Duke told the Russian they would have to go to at least five Gees and explained that he and the craft were in a force field, so he wouldn't feel the acceleration—not the crushing weight, anyway. The thrust force fanned out in a cone. That meant that in addition to the linear thrust, it would have some radial vectors, too. Duke didn't think there'd be any danger, but it might not feel pleasant. He advised sitting as close to the center as possible with one leg on each side of the camera.

The star field on the big screen shifted, jiggled, and blanked out as the cosmonaut settled into position. Finally, a huge fist with a thumb appeared on the screen, with a very blurry torso and helmet in the background.

"I'm going to bring up the thrust gradually. Stop me if

it becomes painful, but we don't have much choice."

Duke counted off the Gee forces as the *Tetra* accelerated. He reached five with no signal from the Russian.

"That's it. Can you endure that for the next fifteen minutes?"

Thumbs up.

"Great! You'll get a brief break when we start decelerating vertically. Based on your leakage rate, that should be when you switch over to your reserve tank, too. Keep your suit pressure as low as you dare. Signal us if anything changes."

Duke pushed back from the table and took a deep breath. He looked at Angie, marveling at how many shocks had been thrown at her in the last few days and how readily she had absorbed them.

"Do you still want to be an astronaut?" he asked.

Angie looked at the big screen. "I know there are risks, but yes, that's what I want—more than ever, now. I don't think either one of us could accept leading an ordinary life."

"No," Duke agreed, "and as soon as we set this guy down, even ordinary people's lives are going to get some excitement."

"Speaking of that…what are we going to do with him when we get him down? We can't bring him here."

"No, absolutely not." Duke didn't want anyone else to see the craft. He thought it would be best to drop their passenger off at the outskirts of a city with a Russian embassy. He could make his way to a road where he would be picked up. Duke's charade would be exposed, but *he* wouldn't.

"Okay, let's see where we're going to land," Angie suggested. "His air supply didn't allow us many choices." She tapped the camera's joystick to rotate it downward. Oddly, the star field remained unchanged, and the white spacesuit stayed visible on the edge of the picture. The cosmonaut began waving frantically.

"Uh oh," Duke said, worry lines forming on his forehead. "Something must have happened." He keyed the microphone. "I'm cutting the thrust," he warned. "The net will keep you from drifting."

"What is it?" Angie asked.

"I don't know. The camera didn't respond to its joystick. Let's see what he can tell us."

He picked up the microphone and asked the cosmonaut to try to communicate what had happened. The man pointed down, repeatedly, but Duke couldn't understand what he was trying to say. Finally, he made a quick twisting motion with his fist. Something was broken.

"Okay. I don't know how you can communicate the details, but use your imagination, please."

The cosmonaut didn't respond right away. Finally, he pointed to his helmet and drew a circle, then placed his index finger forward against the faceplate at an oblique angle.

"Does your helmet represent the sphere containing the camera?" Duke asked.

Thumbs up.

"I get it, I get it!" Angie said. "A broken strut is stuck in the sphere. Right?"

Thumbs up, again.

"All right," Duke sighed. It wasn't good, but it could have been worse. They should still be able to fly. He told the Russian to yell if he saw a tree up ahead. The Russian put his forearm across his faceplate as if to brace for a collision.

The silly bit of humor went a long ways toward reducing the tension.

"All right," Duke said. "I'm going to bring us back up to full thrust manually. Signal if something really bad happens."

He entered commands at the console, and the star field shifted slowly, then stopped. Additional commands resulted in no visual changes, but the console displays began updating. He waited and watched for a moment. When they reached five Gees, Duke asked if everything was holding. The cosmonaut didn't answer immediately, but finally the 'thumbs up' sign appeared. Duke let out a sigh of relief. Playing with the An-G force had been fun when it had only involved him. Having someone's life depend on it was an entirely different experience. "I'm ready for this flight to be over," he told Angie.

"Yeah, well, not quite," she cautioned. They still didn't know where they were, she pointed out. She could calculate an approximate landing point from their orbital data, but it could be way off due to some of her assumptions.

"We're coming up on the turnaround point," Duke advised. "We can rotate so the camera points down then."

"Turnaround point?" Angie asked.

"Whatever you astronauts call it—where we stop accelerating downward and start decelerating. I originally planned some free-fall time then to damp out the pendulum effects, but we don't have a pendulum now that he's hanging onto the framework. We can use the time to rotate the whole structure. Let me get him prepared."

Duke keyed the microphone. "Hello, again. We're going to adjust the angle of descent in a minute or so. I will cut the thrust, and we need you to hang onto the struts so we can rotate. You and the craft will be in free-fall. It will only be for a short time while we get our bearings, then you can go back to the same position as before. How is your air supply? Have you switched to your reserve yet?"

Hand back and forth across camera.

"Good. Stretch it as far as you can, but don't pass out. Free-fall coming in…three, two, one, now."

"All okay?"

A finger pointed off-camera, followed by a 'thumbs up', then to the spacesuit with another thumb.

"Great! We may get you down after all! Hang on a minute. We're turning the camera straight down to see where we are and where we will land. I'll be right back."

The stars began to shift, and a stunning white band scrolled across the screen, followed by the beautiful indigo blue of the ocean. Angie squinted at the nearly featureless panorama.

"Yikes. We're in the middle of nowhere. My calculations put us somewhere over the South Pacific, but I can't spot anything that would help refine that. Wait a minute. I see tiny specks down there that might be islands." She twisted the map around, looking from it to the screen and back.

"Well, Duke, as near as I can tell from the map and my calculations, we're somewhere over French Polynesia right now, moving northeast. We're going to splash down north of the equator about as far from land as possible."

"Down is good; far from land is not. If his air allows us to go farther, what is the closest land?"

The southernmost tip of Baja California was almost

directly ahead, or they could veer east toward the coast of Mexico near Guadalajara. It was about the same distance. That way they could drop the cosmonaut off near Mexico City. Another option would be to turn north and head for home. They could put him down at Phoenix.

"I'm sure he already knows we're Americans from our accents," Duke said. "He also knows that we haven't been able to make any significant course changes, so dropping him off in Phoenix won't suggest that our home base is nearby." Duke preferred to make it easy on themselves and head for home if the Russian's air allowed it. He glanced at the console. "Time to resume deceleration. Is it all right to rotate back?"

"Yeah, I've learned as much as I'm gonna."

Duke tapped the keyboard, then leaned over to the microphone. "You need to get back in position. Same as before. Thrust in about twenty seconds. I'll give you a count-down."

Duke turned to Angie. "Can you do the impossible again? We're going to need a new thrust program to kick in depending on our landing spot. Why don't you tell him what the plan is and see if he has a preference for where we go?"

"Hmm. Don't know where we are. Don't know where we're going. Be ready in five minutes. Now where have I heard that before?" she complained. "Only this time you don't know when, either!"

Duke patted her on the top of her head and grinned. Her teasing eased some of his tension. He gave the cosmo-naut a countdown, then brought the force up slowly, watching the stars on the screen to see if the craft showed any unexpected motion.

"Five Gees," Duke announced. Still no signal from the Russian.

As Angie keyed the microphone to speak, the big screen flashed white. "Uh oh! Duke, did we lose the camera?"

"I don't think so. The screen would go black. He must be blocking our view."

"Are you okay?" she asked. "All we can see is your suit."

No answer. Angie repeated the question. Still no answer. "Duke?"

"I don't know. We can only hope that he didn't pass out. Do you know anything about spacesuits? Would he have to lean over to turn on his emergency air supply?"

"Yes! That's it...I hope," she added, "but what if the valve is on his bad-arm side? What if —"

Duke touched her hand and looked at her. He couldn't afford for her to lose confidence, now.

"Okay, but it's been almost two minutes," she reasoned.

The screen suddenly flashed, and they both looked up to see the cloud-strewn sky again with a big fist and thumb wiggling 'success'.

Angie gave Duke a quick hug. "Whew. I think we're *all* breathing a little easier," she said into the mike. "This is really good. You've stretched your air enough that we have a couple of options where we can land now. Our plan is to drop you off in an unpopulated area, but close enough to a big city that you can get to a Russian consulate. Right now, the best choices are Mexico City and Phoenix, Arizona in the United States. Do you —"

The cosmonaut interrupted and waved his hand rapidly back and forth in front of the camera.

"Is something wrong with the craft?" she asked quickly.

He waved a 'no'.

"No? Then what are you saying 'no' to? The choice of city or the remote location?"

Hand waving, pause, hand waving.

"No to both? I'm sorry, but that's all we can offer you."

His index finger circled forward, then pointed to the camera.

"Go where we are? No. That is totally out of the question. We cannot allow our identity or location to be revealed. You'll have to choose: Mexico or USA, and we need a decision quickly so that we can make a course correction."

Index finger circling forward, then pointing to the camera.

"No. We already had this conversation. You can't come here. Choose a spot, or we will have to choose one for you. Time is running out."

Index finger circling forward, then pointing to the camera.

"Duke," Angie appealed. "Can you talk sense into this guy? I'm getting nowhere."

Duke wheeled over to the microphone.

"My friend, here is the situation. If anyone finds out who or where we are, we will become the most hunted people on Earth. If we bring you here, your life as well as ours will be in danger. If we drop you off, then you won't know any more about us than you do now. It has to be that way."

Finger touching forehead; point at camera.

"You know us? No, you don't. That won't work. No

one knows who we are. No one."

Finger pointing to self, twice, then to forehead, then at camera.

"*You* do? Fine! Who am I?" Duke's face flushed with anger.

Index finger moving down, curving up halfway: 'J'; index finger making circle with thumb: 'O'.

A cold chill ran down Duke's spine as the Russian reached into his zippered bag and pulled out a flashlight. He held it horizontally between his forearms: 'H'. Then he held it with one end in his hand and the other end touching the opposite elbow: a backward 'N'.

"Duke!" Angie's scream echoed crazily around the control room.

Duke looked at her helplessly. His face was an ashen white. "There's no way," he whispered. "No one knows. Not even Gramp."

DOWN

Angie's hand trembled as she took Duke's. He stirred as she touched him, and seemed to come back to reality, but continued to stare across the room at the out-of-focus spacesuit.

"Duke, I love you, and we're going to get through this together."

"Yes." He finally made eye contact. "We are, and I love you." He attempted a smile, but it faded almost before it formed. "This changes everything." His gaze drifted as he thought. "Most of the rooms in this mine don't even have doors. What are we supposed to do—ask the guy to sit quietly while we build a jail to keep him in for the rest of his life?"

Angie massaged his shoulders and neck. "Why don't you take a break while I revise the thrust program?" she suggested.

Duke rubbed his forehead while Angie worked. *Who? How? When?* He'd taken every reasonable precaution. He worked alone, shared his discovery with no one, and kept his records locked in a strongbox in the back of the workshop tunnel. Even Angie hadn't learned of the discovery until she came to the mine. How could anyone—most particularly a Russian—have discovered his secret? He gave up trying to figure it out.

Angie finished her calculations, started the program, and then came to sit on the couch with him. He felt her hand take his, felt her head on his shoulder, and rested his head on hers. Neither spoke for several minutes.

A beep from the console brought both of them to attention. "Two minutes to program end," Angie explained. "Are you going to be okay?"

Duke made a noncommittal shrug. "Okay—yes. Happy—no."

They both returned to their chairs at the console.

"Well, I'm back," Angie told the cosmonaut. "There's going to be a lot of activity in the next few minutes. You don't have to do much, but you need to be prepared. How is your air?"

The Russian put the back of his hand on his forehead, pointed to the box on his chest and made a zero sign with thumb and finger.

"The gauge says zero? Well, I hope it's wrong by at least a couple more minutes. The thrust program ends in... forty seconds. You will go into free-fall briefly while we rotate to a camera-down position. Then we go back to the earlier configuration with you hanging in the net like before. We will go straight down, but it may be another minute or so before we get down to where you can breathe. I'll give you a countdown."

Angie set the microphone back on the table with trembling hands. She looked plaintively at Duke. "We're so close. I know he's going to be a problem, but I want to save him. Can you fly? I don't trust my hands."

The worry lines were deeply etched in his forehead, but he nodded. "We really don't have any choice. We've got to try. I can fly. It's about my turn, anyway."

Angie squeezed his shoulders, then returned to the

microphone. "Ten seconds," she said. Her gaze bounced from the console to the big screen. "Hold onto the net. The rotation will push you away from the craft. Three, two, one, now."

Duke nudged the joystick to start the rotation. He watched the cosmonaut drift away from the craft and into the net. As the rotation slowed and the net stretched, the big screen presented an unflattering view of the cosmonaut's backside. "Oh, give me a break," Duke groused. "He can't see the camera to talk in that position, and worse yet, he won't be able to take off his helmet."

Duke pulled the microphone closer. "Hang on. I'm going to apply a short burst of upward thrust, then cut it. As soon as you start rebounding from the net, see if you can get untangled and roll yourself upright."

The maneuver worked, but as soon as Duke applied a light braking thrust, the net forced the cosmonaut back down on his face.

"See if the net is snagged on something behind you," he instructed. "As soon as I see your hand above your head, I'll do it again."

They watched anxiously, but couldn't see much. Only the elbow moved...and moved. Time was running short. Angie reached for the microphone when his hand finally grabbed the net above his head. Duke quickly touched the joystick, and the Russian tumbled backward, facing the camera. He waved his good arm frantically as the net stretched with his weight.

"I'm here," Angie answered.

He moved his hand in and out over his chest, then made a slashing sign with his finger at his throat.

"Okay, we're at eighty-five hundred meters. There's not much oxygen at that altitude, but it's below Mount Everest. You make the call."

He immediately tore open the latch at his neck and used the crook of his good arm to wrench off his helmet. Crimson blood gushed over his face.

"Duke!" Angie screamed.

"I see it, Angie, but there's nothing we can do about it except get him down as quickly as possible."

She grabbed the microphone. "Are you okay? Can you breathe?"

Several seconds passed before he responded. His hand moved in an out over his chest. Duke noted that he didn't answer her first question.

"Home!" Duke said as he began to recognize landmarks below. He grinned as he pointed to a rock with a chain-link fence on top, surrounded by several dark circles. He could barely see them through the netting near the cosmonaut's left shoulder. "Angie, can you take it from here? I need to be outside to help him when he lands."

"Duke, I'm afraid. What if I drop him or mash him or something?"

"Don't worry. You can use the joystick until you get close, then switch to the console. It gives you very precise control. Here," he moved the landline phone to her table. "I'll call you on my cell."

"Okay, I'm as ready as I'm ever going to be."

Duke dialed his home phone and talked to her as he descended the shaft. "See if you can come down in the flat area between the trailer and the mine. I suspect he's not going to be able to walk very far."

"I see you!" Angie said as Duke exited the mine. He looked up and found the *Tetra* floating above the valley in front of the mine.

"Good. Bring it straight down. I'll tell you when to stop. Then you can bring him in over the treetops."

The craft dropped slowly. "Just right," Duke encouraged. "Another hundred feet or so, then hold it there. Good… good. Now come northeast about two hundred feet."

"I don't know which way is northeast."

"Oh, that's right, you're looking down. All right, aim about forty-five degrees left of where his feet are pointing… left again, a little more. Perfect. Now, let it coast. As soon as you clear the roof of the trailer, stop.

"Nice. Down about ten feet. Slowly. As soon as his butt touches, move sideways a little. Three, two, one, down.

"Excellent job, Angie! Hit the red button and come on down." He paused and looked at the Russian. "Uh, on second thought, can you make a detour first? Would you mind putting extra towels and stuff in the second bathroom? We're going to need them."

Duke had to breathe through his mouth as he approached the cosmonaut. The stench of sweat and urine nearly overwhelmed him. The man's bloodshot eyes stared out from dark sockets. Matted hair twisted in every direction. Most of his face was covered with blood that had dried, crusted and flaked off in places. He held his injured left arm against the front of his suit.

Duke braced himself and stepped forward. "Welcome to Arizona," he said as he helped the cosmonaut get untangled from the net.

"Arizona? Is not Arksaw?"

"No, why? Do you recognize my Arkie accent?"

"No. I recognize voice of Angela Sgambelli who talks constantly of John Wainwright who lives in Arksaw."

Duke mentally sounded out the Cyrillic letters embroidered on his name patch: Б Е Л А Р О В—Belarov.

Angie gritted her teeth, irritated with Duke. She wanted to go down and meet the Russian, not waste time playing maid. Immediately she chided herself. *The guy has been through hell, and I can't take time to get him a bar of soap.*

She hurried down to the living level and gathered everything she thought he might need in the bathroom. She couldn't find a spare comb. *He's probably got a crew cut, anyway. He's going to need something to wear, though.* She went to Duke's dresser and pulled out a sweat suit and socks. Conscience appeased, she headed for the central shaft, only to turn around as she thought of something else. Finally, with a water bottle in her hand, she headed down.

Angie jogged toward the mine entrance, eager to meet the man she had been talking to for the past several hours, but the sight that greeted her there stopped her short. She saw Duke bent over someone who looked like a punk rock star who had been beaten up and stripped down to his long johns. A man with wildly spiked hair sat on the ground near the *Tetra*. He was leaning forward, supporting his head with one hand with the elbow propped on his knee. Disassembled parts of his spacesuit lay scattered nearby. Duke hurried to meet her.

"Good thinking, Angie," Duke said, indicating the water bottle. "That's exactly what he needs." He stood there somewhat awkwardly. "Uh, right now might not be the best time for you to meet him."

Angie wrinkled her nose at the smell that accompanied him. "Yes, I think I agree with you. What can I do to help?"

"I'd like to get *Tetra* out of sight if we can. It barely fits in the workshop tunnel. Do you think you can park it?"

"I'll try. Do you want me to fix something to eat?"

"Something light—just for the two of us. He's not going to feel like eating. I think his nose is broken from when his helmet blew off, and there's a deep cut on one of his cheeks. He's got a really bad headache. We're lucky the pressure in his suit was so low. The rapid decompression could have given him the bends. I'm not sure if his arm is broken or badly bruised, but it's got to hurt. As soon as I get some water in him, I'll bring him up. Once he's cleaned up, I think I'll give him one of my migraine knockout pills and let him sleep a few hours."

Angie and Duke sat at the breakfast table sipping coffee while cinnamon rolls baked in the oven. The wonderful aroma filled the room. Angie reached for Duke's hand.

"It's nice to see you relaxed, Duke. I was afraid you'd be uptight about having to bring him here."

"I was, and still would be, but he relieved my fears a lot yesterday. Hurting as badly as he was, his first request was that I notify our government of the beam weapon the Russians put in orbit. I reassured him there was no longer any need."

"That's great! I can't wait to find out how he knows your name, though."

A voice came from the archway leading to the kitchen. "You told me."

That voice. Angie screamed. Her chair fell sideways as she spun around. "You!"

He barely managed to raise his injured arm out of the way before she crashed into him, laughing, crying, and hugging.

"And *you!*" She pointed an accusing finger at Duke. "You knew all this time!"

Belarov's English had a certain French nasal quality about it, due most likely to his broken nose.

Duke and Angie listened attentively as Ivan—he adamantly insisted on dropping the "Colonel"—related the events leading up to the launch of the *Buran II*.

"I do not know details. Anti-satellite laser project began long ago, was ninety percent complete at time of Soviet Union breakup. After breakup…well, better to spend small money to finish project than waste big money already spent. Two beam weapons were build." Belarov shrugged apologetically.

"When signal from space begins, only Americans reported seeing light when it was near Moon. Craft moved to geosynchronous orbit in Western Hemisphere before signal was reported, before others could confirm it was once anywhere else. Maybe Americans developed weapon of their own, put in orbit before Russia. Panic outbroke." He questioned their understanding with raised eyebrows. Both nodded.

"Russian weapons were to be launched by unmanned rocket, but none were ready. Working around clock, *Buran*

II shuttle might be ready in few weeks or so. I am called back to space center with two comrades. We are told cargo is surveillance satellites. First would investigate source of signals and provide intelligence information on activities in West. Second was to increase intelligence coverage in East."

Belarov paused in his narration. His mood turned dark, and his jaw muscles knotted as he spoke.

"When cargo bay was opened, instead of surveillance satellites, we found high-energy beam weapons. We object, but we were ordered to launch satellites. We had no choice. It was—you say—the rock and the hard place? If we did not obey, it would endanger lives of our families." He shrugged and spread his hands in resignation. "We launched weapon.

"Next five hours were exhausting," he continued. "Arguments, exploding tempers, more threats—but it was same as before. We had no choice. We removed second weapon from cargo bay and released it. Electrical system failure prevented full retraction of deployment arm. My comrades still worked to correct problem—outside safety of shuttle—when ground control fired beam weapon engine. It exploded, cutting shuttle in half and killing my friends."

FOURSOME

Duke pulled a dog-eared business card from his wallet and dialed the phone number, hoping it still worked.

"Yes, I'd like to speak to Dr. Rebecca Coleman, please.... I figured that might be the case. Does she have voice-mail?... Great.... Yes, please."

Duke left a message asking to meet with her at her earliest convenience. He told her he was located a few miles outside of Sedona and would need a few hours lead time, but he'd be there whenever she said. He also asked that they meet somewhere away from the media if possible. He left his phone number. *I'll wait until she calls back to tell her Angie and Ivan are coming, too.*

"Is now a good time to go down there?" Angie asked. "I mean are you okay with taking Col... . uh, Ivan out in public?"

"No, definitely not, but I need to get down there fairly soon. I want to make sure Dr. Coleman doesn't suffer as a result of my irresponsibility."

"I don't think discovering anti-gravity could be considered irresponsible."

"No, but what I did with it certainly could," he said. As to taking Ivan out in public, he didn't have much choice. He couldn't leave him alone in the mine. He trusted Angie's judgment that he was a good guy, but there was too much at risk. He figured he'd always be looking over his shoulder now, but at least no one was looking for him. If they were, there was no reason they should look here. He thought it would be safe.

"We'll need to come up with a name and background for him, though. Let's go see if he has any ideas."

"Not to worry," Ivan assured them when they found him in the library. "I was thinking of this problem coming down from *Buran*."

"What? How could you possibly think about an alias at a time like that?" Duke asked.

"I had much time to think. As soon as I heard Angela speak *'Vnimaniye Buran'*, I know I will be coming here. I could not go back to Russia. Belarov was dead. I was on my way to America. I would need American name. I am Nick Constantine."

"How did you come up with that name?" Angie asked.

"Nick was cousin—like twin. We have same birthday, and many people said we looked alike at least when we were young. He was—black sheep? He ran away to Alaska. He would write each few years. Last letter came few months ago. It was from someone else—in English. I had to read it to my aunt. Nick went out on boat with friends. Wreckage of boat was found some days later. I will be my cousin."

Angie looked questioningly at Duke. "What do you think, Duke?" she asked.

"It's better than anything I can think of. I'm not sure how we're going to get papers to go with the name, though."

TUCSON, ARIZONA:
Duke parked the truck and then led the way diagonally

across the street from the Steward Observatory complex on the University of Arizona campus. "This is where I worked with Dr. Coleman a couple of years ago," he explained. "She thought it would be a good place to get away from the media. There are still too many people, though." He glanced nervously at Ivan.

The Russian wore blue jeans, one of Duke's oversized sweatshirts, and an Atlanta Braves baseball cap, but too much of his face showed, and the arm sling drew too much attention. Duke already regretted that they brought him along, although he hadn't had much choice.

He spotted Becca as they entered the building, and he led the way.

"Hi, John. Good to see you again." Becca reached to shake his hand, looking at his companions as she did so.

"Likewise," Duke responded. "Uh...Angie, I'd like you to meet Dr. Rebecca Coleman. Dr. Coleman, this is my fiancée Angela Sgambelli."

"Oh, please—just Becca. It's nice to meet you...and congratulations."

Angie beamed and took Duke's hand.

Becca turned to Ivan and offered her hand. "Hi, I'm Becca Coleman. You look very familiar. Have we met before?"

"No, I do not think so," he responded. "I am sure I would remember. I am Nick Constantine. Pleased to meet you."

"Hmm. Interesting accent," Becca observed. "Russian?"

"Greek, Turk, Russian, American—take your pick. I am mongrel."

Becca laughed so loud that several students across

the foyer looked up. "Well, it's nice to meet you wherever you're from. Come on, everyone," she said as she herded them toward the CCD Laboratory.

She closed the door behind them and waved them toward a round conference table. Suddenly she snapped her fingers, turned and pointed at Ivan. "Colonel Belarov, the Russian cosmonaut."

Angie sucked in her breath audibly. Duke and Nick froze.

"What? Sorry. I didn't mean to startle you. That's who you remind me of. Belarov. His picture was on the news less than an hour ago. It's mostly your eyes, but your voice is similar, too. They showed some video clips. He was speaking Russian, though."

Duke sank into a chair without waiting to be invited. His legs were rubbery and his stomach queasy. *What a scare!*

"So, John, what brings you down to Tucson? Your message had a note of urgency in it."

Duke took time to slow his breathing. "Uh, why don't you call me Duke? Everyone else does."

Becca studied his face, then nodded. "Wainwright—Wayne, huh? Fits."

"As to the urgency," Duke explained, "I heard you were leaving the Peak. I was hoping to catch you before you made a commitment for another job."

"No problem there." She laughed. "I'm ready for a vacation. I'm curious to hear what you have in mind, though. Money comes in handy now and then."

"Well, simply put, I'd like to encourage you to keep on doing what you've been doing. Nobody really believes that you were talking to an alien out there, but what if? We're totally unprepared to communicate with another intelligence."

"Well, I have to admit that I was enjoying myself, at least until the NSA showed up. It looks like our friend has disappeared, though. Who would I talk to, and for that matter, what would I talk with?"

"That's where I think I might be able to help. I'm a big contributor to SETI's funding, so they have to listen to my suggestions. I think they might agree to sponsor practice conversations if you're interested."

"Hmm. Well, I'm definitely interested. Do you really think they would put me on a project like that?"

"Absolutely. You're good at it. I followed the exchanges on the news and was really impressed with how fast you responded to the messages and your innovations in developing new vocabulary."

"Yeah." Becca laughed. "Jeanette and I were pretty proud of ourselves, keeping pace with a superior intelligence." Her eyes twinkled mischievously as she stared directly at Duke. "So what made you choose the base-twelve number system?"

"I just thought it —" Duke caught himself, but too late.

"Gotcha you sneaky bastard!" Becca pounded the table with her fist.

"Duke!" Angie yelled.

Duke sat frozen in his chair, speechless.

"Go easy on him, Honey," Becca advised. "I was ninety-nine percent sure before you got here. The minute I got his voice-mail, I got suspicious. The signal had to be man-made, sent by someone who knew Kitt Peak's current operations, and it couldn't be from a space agency. I didn't know how, but the who was pretty easy."

Duke's whole body tingled, buzzed, and burned. He covered his face with his hands and rested his elbows on the table. Angie touched his shoulder, and he looked up, shaking his head in disgust.

"I guess we have a new member on our team," she observed.

"Two," Becca corrected, "unless Nick already knew."

Duke took a deep breath and let it out slowly. "If you know that much ..." He looked at Nick and shrugged. "Do you want to do the honors?"

Nick stood, bowed slightly in Becca's direction, then straightened. "Ivan Davidovich Belarov at your service."

"*What?* You *are* him? The news said you were dead! How the hell do *you* fit into this picture?"

"It's a long and interesting story," Duke said. "One I think we'd best not share with you here. If you recognized him, someone else might. We need to get him back where there's nothing but cactus and coyotes. Would you be able to come up to Sedona for a few days?"

"I guess I don't have a choice, do I? You're not going to leave me with all these loose ends dangling." She turned to Belarov. "So do I call you Ivan or Nick?"

"Nick, please. As you already heard on news, Col. Ivan Belarov is dead."

"Wow," Angie said as soon as they were all back in the truck. "She certainly doesn't fit the stereotype image of an astronomer. Do you like her?" she asked skeptically.

"It took a while, but, yeah, I guess so," he acknowledged. "Don't you?"

"I don't *dis*like her," she replied, "but she doesn't exactly exude charisma. Maybe I'll like her later."

"I hope so," he said as he started the truck. "Thanks to me, it's going to be important that we all get along."

Duke was not in a talkative mood on the way back to Sedona. He was angry with himself. He wasn't upset that Becca discovered their secret—he felt that he could trust her. He was upset because he couldn't trust himself. His blunder could have put them all in jeopardy.

Becca arrived late in the afternoon, and Duke gave her a quick tour of the mine. "Man, this is awesome," she exclaimed. "You've got better equipment here than we had at the Peak."

Duke smiled his appreciation. *Hmm. I wonder if I could talk her into joining us here. Angie and I could sleep in the trailer. She's between jobs, and she likely knows a lot more about physics than I do.*

Duke scrolled through the log, looking for the right timestamp while the other three watched snow on the big screen.

"All right, everybody. I'm going to re-play from the time we saw the explosion. We'll fast-forward over the parts where nothing special was happening. I already explained how the sounds you'll hear were generated. Our voices weren't recorded unless we were speaking into the microphone, so Angie and I will narrate as we go."

He found the timestamp, and the big screen flickered into life, showing the barely discernible features of the darkened Southwest sprinkled with pinpoints of light.

Soft sounds of space sighed and mumbled from speakers spaced around the room. The low, regular groan of radar could easily be mistaken for the sound of a porch swing on a warm summer night. A light flared far below, and the speakers hissed briefly.

"That was the explosion," Duke said quietly, not wanting to interrupt the mood.

Angie took over. "We made a wild guess that they had launched something to come investigate the signal craft. Duke, you can fast-forward through this. I was programming the trajectory for us to go down to the site of the explosion," she explained to Nick and Becca.

Duke re-started the playback as the *Tetra* began its downward pitch.

B-b-baw! B-b-baw! B-b-baw!

Angie and Duke jumped as much as Becca and Nick. Duke let the re-play proceed without speaking. When the wildly spinning debris of the beam weapon filled the screen, he paused the re-play.

"Things happened pretty fast there, so I'll re-run it and explain." He turned down the speakers as the craft reappeared on the screen.

"The disk on that arm was obviously radar," he pointed to the screen, "but the tube on the other arm was something else. It looked too much like a gun. I decided to shoot first and ask questions later." He paused the re-play again as the smoke puffed in front of the camera and the other craft lost its middle.

"The smoke shows that he got me. The picture shows that I got him. It was *that* close." Duke pinched his thumb and index finger together.

Belarov frowned. "Where is middle of craft?"

Duke just shrugged and shook his head. "Somewhere else," he said.

The room was deathly quiet as Duke searched forward on the recording. Only the muted click of the keys on the control console disturbed the silence. He resumed the display at the point where the *Tetra* arrived at the site of the explosion, then turned up the sound again.

"We'll be able to hear anything we said to Nick. I'll let it play without talking unless someone has a question. The camera's focus is stuck on infinity as a result of the laser beam hit, so close-up pictures will be a little fuzzy."

The mood in the room changed immediately as Angie's voice came over the speakers. "*Vnimaniye, Buran. Vnimaniye, Buran.*"

"Boo-rawn," Nick said, imitating Angie's pronunciation. "I knew it was Angela Sgambelli when I heard her say it." He looked affectionately in Angie's direction.

The replay was as exciting for the three key players as it was for Becca. Nick kept a running commentary going and translated for Becca when Angie or Duke spoke Russian. They skipped over the long flight from the Gulf of California, resuming when the shaft on top of the mine was visible.

"Man! I'm worn out merely from *watching*," Becca said as the screen went blank, "and you've got about two seconds to start talking before I throttle you. What the hell happened to that laser weapon, and how in hell does your craft have the ability to hover? Give!" She snapped her fingers impatiently.

Duke laughed somewhat nervously. *She's big enough*

that she probably could *throttle me.* "That's what I want you to tell me," he said defensively. "I'm in way over my head here. I don't know what I've got. I do know that it's too big, too important, too dangerous to be left in my hands when I have so little knowledge of what I'm dealing with."

"I'd like to take the rest of the evening off—fix a nice supper, have a drink or two and relax. I want all of your brains fresh in the morning. If everybody's agreeable, we'll have a real quick course in applied non-Newtonian physics, then."

Nick's head jerked around. "You would share this information with *me*?" he asked incredulously.

Duke spread his arms in an expression of helplessness. "Sharing with anyone is a risk, Nick. Angie trusts you, and I trust her judgment. We're all in this together. If you're willing to share the responsibility, I'm willing to share the knowledge."

Dinner was simple: lasagna and a big bowl of Caesar salad. A fat-bottomed bottle of chianti encased in woven straw helped everyone relax and get acquainted. Duke and Angie were surprised, but pleased to see how well Becca and Nick hit it off—nothing intimate, but friendly, nonetheless.

SOCRATES

The next morning, Duke gathered his small class into the library. They had to wheel in swivel chairs from the control room, as the sofa and desk chair were the only other places to sit. Duke's books were in disarray—some vertical, some stacked horizontally, although he had packed and unpacked them by category, so they were at least organized by bookcase. Between the recently disturbed books, the red cedar plank table, and the cowhide on the floor, the room smelled...interesting. Duke hardly noticed it. He had other things on his mind.

"This is going to be one of the strangest college courses any of us has participated in," he warned. He stood, while the other three sat at the table, their faces bright with anticipation. "Within a very few minutes, the students are going to know every bit as much as the instructor," he explained. "At that point, I confess my own ignorance and look to you for a logical explanation of the phenomena."

"Just like Socrates," Nick observed.

"Yes, I guess you're right. Well, then, let's do him honor."

Duke went to the whiteboard and drew three short vertical lines side by side. "This is a cross-section of a ribbon—a sandwich of flat optical fiber between two strips of recording tape. The edges of the tapes are magnetized with opposite polarities, so they attract each other, trapping the optical layer between."

Under the three lines, he drew a large spiral and sketched a light bulb at its center. "The light bulb is symbolic," he explained. "Ordinary light won't work. It has to be monochromatic and coherent—the kind of light a laser produces—and polarized. That's the reason for the flat ribbon fiber as opposed to round. You with me so far?

The three students nodded.

"Okay, pay attention, 'cause it's going to be quick." He turned back to the board.

"Laser light goes in here," he pointed to the bulb at the center, "and," he spread his fingers over the spiral and moved his hand away from the white board, "anti-gravity comes out here."

"Anti-gravity!" Becca shouted. "No fucking way! I mean…it couldn't be that simple. Surely there must be something else going on."

Angie nodded. "That's what I said when he explained it to me."

"And I agree," Duke said. "It's too easy, too simple, and too unbelievable. But there's no denying that it works."

He looked around the group, waiting for more questions or comments, but no one spoke. Becca and Nick's faces showed a mixture of shock and stunned disbelief.

"Okay, here's what I think I know." Duke referred to a paper and wrote bullets on the board, elaborating as he wrote.

"First, it's not a wave. The force field just suddenly exists—at infinitely distant points and all points in between."

"Infinitely?" Becca challenged.

Duke shrugged. "I put *Tetra* on the Moon, aimed an An-G beam at it, and it sent a beam back. The only elapsed time was the few milliseconds used by the electronics aboard *Tetra*."

Becca compressed her lips, but said nothing further.

Duke continued. "Number two is a big one—the force is proportional to the amount of light going through the fiber, but the proportionality factor is a very, very, *very* large number." He looked at Angie. "I wasn't kidding when I told you that a child could knock the Moon out of its orbit." He turned to Nick. "You asked where the middle section of the beam weapon was. I suspect that it was moving out of our solar system faster than any of us can imagine." He paused to let them absorb what he had said.

Nick said something in Russian, his face a paradoxical mixture of belief and skepticism.

"I don't know what you said, but you can say it again," Becca grumbled.

"Okay, brace yourselves, 'cause I saved the best for last, and I'm going to take a moment to let its significance in," Duke said, as he wrote on the board, "Bullet number three is—there's no equal and opposite reaction. Whatever this force is, it doesn't obey Newton's third law of motion."

"Holy shit!" Becca yelled. "You can't be serious. That would mean …"

"Yes." He nodded. "Everything from Pandora's box— both the good and the bad. Now you know why I built the *Tetra*. I want the world to know about the discovery, but I'm scared to death to tell them."

"Holy shit," Becca repeated, this time barely audible.

"All right." Duke broke the silence. "This is my theory—and so far the experiments back it up." He summarized the discovery in much the same way as he had for Angie—

that Earth was in some kind of energy field. They couldn't feel it, like they couldn't feel the magnetic field they were in. The optical coil didn't actually generate anti-gravity—it acted like a window. It let a repelling force come through, and at the same time modulated and directed it. The right-hand rule applied—light moving counter-clockwise directed the An-G force upward. If they constructed a disk—a flat spiral of the ribbon—and passed light through it, the amount of the force that was released depended on the angle of the disk's plane relative to the surrounding energy field, so if the disk was turned edge-wise to the field, they would get nothing. Otherwise they'd get *lots*.

"That's it, folks. It's not much to work with, I know, but that's why I need your help. Socrates takes over from here." Duke bowed modestly and sat down.

"Not much!" Becca practically exploded. "Any one of those phenomena would blow a physicist's mind, and you've got three!"

Duke merely looked at her, eyebrows raised, a patient expression on his face.

"What? You expect me to explain this?" she asked.

"You, me, Angie, and Nick," Duke answered. "I'm hoping that one of you knows more about physics than I do."

"Classical physics, maybe—not this kind," Becca waved at the board.

"Perhaps they are same thing," Nick spoke up. "What if equal and opposite reaction occurs on other side of window?"

"I don't know," Becca answered. "It's possible, I guess. The latest thinking is that there are several more dimensions to space than the three we are familiar with. The reaction could be happening in another dimension—whatever that means."

"Yes!" Duke shook his fist. "That's exactly the kind of ideas I'm looking for—how to explain the observations within the existing laws of physics. We may have to modify them to accommodate new concepts, like what the other side of the window means, but the laws still hold. Can we do that with the next one—instantly infinite?"

"I'm not sure it actually contradicts any laws," Becca admitted. "In fact, instantly infinite was the way Newton thought gravity worked, but supposedly Einstein proved it was a wave, which means it would take time to propagate from one point to another."

"Wait a minute," Duke interrupted. "Didn't there used to be an experiment that was looking for gravity waves? Fido or something like that?"

"LIGO," Becca corrected, chuckling. "Stands for Laser Interferometer Gravitational-Wave Observatory." They lost their funding in the Q of L debacle.

Duke ignored the explanation. "Well, they hadn't found any waves up to that point, if I remember correctly. So if they haven't found gravity waves, then maybe Newton was right. If *anti*-gravity isn't a wave, then maybe gravity isn't either."

"Unlikely," she answered. "The properties of gravity have to correlate with the observable facts. Newton's version did a good job for a long time, but then we discovered that the universe is expanding, and after that we found that the expansion rate is accelerating. Any gravitational theory will have to explain that."

"Becca," Angie said, hesitantly. "Wouldn't instant gravity explain the accelerated rate? Mass gets converted to energy inside of stars, right? When the mass disappears, gravity would disappear and stop pulling on distant objects immediately, whereas light-speed gravity would continue pulling for a long time."

"Good thinking, Angie, but the mass doesn't disappear. It just changes form—into energy—and all forms of energy act as a source of gravity."

"I never knew that. Gravity is a property of energy, too?" Angie asked.

"I didn't know that either," Duke said. "Has that been verified experimentally? Or is it just someone's theory like the gravitational waves? I'm beginning to wonder exactly how much we really know about physics. Someone comes up with a theory, but it doesn't match reality, so they invent something else, like dark matter, to explain the discrepancy. Maybe the theory is wrong."

Becca sat shaking her head. "I don't know the answer to your questions, Duke. I'm not a cosmologist, and I haven't kept up with their experiments, so I don't know what is theory and what is fact. Your discovery obviously proves that they don't know everything. I can't believe the historical significance of this. You're gonna win the Nobel Prize!"

"Not me," Duke stated flatly. "I've had my fill of being patted on the head. Besides, tying my name to anti-gravity is the last thing I want to happen. I'm more scared of what I may have unleashed than proud of what I've discovered."

The rest of the morning passed with a flurry of questions, but few answers. Duke's prediction was correct—soon the students knew as much as the instructor. No one lacked enthusiasm. Everyone contributed questions and ideas—

some far-fetched, but most were sensible. Ideas were still coming, but with longer pauses between them when Nick's tummy growled so loudly that everyone laughed.

"That's the best idea I've heard in a while," Duke joked. "Let's take a lunch break and tackle a different problem when we come back."

Angie was deep in thought as she followed Duke down the spiral stairs, but not about anti-gravity. When she heard him tell Becca he'd had his fill of being patted on the head, she realized they had more in common than she previously imagined. She'd been teased and ridiculed because of her intelligence. He'd been praised and fawned over for his. Though opposite in nature, their treatment by others had driven them both in the same direction—to be humble, yet self-reliant and determined. All of those were characteristics she would need to consider before making any decision about her relationship with Duke. Maybe Mamma would help her when she got home *and* if they were on speaking terms. Mamma's sense of morality had been stretched to its limit when Angie told her where she was and who she was with.

Holy shit! The two words cycled in a tight loop in Becca's mind. She knew enough about physics and human nature to recognize just how dangerous Duke's discovery could be. Learning that he was the guy behind the signals from space had already made her question how responsible a person he was. His decision to share not only the discovery, but also the *details* of it with Nick left her questioning his judgment. She *liked* Nick. That wasn't the problem, but c'mon—a few days ago, the guy was top dog in the Russian space program! And Angie…wasn't the situation complicated enough without tossing in a love-struck hormonal teenager? No, that wasn't fair. Becca didn't know Angie *or* Duke well enough to be judgmental. Nevertheless, she still felt it was a good thing the NSA had taken over at the Peak. She needed to stay here and keep the lid on things.

Nick didn't believe in God, but neither did he believe in coincidences. Whether it was Fate, Karma, or some supernatural power, *something* brought him to this particular place with these particular people. The discovery Duke had shared with them would affect every person's life on the planet. The decisions the four of them made would likely shape the course of history of the entire world. He accepted his new role with the same stoicism he had accepted his old life. The new turn of events certainly promised to be interesting.

After lunch, Becca found Duke out by the central shaft. "John," she began, "I mean Duke, I don't have any bars. Can you use a cell phone inside all of this rock?"

"Well, I could when I first moved here, but for some reason, the satellites have been messed up lately. You're welcome to use the landline in the living room, though."

"Oh, thanks. I have to check on my new job opportunity. I took your advice and contacted SETI before I drove up here. They're supposed to get their budget allocation sometime this week."

"Really? So the rumors are true? You're not going to work at the observatory any more?"

"Nope. Actually, I turned in my notice the day before you stopped sending signals. Dr. Howards was pissed, the NSA was taking over everything, and I figured it was only a matter of time before the job disappeared. I never did understand how my piddlin' project at the Peak kept its funding when everything else was being dropped."

"Do you know where the funding came from?" Duke asked.

"Yeah, I had to fill out all of the budget paperwork. J. W. Duke Research Group, I think—. Son of a bitch!" she exploded. "*You*, again! I oughtta kick your sorry ass down that mine shaft."

"That wouldn't look too good on the reference from your previous employer," Duke laughed as he back stepped to put some distance between himself and Becca, "or your new employer, either" he added. "I have my fingers pretty deep in the SETI pie, too. I've always been fascinated with the idea that we're not alone in this universe."

"Well, I'll be damned," Becca replied, shaking her head. "So, if I kiss up to you, do I get the SETI job?"

"After that 'sorry ass' remark? Fat chance," Duke teased.

"Me and my big mouth! Where's Jeanette when I need her?" she moaned.

Duke waited until everyone got settled in the library again—Becca and Nick on the sofa, Angie in a swivel chair, and he sitting sideways on a chair next to the table.

"Are you totally brain-dead from this morning?" he asked. "If not, then I'd like to get your help in finding answers to several more questions."

The three "students" looked at each other hesitantly.

"As long as it doesn't have anything to do with New Physics," Becca answered for the others.

"No. No physics," he reassured her, "but the questions are just as hard. We have the power of a black hole that can be held in your hands. What do we do with it? Something more intelligent than *I* came up with, certainly. What *can* we do with it in a world that can't handle the technology it already has?

"Next, we're going to need help. We need a partner company or companies that can work in the open to provide the manpower, expertise, services and equipment we will need. And *security*. Who can we trust?

"And last, at least for now, how do we pay for it? Whatever we agree to do is going to cost money and lots of it."

"She-*it!*" Becca shook her head slowly. "You don't mess with trivia, do you?"

QUESTIONS

Duke wrote each question at the top of the whiteboard: What to do? Who to help? How to pay? Angie and Nick answered the first one immediately—space travel. Becca agreed, but for a different reason. She feared the force might be too dangerous to use on Earth, based on what Duke had told them.

"Not only on Earth, but in near space, too," he added. "*Tetra* has seventeen main and auxiliary thrust disks. Each of those An-G fields has to be monitored to make sure it's not pointed at Earth or anything else that's critical. More vehicles will make the monitoring task exponentially more difficult. Deep space may be the only safe place to use it."

He wrote 'space travel' beside the first question, pleased at how quickly they had reached a consensus, but not surprised. Belarov had been in the Russian space program most of his adult life, Angie aspired to do the same, and Becca spent her time looking into space via Kitt Peak's telescope. Using the An-G force, they now had the means to explore it in person. Duke even felt that the 'instantly infinite' quality of the force offered possibilities of faster-than-light travel.

The answer to the next question, 'who to help', was of huge importance. Revamping the U.S. space program to incorporate the An-G force would require hundreds of thousands of workers. Duke's tiny group couldn't accomplish even a fraction of the work that would be required. They needed an aerospace company—a huge one, and one with absolutely fail-safe security. *Everyone*—individuals, companies, and governments—would want the secret once anti-gravity was announced.

"Most aerospace companies have gone defunct, thanks to Q of L," Becca observed. "Who's left, and which ones can we trust?"

"Well," Duke said, "if Gramp was still CEO of McLean Precision, I'd choose them, but I don't know much about the new guy in charge since Gramp retired."

"But you *do* know a lot about Gramp," Angie pointed out.

Duke's face lit up. "Angie, I *like* that idea. Gramp would come out of retirement in a heartbeat for something like this. Perfect!" He wrote 'Gramp' on the board and underlined it.

"All right, the last one may be the hardest. 'How to pay' not only means where does the money come from, but how do we get it to our creditors? We can't sign contracts, transfer funds, or meet with anyone in person."

The room remained silent so long, Duke began to think the challenge was beyond their capacity. Finally Nick spoke up.

"I seem to be temporarily short of funds," he lamented, "but I was wondering—how much is worth a cubic kilometer of nickel-iron alloy? We go to asteroid belt, bring back small one, use to pay bills." He looked around the room.

The reaction was immediate and enthusiastic with everyone talking at once. When the tumult finally died down, Duke went back to the whiteboard.

"So, we explore space, get McLean to build whatever

196 :: BEYOND HERCULES

we need, and drop a small asteroid in their parking lot from time to time."

"That's going to scare shit out of the natives," Becca predicted.

Duke grinned. "We'll have to let the world know what's going on, but they'll want us to share the technology, and I don't think it's safe to do that. That's the problem I've been struggling with for over a year. How do we tell the world that we've discovered anti-gravity without revealing the technology, our identities, or our whereabouts?"

"Hold it, Buster," Becca interrupted. "You're sneaking in another question on us."

"True," Duke admitted, "but it has to be answered"

He had considered dealing with the U.N., but they would be buried in bureaucracy over every simple thing. Angie suggested they continue sending messages to Kitt Peak, since news coverage was already international. It wasn't the whole world, but neither was the U.N., and their anonymity would be safe. Duke looked at Becca and Nick, raising his eyebrows.

"Not with the vocabulary *we* developed," Becca answered.

"No," Duke agreed. "I think it's time we came out of the closet. Let's switch to English."

"We must be careful," Nick warned. "One can identify my native language from my accent and sentence structure."

Duke squelched the idea of voice communication immediately. They would send pictures and text only. Even then they would have to be extremely careful about the wording.

"So what do we tell them?" Angie asked.

"Whoa," Duke interrupted. "That's yet *another* question and an all-day project in itself. World peace will have to wait one more day. My brain is tired. Let's go do something else."

No one voiced objections. They all headed for the central shaft. As they neared the lower level, Nick spoke.

"If you look for suggestions of something else, may I offer one?"

"Sure," Duke answered.

"I would like to assist in the repair of your space craft. I am very eager to learn to fly—if that would be permitted."

"Me, too," Becca agreed. "I mean—not the flying part—I just want to *see* it."

"Hey, that's right," Angie said. "You only saw what the camera showed. I can't wait to see your reaction!"

"Watch your step, everybody," Duke cautioned at the bottom of the spiral stairs. "I still have some work to do on the landing."

They all trooped through the horizontal mineshaft, squinting as they exited into the bright afternoon sunshine. The *Tetra* was still parked in the other tunnel with only inches of clearance between the corners of the tetrahedron and the mineshaft walls. It looked small tucked away in the darkness.

Becca's expression changed from excited anticipation to disappointment, then to awe. "My God," she whispered, looking back and forth between the craft and the three people standing nearby. "You came down on *that*?" she said to Nick, "and you *got* him down on that?" She looked at Duke and Angie. "Awesome," she said, still in a subdued voice. The four of them stood in awkward silence until Becca spoke again.

"Sorry. I didn't mean to go sober on you. Can I help do something?" she asked.

"Sure," Duke responded, happy for the change of mood. "If you and Nick can grab the two front corners, I'll slide under to get to the one behind. Angie, you can stand out front and direct us."

They set the *Tetra* on blocks that Angie retrieved from the workshop, and gathered in front of the sphere that had been seared by the laser beam. Duke looked closely at the damage.

"I made spares for everything except the camera sphere," he said. "We can leave it locked in home position. We still won't be able to focus on anything close, but that won't keep you from flying. We can probably have everything fixed in a couple of hours," he said to Nick.

"Well, if you men are going to be playing in the workshop, we women may as well go shopping," Becca announced. "I need to pick up a few things."

"I wonder if you would pick up a few *more* things while you're in town," Duke inquired. "If Nick doesn't mind, I'd like to see if we can change his appearance so that he can go out in public without being recognized. He's probably getting tired of looking at these sandstone walls."

"Thank you, yes," Nick agreed immediately. "I would like that very much."

Becca smiled impishly. She framed Nick's face like a movie director setting up a scene. "Whattaya think, Angie? Blond? Moustache and sideburns? Maybe an earring?"

Nick stiffened.

"Okay, no earring," she patted his arm, "but lots of tanning lotion. You stand out like a ghost in a ghetto, Sweetie."

The two women took off for town while the men began dismantling the damaged parts of the *Tetra*.

Replacing the broken strut required the removal of the thrust/sensor spheres on each end. Duke removed the undamaged one first and handed it to Nick to put on the workbench. Nick carried it as if it were a glass globe filled with nitroglycerin.

Duke smiled at him. "I handled it the same way when I first started experimenting with the ribbon. I was scared to death that I might accidentally set off an earthquake or something," he admitted. "Think of it like it's a video camera or a laptop," he suggested. "It helps."

Duke turned a small recessed tab on the camera sphere to release the access panel. He peered inside, shining a flashlight around to reveal the camera, lasers, and a small electronics package toward the back. One side of the camera was spattered with gobbets of melted plastic.

"I think I see the problem." He stood aside so Nick could see. With a small screwdriver, he popped out a piece of plastic that was stuck between the rotating rings on the camera lens. "Now we should be able to focus the camera."

They finished the repairs well ahead of schedule and were up in the control room going over the joystick functions when the women returned.

Nick was definitely not a blond. The two women worked on him all morning. After enduring an hour of bleaching, trimming, combing, and criticizing, they all agreed—not blond. A short time later they ruled out red. Brunette was too close to his natural color, so they took the only option left.

"Yes!" Angie declared as she stepped back to view the results. Nick's newly shaved head shone in the light. The broken nose and scar on his cheek added their effects to the overall picture. "He looks like death warmed over, but this is it."

"I'll take care of that," Becca promised. "You go find something to do for an hour or so."

Angie left them alone—wondering if Becca was actually flirting with Nick. Whatever. She was happy for them and happy for herself.

"Ta-daaa," Becca tooted as she bowed and ushered Nick into the room with a sweeping wave of her arm. He was tan, wearing loafers, khaki slacks, and a short-sleeved turtleneck sweater that accented his muscular arms.

"I still think he needs an earring, but we'll let it slide for now."

RIBBONS

"You two behave up there," Duke admonished as Angie and Nick headed up to the control room for flying lessons.

"I don't think he meant it *that* way," Angie reassured Nick when she saw the look on his face.

"No," Duke laughed. "I meant *way* up there. I don't want to see the *Tetra* show up on the evening news."

"Rats!" Angie feigned disappointment. "I was going to buzz Roswell."

She and Nick disappeared down the arched hallway with Angie explaining about Roswell, Area 51, and UFOs. They had been waiting all day to go practice flying, but Duke had insisted that they wait until dark.

Becca had volunteered to cook dinner, and Duke was enjoying the luxury of having nothing to do. He lounged at the small kitchen table, directing her to the right cabinet when she needed a utensil or ingredient.

The kitchen, like all other rooms in the mine, was circular, but Duke had erected a partition that sliced off a segment which served as a pantry. The major appliances were arranged in an 'L' along the partition and the adjacent sandstone wall, leaving the rest of the room open for the table and chairs.

"Becca, can I ask your advice about a problem while you cook? Angie and I can't seem to come up with any ideas."

"Sure. Shoot."

"It's Nick. When we brought him down, he was hurting pretty badly. I keep wondering what we would have done if he had been really seriously injured. His picture has been in the world news, he has no ID, and he speaks with a Russian accent. It's like this giant finger is pointing right at him—and at us. You two did a great job changing his appearance, but we don't have the first clue what to do about his ID," he explained.

"Yeah," she nodded. "The problem had already occurred to me." She twisted her mouth sideways, frowning. "I know some people who know some people who know some people," she admitted. "I do volunteer work in a Hispanic community outside of Tucson," she explained. "False papers are always available for a price. The question is—can they generate a set of papers that will work for Nick. A six-foot Juan Gonzales would raise some eyebrows."

"It's a little more complicated than that," Duke pointed out. "He says that his cousin—the real Nick—became a U.S. citizen, so he had legitimate papers. The problem is—we don't know how to put Nick and the papers together."

"Understood," Becca said, still pensive. "When I go back home, I'll ask around. You may need to bring him down if things look promising."

"Great! That would be a big load off my mind."

"Ehhh. What's up, Doc?"

Becca splattered picante sauce on the stove and countertop when Angie's voice came booming through the kitchen.

A few seconds later at a lower volume, "Take me to

your leader," followed by Angie's characteristic giggle.

"Someone is going to go without her supper tonight," Becca predicted as she wiped off the countertop. "I thought you told her to behave."

"Sorry, Becca," Duke said, laughing. "I forgot that the microphone was still connected. I've got an errand that I can send them on that should keep them out of your hair. I'll be back in a few minutes." He headed for the central shaft. *Angie and Becca are getting along, but I'll have to remind her not to rock the boat.*

They appeared to be expecting him when he got to the control room. Angie was still giggling.

"Nick, I'm putting you in charge up here," Duke said. "Otherwise we may be eating peanut butter and jelly sandwiches tonight."

Angie stuck her tongue out at him.

"Also, I have something for you two to do that will help keep you out of trouble, challenge your flying skills, and accomplish something worthwhile at the same time." He squatted down to pull a small control box out from under the table, throwing one of the toggle switches as he placed the box in front of the console.

"Bring the *Tetra* down in front of the workshop and hover it there a few minutes," Duke instructed. "When you see me give you a 'thumbs up' signal, throw this switch, then wait for me to come back up." He headed for the shaft again.

The *Tetra* was waiting outside the workshop by the time Duke got down there. *Either Nick's a quick learner, or Angie's still flying.* He walked to the very back of the workshop. A wheeled cart supported what looked like a huge wrecking ball with a seam around the middle. He pulled the cart carefully through the tunnel and stopped outside in front of the *Tetra*. The moveable thrust disk had pivoted to the back of the strut, and a pincer-like clamp on the end of a short arm now occupied its place. He maneuvered the ring on the ball until it was inside of the clamp, then stepped back and signaled with his thumb. The clamp snapped shut.

Back in the control room, Duke outlined the task. "I need this sphere to be placed in orbit in the same place we orbited before—over the hundred eleventh parallel. I could probably do it myself, but it would take me three or four times as long. I confess—my navigation skills are pretty primitive.

"This is an optical ribbon-making machine—or more accurately that's what's inside the sphere. It has to operate in a vacuum and it's a real pain to have to shut it down every time the ribbon roll gets full. I'd like to put it in orbit where I can open it up. That way it can run more or less continuously. When you get it in position, this toggle switch releases the clamp. Any questions?"

"How much does the sphere weigh?" Angie asked.

"A little over fifty pounds. You can determine the mass the same way we did when we measured Nick's mass before bringing him down."

"Do you want us to call you before we release it?" Angie asked.

"Nope. I trust you. If the best teacher and the best student in the world can't do the job, then no one can."

Angie beamed, and Nick sat up straighter with a glimmer of pride showing on his face.

"On second thought, I *do* want you to call me," Duke

amended. "As soon as you release it, I'll need to open the sphere and activate the machine. I want to watch it to make sure it's working correctly."

Duke headed back down to the living level. *That will keep them busy for a while.* He chuckled to himself.

"What kind of volunteer work do you do in the Hispanic community?" Duke asked, as Becca continued to prepare dinner. She explained that she worked with teenage girls—young women—helping them learn to speak and read English—anything that would allow them to consider options other than getting married and having babies. She wasn't against either one of those, but she saw too many abusive marriages and too many unwanted pregnancies. She wanted to give them some choices.

"That's a long way from astronomy," Duke observed.

"Yeah, I guess so. It's sort of a payback," she said. She grew up in a barrio—mostly Hispanics—with a few others like herself mixed in—all of them going nowhere. Her mom was a waitress; her father disappeared before she could remember. She had a teacher in high school, who was one of those truly dedicated people. He kicked their butts and made them use the skills he knew they all had. Anyone who showed real potential got more attention. He dug around and found grants, scholarships, financial aid—whatever it took. Thanks to him, Becca got her Bachelor's degree. After that, she was able to help herself.

"Nice success story," Duke commented.

"No complaints. What about you?"

Duke gave her the Cliff's Notes version of his life—his early aptitude, fast-track through school, easy money from his inventions, and popularity. When the Q of L movement wiped out the science budget at the high school in Haysville, he started volunteering his time to teach science—not officially, but after school.

"Angie moved in across the street around that time," Duke continued. "Her story is similar to yours with a few extra twists. She was a kid with a phenomenal potential, going nowhere. I sort of took her under my wing. I sent her to Russia to take some courses she couldn't get here. Nick was one of her instructors. Then —"

"What! No one told me *that* part. Oh, this is just too weird. Now I begin to understand."

"Understand what?"

"Well, it surprised me as much as it did Nick when you included him in the New Physics class. I thought you'd only known him for a few days. It makes a lot more sense now."

"Do you think including him was a mistake?" Duke asked anxiously.

"No. He has expressed only the utmost respect and gratitude for the both of you. I don't think you have to worry about his loyalty."

The last word was stressed enough to catch Duke's attention. "Is there something you think we *should* worry about?"

"I wish I could tell you for sure. One second he was on top of the world, a national idol with a bright and beautiful future. Next second, he was a man without a country, staring death in the face—already dead, in fact, with respect to his previous life. I'm not saying that he's about to go off the deep end, but he's bound to harbor some pent-up emotions that he will have to express or internalize. Is he the same guy he was in Russia? Probably not. Is he still basically trustworthy? I think so, but I don't know for sure."

Duke sighed heavily. "Why did I ever —"

"Oh, shit!" Becca interrupted. Her expletive changed the mood abruptly. "I was so absorbed in talking to you that I almost forgot about dinner." She began lifting lids and checking the contents of each pot and pan. "Better give them a yell," she advised. "This will be ready in just a few minutes."

Duke hoped that Angie and Nick would still be working on the thrust program. It would not do to leave the *Tetra* flying with no one at the helm. He was reluctant to interrupt them, but they didn't really have a deadline, so they could resume after dinner.

Angie threw a wadded paper at him when he walked into the control room.

"Does that mean I'm sleeping in the doghouse tonight?" he asked. The problem he'd given them must have been more of a challenge than he anticipated.

"Not yet," she replied, but the raised eyebrows told him not to press his luck.

"Becca says dinner is almost ready. Can you take a break?"

Duke was in bed—alone, but not in the doghouse. Angie would come later. She told him not to wait for her, since it would be well after midnight before she and Nick got the *Tetra* in position and stabilized. Duke suggested that they leave it there overnight. They could release the sphere the next day.

He didn't notice the time when Angie came to bed—
he only noticed the warmth of her breath as she nuzzled his
neck. They fell asleep in each other's arms.

ALLEGRO

MILKY WAY GALAXY, LOCAL ARM:

Philosophers might ask whether the sentinel qualified as an intelligent being. It was aware. Was it *self*-aware? Did it think? What *is* thinking? Consciousness? Was it exercising free will? Was it innovating?

If the philosophers thought of it, they would all be surprised to note what a model citizen the sentinel would make in any society. Except for that one tragic programming error, Brother Kirrt and Lord Chizek could have been proud of their creation. It followed the rules, minded its own business, performed its job efficiently, and found satisfaction in doing so.

<I have sung loudly. I have sung softly. Now I will sing quickly.>

ANNOUNCEMENT

Angie and Nick released the ribbon generator early in the morning, then sat and drummed their fingers while Duke activated it and checked its operation. As soon as he gave the okay, they were off—challenging each other's flying skills, fighting over the joystick. Watching the big screen while they did barrel rolls made Duke nauseated. He left the control room with his stomach turning flip-flops.

When it began to get dark, Duke called to them from the hall. "It's time for you kids to put your toys away and come in, now." Reluctantly they parked the *Tetra* within a few meters of the ribbon generator, lasers aimed at Kitt Peak once again.

Becca had declared herself Encryption Officer and had dedicated several hours, carefully wording the message so it would reveal only what the foursome wanted to reveal. It finally met everyone's approval.

"All right, everybody—one last time. Any second thoughts?" Duke looked around the room. "This is the point of no return. Once we tell them that we've got anti-gravity, the search for us begins. Our lives will never be the same again."

No one said anything. Duke expected that. They had already made the decision together. He looked at Becca, shrugged his shoulders and said "Go."

Becca transmitted the scanned image of the document

to *Tetra*, and its lasers beamed the picture down to Kitt Peak.

Good evening.

We end the charade. It caused fear, mistrust, and bloodshed.

We will communicate in English. We request translation and worldwide sharing of all messages.

We are a multi-national group. Our identities and locations will not be revealed for security reasons.

We announce discovering anti-gravity.

Our goal is to share benefits with all. First priority will be prevention of misuse. We invite suggestions of how to realize goal and meet restrictions.

Details of discovery will be provided in next communication.

Good evening.

"Now that was terse," Angie exclaimed. "Just like one of the Colonel's lectures." She smiled at Nick. "Every word counts."

It took less than a half-hour for the answer to arrive. "Whoa, that was fast." Duke glanced at the first few sentences of the response on the screen, then walked away, shaking his head in disgust. "Obviously the NSA still controls communications at Kitt Peak. Do this! Don't do that! Maybe *they* think they're in charge here, but I've got a surprise for them." He fumed a little while longer, then cooled down. "Would one of you mind reviewing their response? They might actually have some good ideas, and I don't think I can be open-minded enough to recognize one if I see it."

"I will do this," Nick volunteered. "I am not open-minded, too, but I am familiar with security...*sklad uma*," he said, looking to Angie for help.

"... mentality," she supplied.

Duke opened a window on the big screen so they could watch the news coverage on TV. It began almost as quickly as the response from Kitt Peak.

"The media must still be camped out on the access roads," Becca commented. "The NSA kicked them out of the dome before I left, but anyone within miles can still see the laser beams."

The media analyzed each sentence of the announcement one by one, speculating on its significance and implications. They interviewed "experts" who further analyzed and speculated. When they ran out of experts, they called in science fiction writers. Duke finally interrupted the marathon to scan other channels.

"Well, good," he said after running through the channels. "At least the news media are doing what we asked. I counted seven different languages. By the time we make the next announcement, the whole world will be tuned in."

"Speaking of...," Angie began, "... what 'details' do you plan to provide them? That sounds dangerous."

"It is, but we're the ones in control. No matter what we tell them, it will be less than what they want. Let's go to bed. This coverage will last all night."

WHITE HOUSE, OVAL OFFICE:

"My fellow Americans... ."

Carlton Tate felt ridiculous beginning his address to the nation with the same hackneyed phrase that could have originated with George Washington, except they didn't call themselves Americans back then. Nevertheless, Tate was in a good mood. The previous evening's announcement had removed the bull's eye painted on his back, and now it was someone else's turn to squirm.

First of all, the group that had discovered anti-gravity *had* to be responsible for the atmospheric and near-space disturbances. The coincidence was too obvious. That transferred the target to their backs, but even better, it created a situation that could easily be labelled a national emergency. He would get access to emergency funds. They could send up a shuttle, grab the sons-of-bitches who were sending the signal, and wring the anti-gravity technology out of them. The acquisition would forever be associated with his term in office.

Second, it defused the ticking bomb between the U.S. and Russia, which had come dangerously close to exploding, especially when debris falling from the sky had been unequivocally identified as Russian in origin. President Rostov still hadn't given a satisfactory answer for that.

Finally, there was the discovery itself. Anti-gravity! It would revolutionize *everything*. The economy would grow like a Ponzi scheme. No, he'd have to find a better metaphor, or was it simile? Whatever. That's what he had speechwriters for. But with plenty of money, he could finally show those nay-sayers that the Quality Of Life Movement was a good idea after all.

Yes, life was looking good again for Carlton Tate.

"Hot damn, I love it!" Becca exclaimed when the second message finally received everyone's approval. "Interface Window! We tell them what it does, but don't give them Jack to work with."

"It sounds clunky," Angie complained.

"Yeah," Duke agreed, "but I think it's the effect we're looking for. We want to make it look as if each sentence was written by a committee whose members only speak English as a second language. It communicates, but it tells them only what we want them to know."

"You're still worried about someone identifying who or where we are?"

"Angie, I'm terrified. If I directed the *Tetra*'s thrust disk straight down, I could probably cause molten iron from Earth's core to erupt on the other side of the planet. I could have done exactly that in Haysville if the angle had been slightly different. Who do you think would like to have that kind of power, and to what lengths do you think they would go to get it?"

In the silence that followed, Duke could hear the sound of wind sighing in the central shaft.

"Sorry. I don't want anyone getting paranoid because of what I just said. I think we're doing the right thing, but I want those thoughts to be tickling the back of our minds, subconsciously influencing and guiding every decision we make and every word we communicate.

"Let's do it," he said quickly to change the mood. "Becca, do you want to do the honors again?"

Good evening.

Thank you for comments and suggestions. Outlined below are major details of discovery.

Genesis Field — vectored field of unknown nature, origin, or extent, but with uniform intensity and direction observed throughout Earth's orbit.

Interface Window — device through which energy in Genesis Field is transformed into repelling force. Magnitude of force is proportional to sine of angle between Interface Window plane and Genesis Field vector. Direction of force is perpendicular to plane of Interface Window.

Anti-gravity — repelling force field that acts instantaneously at infinite distances with no equal and opposite reaction.

Please consider social impact of information provided above. We welcome suggestions that meet conditions imposed earlier: share benefits; prevent misuse.

POSTSCRIPT: We deny responsibility for the strange behavior of satellites and weather. We join you in seeking the cause.

Good evening.

"They've been thinking since our last announcement," Becca observed after reading the response from Kitt Peak.

"Give us the secret; we'll protect it for you," she paraphrased.

"Yeah, right," Duke added derisively. "I'm getting sick of dealing with those guys. We need to figure out how to talk to someone else."

"How to talk is easy," Becca responded. "All of the major networks have their own receivers on the mountain now. How to get an answer is the real problem. None of them is set up to transmit laser signals and if they were, we wouldn't be able to distinguish their signal from the one from the Peak."

"What about the internet?" Angie suggested. "Most of the networks already have webpages or blogs dedicated to the topic. They could post their response there and we could read it at our leisure."

"I like that idea, Angie. Can we set up our own web-page and scrap the laser signals altogether?"

"No...I mean yes we can, but the location of the web server can be traced."

"How do you communicate with signal craft?" Nick asked.

"Good thinking, Nick," Duke said. "I use a digitized An-G beam. The media can set up a simple vibration detector, and we can send them a beam from *Tetra*. We can work out the details with them tomorrow."

The details took two days and two more messages to work out, but resulted in a very satisfactory arrangement—satisfactory to Duke's group— not to the NSA, which lost its monopoly on the conversations. Several news agencies including AFP, Reuters Group, ITAR-TASS, and CNN as well as the United Nations competed to receive the messages and provide the requested communication services. Although the U.N. offered the most extensive translation services, CNN came in a close second and offered faster response, polling services and imaging capability.

Duke felt certain they made the right decision to go with CNN when he saw the first webpage summarizing public reaction to the announcement. Pie charts showed that thirty percent of the people believed they had discovered anti-gravity, twenty-nine percent did not, and the other forty-one were undecided. Additional charts broke down the believers and non-believers by demographic groups and summarized their reactions. There were demands to turn over the technology to the U.N., proofs by renowned physicists that anti-gravity could not exist, doomsayers predicting the Apocalypse, etc., etc. The most serious reaction was Russia's insistence that the U.S. was testing a beam weapon that they said was launched two days before the messages began.

"This is serious situation," Nick warned. "They truly believe this, and President Rostov is hothead. They may do something foolish. We must act to reduce tensions."

Duke rested his forehead on the heels of his hands. "I should have dropped the whole experiment down the hole in my garage floor and poured concrete over it," he moaned. "All right. Nick, we're going to need your help with the details."

Angie clicked CNN's website. "They got it," she announced. "They added a headline and stuck in the articles that we so carefully left out, but the message looks the same."

BEAM WEAPONS IN SPACE
RUSSIAN, NOT AMERICAN

A high-energy beam weapon was placed in geosynchronous orbit over the one hundred eleventh parallel by the crew of the Russian spacecraft, *Buran II*. We destroyed it. A second weapon exploded in low Earth orbit immediately after it was released. It cut the shuttle in half and killed two cosmonauts who had not returned to the safety of the cabin. A third cosmonaut was injured, but not immediately killed in the explosion. Our unmanned signal craft, *Tetra*, arrived in time to communicate briefly with the survivor before his air ran out. Cosmonauts Belarov, Kalinova and Yabin did not die in a plane crash as reported by the Russian news agency. Debris falling from the sky is from the two weapons and the *Buran II*.

Two additional transmissions provided pictures—one, a short clip, showed the brief battle between the *Tetra* and the beam weapon, the other showed the tumbling nose and tail sections of the *Buran II* and the final close-ups of the cabin window with Belarov waving.

"That ought to shut their yaps," Becca said. Duke looked unconvinced. Nick stood stiffly behind the other three, his jaw muscles clenched tightly.

ADAGIO

MILKY WAY GALAXY, LOCAL ARM:

<*I have sung loudly. I have sung softly. I have sung quickly. Now I will sing slowly.*>

The sentinel's makers had given it optical sensors with which to see the giant planet above which it orbited. Although it could perceive the full spectrum of visible light, beauty might have been a concept beyond its ability to grasp—or not. Nevertheless, it could certainly wonder at the marvel below.

Long chains of salmon and cream swirled together in interlocking paisley patterns trapped between bands of solid white and solid rust. Freckles, rings and dots peppered the huge marble from pole to pole, fuzzing and fading to blue on the sunward side, black on the other. Giant ovals floated here and there, red-brown curled with blue and white in yin and yang oneness. With a regularity the sentinel noted, black elliptical shadows moved across the scene, outpacing the fastest of the clouds.

Alas, the sentinel's attention was centered elsewhere— the sensual tickle from an audience far away. It sang to that audience, slowly.

HERCULES

"Something's wrong," Angie said the moment she sat down at *Tetra's* control console. "It's not where we left it. It's drifted out of position."

Nick sat at the table beside her, and the two of them began discussing the current console readings compared with the notes they had recorded when they released the ribbon generator. Neither one seemed to realize that they had slipped back into Russian.

"We stabilized it," she insisted, speaking English again. "It didn't move a centimeter for twenty minutes last night. Now it's more than a meter out of position!"

"Easy, Angie," Duke reassured. "You or Nick making a mistake is the *last* thing I would suspect. The fact that he's sitting here beside you right now is proof of both of your skills. Maybe the Earth passed through another wave of dark matter that moved it. Let's put it back in position and see what the news says," he suggested.

Angie insisted on doing it herself. Her hands were trembling by the time the craft was stabilized.

"Why don't you pilots take a well-deserved break?" Becca suggested, and Duke quickly seconded the motion. "If you get bored, then work on the next message for CNN," she told them as she shooed them out of the control room.

Duke went to the console and called up the log file. He scrolled through it and highlighted a long section to send to the printer.

"We'll have to do quite a few calculations," he said, "but the log should tell us what happened and when."

Duke explained what each of the data items represented, and they discussed the approach they would take.

"Can you dump all of this into a file instead of on paper?" Becca asked. "I can write a program to do the calculations. I need to practice my programming skills, anyway," she reasoned.

Becca skipped dinner. Her analysis of the log file vindicated Angie and Nick—the ribbon generator was stationary when they left it. Sometime during the night, it began drifting infinitesimally southward away from the equator. She spent the afternoon and early evening analyzing the magnitude and direction of the force that was pushing it out of orbit. When she came down to the living room, her cheeks were flushed, and she had a smile on her face.

Angie sat at the table with Nick, looking over a piece of paper. "Perfect timing, Becca. We just finished the next message. How's this sound?"

Angie read the message, imitating a monotone computer voice.

"Well, I guess it's okay, but I think you left out the most important part," Becca answered indifferently.

"What part is that?" Angie sounded miffed.

"The part about the signal from Hercules," Becca responded in a matter-of-fact tone.

"Hercules? Becca, what are you talking about?"

"You guys didn't do anything wrong when you positioned the ribbon generator," Becca explained. "Somebody pushed it out of orbit—somebody far, far away."

"Becca—," Angie began, but Becca resumed before she could finish.

"I analyzed the log file and found that the craft was being pushed by a periodic force—a force that came in pulses with a very interesting and familiar pattern. Someone in the constellation of Hercules is sending us a message."

"You're kidding!" Angie screamed. "For real?"

"Yep. For real." She grinned.

Everyone gathered around Becca and waited for details.

"Well, what did they say?" Duke finally asked.

"Not much, but they're obviously more intelligent than we are—or at least more than *you*. They can count all the way to fifteen!" She grinned again. "The signal is nearly identical to the one you sent—binary integers counting from fifteen down to zero. The digits are spaced out really far, though."

"Is there any chance that they intercepted our laser signals and patterned their signal after ours? That would mean that they're pretty close, wouldn't it?" Duke asked.

"That was my first question, too, but no—your beam always hit Earth. Although my reply from Kitt Peak went out into space, I never sent a countdown of numbers, so it's not likely a copycat signal.

"As to them being close—no. I analyzed the deflections in the motion of the sphere and found that a very tiny force—actually two different levels of force—was periodically pushing it out of orbit. All of the nudges came from the northern part of the Hercules constellation."

The significance of her statements slowly revealed itself on the faces of the other three.

"We're not alone," Duke said in a subdued voice.

Becca nodded, uncharacteristically quiet. "Not only does life exist elsewhere in the universe, but *intelligent* life. We're actually receiving a message from them."

"Oh, my God, Becca! Can you see them? I mean…is there a star where the message is coming from?" Angie grabbed Duke's arm as if he were the messenger.

Becca shook her head. "My calculations aren't accurate enough to pinpoint the source that precisely. My best guess would be a star system somewhere in the local arm of our galaxy."

The room went silent again.

"Angie, I think I've got a bottle of champagne in the back of the pantry. It's warm, but we can still drink it," Duke said.

"I'll get glasses," she replied.

The glasses Angie brought were for margaritas, but no one complained.

Duke thought carefully for a moment, then raised his glass. "To life, both here and there," he offered.

"Nice," Becca said as she clinked glasses with him and the others.

Although it required more than one swallow, Nick downed his glass in the Russian tradition. "You must drain your glass to indicate your full support," he admonished. "I pour," he said as the others emptied their glasses. He poured each person a smaller serving, reducing his own only slightly.

"For *my* life." He held his glass first in front of Duke, then Angie. "*Za vas,*" he said simply, but with utmost sincerity in his eyes.

"Yes," Becca agreed, "I'll certainly give that one my full support." She clinked glasses with Nick. "I guess I'm next." She poured and returned to Nick's side.

"Hmm. Okay. To love—may it be the strongest force of all."

Angie darted a glance at Duke. Was Becca just being philosophical? Duke dismissed it with a slight shrug and smile, then pointed to her.

"Well, this one is so over-done that it sounds corny, but I mean it all the same—to world peace. May life, love, and knowledge bring us together in peace on our world and across the universe."

Duke slept late, but was still the first one up the next morning. It was nine-thirty when Becca came shuffling through the living room in her bathrobe and slippers, wet hair piled atop her head in a turban. She glanced at the TV, which displayed nothing but snow. "Cable out?"

"Yeah. I called and got a recorded message. Whatever happened to the satellites before is happening again. That mumbo-jumbo about dark matter. They don't have any estimate when it'll be fixed."

"If it's moving the satellites again, God knows what it's doing to the atmosphere. We're in for some hellacious storms, I'll bet."

Duke went into the kitchen, started a pot of coffee, and made a batch of Bloody Marys. If everyone else felt like he did, they would need it. The others trickled in and took seats at the table. "Who wants what for breakfast?" he asked.

Breakfast was a quiet affair with people speaking in

whispers, if at all. Becca topped off everyone's cup with the last of the coffee and took a big sip.

"Mm...mm...mm!"

Duke thought she had burned her mouth judging by the pained expression on her face. She banged her cup down hard on the table, spilling a good bit of it, and swallowed.

"The satellites!" she yelled, and then winced, holding her head. "It's not dark matter pushing them out of orbit! It's the message pulses. That's why there's no TV, and that's what's screwing up the weather. They must have been sending the message for months!"

"They don't believe us," Angie said as soon as CNN's webpage displayed. "Barely half of the people believe we have anti-gravity, but now they think *we've* been pushing the satellites out of orbit—that we will use them to extort money. They said if an anti-gravity signal was coming from Hercules, the European gravity wave experiments would have detected it."

"Here we go again," Duke said, shaking his head.

> You do not believe us again. We do not lie again. You look for a wave. Anti-gravity is not a wave. Perhaps gravity is also not. Look for a force. Binary number 1011 will be received at 2130:23:47.8 UT. The force will be greater for the one bit and less for the zero bit.
>
> We request your counsel on sending a response to the signal.

"I'm going for a walk," Becca said quietly from the doorway. Nick was in a foul mood and had been unresponsive to her attempts at conversation after Duke and Angie went down to the trailer for the evening. She was concerned about his increased moodiness and wanted to talk to Duke and Angie before they went to bed.

Lobo barked as Becca exited the mineshaft, but recognized her quickly and came to walk beside her.

Duke had the door open before they reached the trailer. "I wondered what he was barking at. Come in."

Angie was curled up on the couch, so Becca squeezed in by the dining table.

"Trouble?" Duke asked with the furrows already forming on his forehead.

"No emergency," Becca answered, "but something's eating away at Nick. It's hard to read him. I can't tell if he's depressed because the messages keep reminding him of his loss or if he's angry at some guy who pushed a button."

"I don't want him angry at *anyone*," Duke moaned. "Not with the knowledge he has."

"Sorry. I'm not trying to dump this in your lap. I'm only looking for some diversion that will take his mind off his problems."

Duke twisted his mouth sideways. "The problem with diversions is that most of them involve going out in public. I'm worried about him not having any ID."

"Actually, there's some good news on that front. We've located his—that is the *real* Nick's—landlady in Nome. We haven't contacted her. We'll have to figure out how to do that carefully, but all we need is a social security number and we can get the rest."

"Hmm. Nick *with* ID. Suddenly it doesn't sound like such a great idea after all." Duke massaged his forehead.

SUBTERFUGE

"I don't understand it," Angie complained. "We've discovered intelligent life right here in our own galaxy. You'd think that would generate a little excitement. Nothing. CNN says only nineteen percent think we're telling the truth, but the majority don't want to answer back. What's wrong with these people?"

"Momentum," Nick answered. "Every major discovery has met this same resistance to change. One cannot look to the masses for wisdom or guidance."

Duke shook his head. "I guess you're right, Nick. I've been expecting someone else to solve the problem and someone else to accept the responsibility. It's not going to happen. I may as well declare myself 'Benevolent Dictator for Life' and be done with it."

He sighed. "All right, I think the potential benefits of responding outweigh the risks. I'm inclined to answer back. What do the rest of you think?"

"A dictator would not ask," Nick observed.

"You're right!" Duke banged his fist on the table. "Encryption Officer," he said, looking at Becca, "prepare to respond!"

Nick applauded quietly.

"You approve of a dictatorship?" Becca asked.

"In this case, yes," he answered. "Democracy is a luxury—affordable only by those rich with time. It is wonderful form of government so long as no urgency exists."

"Hmm. I think I want to disagree with you, but you make a good point."

"Your democracy agrees with me," Nick argued. "What happens in state of emergency? Leader becomes dictator; individual rights are suspended."

Becca threw up her hands in resignation, and Angie laughed. "Don't even try, Becca," she advised. "I've been there."

"All right, everyone. We've got our work cut out for us," Duke said. "We need to bring the *Tetra* back down to the workshop. The camera and the moveable thrust disk have to be aligned perfectly if we're going to send signals back to Hercules."

"Becca, would you send a message to CNN saying we'll be out of touch for a couple of days? Angie, as soon as she's sent the message, bring the *Tetra* up to our latitude and hover there. When it gets dark, you can bring it down. Nick, I'm going to need your help in the workshop."

Angie drummed her fingers loudly enough to get a disapproving look from Becca. She had programmed the *Tetra* to hover high above Arizona and was waiting for dark to bring it down, but dark was several hours away. Becca was giving Nick a "tour" of the Grand Canyon, pointing out its features on the big screen. The news was on in a small window of the screen.

"Uh oh," Angie said. She sat up. "How many people are on the space station?"

"Seven, I believe," Nick answered.

"What's up?" Duke asked.

Angie pointed to the screen. "*Atlantis*' on-board computer failed. They're running on backup. They were supposed to re-supply the space station and bring the American team down. They just announced that the mission is being aborted. They're coming back right now."

"They can always send up an unmanned vehicle to get the supplies to them, but the people will have to stay," Duke said.

"No," Nick disagreed. "We have very reliable alternative transportation, I think. Only need sleeping nets." Everyone laughed.

"Changing the subject," Becca said, "do you think it's a good idea to use the moveable thrust disk on *Tetra* to talk to both CNN and Hercules? It will have to be constantly adjusted. I was wondering if we could have one for CNN set up here on the ground."

"Good idea, Becca," Duke answered, then frowned. "Dammit! I wish my head was screwed on better."

"What's wrong?" Angie asked.

"We need the ribbon from the ribbon generator so we can make more thrust disks. I should have thought of that when the *Tetra* was parked right next to it. Angie, I know how much you hate flying. Would you mind going back?"

Angie sighed heavily, then grinned. Nick slid into the chair beside her.

"Duke, it's not there!" Her face reflected the anguish in her voice. Nick's look of concern told Duke that the search had been thorough. "It didn't just drift out of position this time. It's not there at all!"

"Take it easy, Angie. It's got an An-G homing beacon the same as the *Tetra*. Becca's already got a program set up to locate the source of an An-G beam. It couldn't have gone far. We'll find it," he reassured.

"Them sons of bitches!" Becca threw her pencil down on the table where she had sketched the trajectory. "Computer failure, my ass!" She looked at Duke. "Your ribbon generator is on board the *Atlantis*."

Duke blanched. "You're sure?" he asked, but knew what her answer would be.

"It sure as hell didn't *fall* along that trajectory. How else?" she asked.

Duke's eyes darted all over the control room as his mind raced. *A diversion of this magnitude has to involve NSA, the Air Force, and probably required the President's approval. Anti-gravity technology in the hands of the U.S. government and enough ribbon to blow the Earth apart!*

"Where are they now?" he demanded.

"The news will probably tell us faster than I can figure out."

Duke grabbed the remote and flipped channels until he found one covering the shuttle's "emergency landing" at Edwards Air Force Base.

"Let me in here, please," he said to Nick and Angie. Nick rose quickly and held his chair for Duke.

Angie rolled to one side. "What are you going to do?" she asked.

Duke didn't answer her. His fingers fairly flew over the keyboard, and the camera pitched upward. The view on the big screen was beautiful and serene as always, but Duke had no time for beauty, and he was anything but serene. He barely glanced at the screen to verify that the craft was responding to his commands, then rummaged through the drawer to find a map. More slowly now, he entered additional commands, and the view yawed slightly to the left.

"Duke—," Angie began, but Nick touched her arm and shook his head.

The clouds streaming off the bottom of the screen began to slow. Duke's eyes shifted back and forth between the console and the news. "... *should be coming into view at any moment...,*" the announcer said.

The console beeped, and Duke typed rapidly again. Southern California suddenly loomed on the screen and grew in detail as the *Tetra* dropped. A dry lake, buildings, roads, and runways began to take shape.

"... *and there's the drag chute. A welcome sight after hours of....*" Duke didn't listen to the rest. He could see the shuttle on the big screen now. He watched as it rolled to a stop nearly a half-mile from the nearest building.

The hazmat trucks arrived first, closely followed by other recovery vehicles. More equipment approached in the distance. When the portable steps were raised into position on the side of the cabin, Duke zoomed in on the nose of the *Atlantis.*

"Come on, come on, hurry up," he mumbled as tiny white blobs moved slowly down the steps and into what looked like a motor home. He waited until the vehicle had gone only a few hundred feet, then hit the ENTER key.

"Duke!" Angie screamed.

Nick, standing behind the others, raised an eyebrow and nodded imperceptibly.

Windows shattered, scattering glass everywhere. Steel

desks jumped and crashed down again. Filing cabinets top-
pled. The sound was deafening—felt as much as heard.

Military training and discipline gradually brought the
stunned personnel out of their paralysis.

"Is anyone hurt?"

Everyone began talking at once.

"Was that an earthquake or an explosion?" someone
asked.

All eyes turned to look out the broken windows toward
the runway. Dust and debris billowed a half-mile away.

"What the hell? Where is *Atlantis*?"

"Get me a jeep!" an officer yelled as he ran for the door,
the rest of the personnel at his heels.

Two fire trucks tore down the runway, trailed by an
SUV and four jeeps, all headed toward the spot where the
shuttle had been parked. One fire truck, well ahead of the
other vehicles suddenly braked hard. Its tires squealed and
smoked. A deep, curving chasm spanned the entire width
of the runway. The vehicle's momentum carried it frighten-
ingly close to the precipitous edge.

With no more warning than a muffled crack, the section of concrete bearing the truck dropped downward as
the supporting ground slumped into the hole.

Men poured out of the vehicles as they arrived on
the scene. "Grab a rope and tie it to the truck," a fireman
ordered as he struggled into a harness. "You got me?" he
asked before leaning out over the edge of the hole. He had
to lean out a long way. "I don't believe it," he said as he
pulled himself back. "They're just sittin' there like they went
down on a goddamned elevator. Break out some more harnesses. Let's get them out of there before the sides cave in."

NSA

"I can't believe you did that!" Angie shouted. "You could have killed someone. That was the only shuttle we had left. They'll never fund a replacement. You just wiped out the entire American space program!" With each sentence her pitch became higher and her voice louder. She stood trembling, glaring at Duke, stiff arms at her sides, fists tightly clenched.

Duke didn't answer her immediately. He looked instead at the big screen and watched the landscape shrink as the *Tetra* ascended rapidly. When the altimeter showed 20km, he activated the hover program.

"Let's all go to the library where we can get comfortable," he suggested. Angie was the last one to follow.

"Nick pretty much summed it up," Duke began. "There's no time for voting during an emergency. I hope no one got hurt or killed. That's the last thing I want to happen. However, the lives of six billion people are at stake. I'm going to do whatever I have to do."

He looked at Angie. "The American space program was dead before I destroyed the *Atlantis*. Anti-gravity killed it in more ways than one. There will be a new space program based on new technology, and we will be at the heart of it. You're still going to be an astronaut—probably sooner than you would have been otherwise."

The fire in her eyes faded as the truth of his words sunk in. She hung her head as she went to him and hugged him without making eye contact. "I'm sorry," she mumbled. "You're right. I saw my ride into space disappear, and I didn't think. I just got angry. I guess you did the only thing you could."

"The problem is—I shouldn't have had to do *anything*. It was really stupid for me to put the ribbon generator in orbit right where they would logically come to look for something. I need the rest of you to help keep me from making that kind of blunder. Sorry, Nick. I'm not cut out to be a dictator. I need advisors, critics, and Devil's advocates—whatever.

"All right, enough politics. We're right back where we started. We need to send another message to the NSA, bring the *Tetra* down, and figure out how we can communicate with Hercules and CNN at the same time."

"What's the message this time?" Becca asked.

"It's real simple—no encryption required—Thou shalt not steal."

"Got any more champagne?" Becca asked as she entered the kitchen.

"I don't think so," Duke answered. "Why? What are we celebrating this time?"

"Same old stuff. Another message from another intelligence in another arm of the galaxy."

Duke looked at her to see if she was serious or not.

"It's very similar to the one from Hercules," she explained, "but much faster. It goes fifteen to zero, repeated four times, followed by a long string of alternating ones and zeroes. It's an interesting pattern."

"*Interesting?* Becca, how can you be so calm? You're actually communicating with another intelligence!"

"Well...not quite communicating, but you're right. When they respond back to something I send them, *then* you'll see some excitement. I wonder how many more we're going to hear from. Life—even intelligent life—must be much more common than anyone thought."

Worry lines crept across Duke's forehead. "I'm beginning to wonder if we might hear from the anti-gravity police...seriously," he said. "We've been spraying An-G beams every which direction. Who knows? We may be breaking all sorts of inter-galactic laws."

"All the more reason to get a conversation going," Becca reasoned.

"I agree. Tomorrow we make that our number one priority."

"All right, Becca, it's all yours," Duke said as he made the last connection. "Sorry, but I had to nix the idea of a separate communication disk for talking to CNN. It might give away our location. Now you've got all of the programs I developed to communicate with you at Kitt Peak. So what are you waiting for?" he said with a grin.

"I thought you gave up being a dictator," she said sarcastically. "Okay, Nick wants me to show him how I detected the message. I'll send him down as soon as we're done."

"Done *what?*" Angie asked as soon as they were out of earshot. They headed down the spiral stairway toward the trailer.

"I don't care as long as they're together and it doesn't

have anything to do with new physics," Duke answered, frowning. "Becca senses a change in him, but she can't get him to open up. I'm afraid something bad's going to happen."

"Like what?"

"I don't know. He knows everything we know. He can fly the *Tetra* almost as well as you. He's got more space experience than anyone, and he's carrying a grudge. I don't know who he —"

Duke stopped in mid-sentence near the tunnel entrance and held his arm in front of Angie. A man stepped out of the trailer talking on a cell phone.

"Stay back in the tunnel where he can't see you," Duke hissed. He walked quickly, but quietly toward the daylight.

The man finished talking on the phone, folded it, and turned toward a van parked near the trailer. He froze as Lobo appeared from behind the van, bristling and baring his teeth.

Duke saw the gun come out and he burst from the mineshaft running full speed. As the man's arms came up to take aim, Duke shouted and lunged into a flying tackle.

The gun fired, and Lobo spun in midair, yelping and biting at his flank.

Angie screamed as the two men smashed into the ground with a grinding crunch.

Duke recovered quickly. He found an arm below him and grabbed it, twisting as he sat up.

"Who are you and what were you doing in my trailer?" he demanded.

The man pumped air rapidly between clenched teeth. "John...Wain...wright?"

Duke twisted harder, and the man cried out as something popped. "I asked you *your* name. Now!"

"Lopez!" he shouted. "NSA."

Duke's heart skipped a beat. He was afraid to ask the next question. "What are you doing here?"

"I'm supposed...to bring you back...with me."

"What for?"

"Please, mister. I don't know," he groaned. "They were supposed to call you. You've got a message on your answering machine."

Duke let go. The man cried out again when his useless arm fell on his broken ribs. His gun lay on the ground a few feet away. Duke picked it up, glancing back at the man, then joined Angie who was bent over Lobo, pressing something against his thigh.

She cried and tried to make reassuring sounds to Lobo at the same time. "I think he's going to be okay," she blubbered as Duke knelt beside them. He examined the wound. The bullet had creased the upper thigh and cut a gash, but hadn't lodged in the flesh.

"Mr. Satterfield?...John Wainwright.... Yes and no—I got the message, but a little too late. I'm afraid I might have damaged one of your agents.... Yes, that's the one. He invited himself into my trailer when I wasn't home and shot and wounded my dog.... You tell *me!*...That won't be necessary. I'm sure he will recover much sooner than your man.... All right, forget about that. Let's get to the point of the call. Lopez said he was supposed to bring me back. Where and why? Your message was a little cryptic."

Duke listened to the reply, frowned, but finally nodded his head. "All right. I'll be ready."

Duke was afraid he already knew the 'why'. Somehow they had connected him to the signals from space. If so, the 'where' hardly mattered. He would simply disappear—to wherever people who crossed the NSA went. There was no point in trying to run or hide. They'd found him here; they would find him somewhere else. He was so preoccupied with his impending doom, he almost failed to listen to Satterfield's answer, and then so relieved, he could hardly speak.

"I...I...yes, I guess I can do that... . Yes, I'll be ready."

Duke blew air from puffed cheeks and sank into a kitchen chair.

"What?" Angie nearly screamed with impatience.

"They want me to take part in a think tank. One day for now. Maybe more later. They're sending a chopper tomorrow morning, early."

"Who's 'they'?" Becca asked.

"National Security Agency. Satterfield is fairly high up. I met him once when I worked on a classified project at McLean Precision."

"Surely you do not trust this man," Nick said apprehensively.

"Not the man nor the organization," Duke affirmed.

"Then why are you going, Duke? I don't want you to go. What if they don't let you come home?" Angie held his arm.

Duke was over his initial scare, but understood her fear.

"Angie, the NSA would not make a courtesy call before coming to pick me up for interrogation. They *would* make a courtesy call if they needed something from me and wanted my cooperation. I'm going because *not* going would look suspicious. I'm going so I can find out what they know and what they're going to do. I'll be all right."

"*I* won't," Angie complained. Duke squeezed her shoulders.

"Becca, how are you doing with the new signal source?" he asked to change the subject.

"I'm snowed under. As soon as I sent a response, they came back with a stream that hasn't stopped yet. They seem to be in a hurry. I'm analyzing it as fast as I can, but maybe it's a good thing that you'll be gone for a while. I could use Nick and Angie's help.

"They're sending two- and three-dimensional matrices like you and I used. I finally figured out that some of the two-dimensional grids represent the sides of a cube. They project what's inside the cube onto each surface—sort of a shorthand description of the cube's contents. As soon as I figure out which surface goes where, I'll be able to reconstruct the picture."

"Great! Good job, Becca. Exciting, huh?"

"Yeah, it is. I'm wondering if we should let CNN know."

"Based on the poor response we got from the first announcement, I'd say don't bother. They've got a vibration detector that can pick up the same signal that you're getting. If they notice it, fine. If not, that's fine, too. You've got your hands full."

"Okay. See you in the morning. I'm going to finish up here and then hit the sack."

Nick padded softly toward the central shaft in his stocking feet. He stopped and listened carefully, proceeding only after he heard the faint sound of Becca's even breathing coming from the other bedroom. He quickly wound his way up the spiral stairs to the control room and slipped into the chair at the console. The big screen was nearly dark—it was midnight in Arizona. He shut off the sound and left only the monitor speaker active. With the flip of a switch, he transferred control of the *Tetra* to the joysticks.

The screen brightened as the edge of Earth, its atmosphere backlit by the sun, blotted out the dimmer landscape below. Slowly at first, but with quickening pace, the brightness grew as the *Tetra* flew due north over the top of the world. Features disappeared in the glaring white. The Arctic Ocean was locked in the clutches of winter.

Nick glanced away to find one of Duke's maps he had placed in a drawer earlier. He put the map on the table and turned it to match its orientation to the view from the *Tetra*.

Greenland crept down along the right side of the screen. It slowly inched its way toward the bottom, then an island appeared. His finger moved on the map as the features moved on the screen, touching first Svalbard, then a smaller group of islands, Franz Josef Land, which appeared at the top of the screen. He waited patiently until the unmistakable long, curved finger of Novaya Zemlya filled the screen. He touched the controls briefly to decelerate and turn *Tetra* parallel to the island, which pointed directly at Moscow. He carefully noted his speed and heading. It was nearly impossible to make out distinguishable features in the vast expanse of whiteness.

An unconscious smile tinged with sadness touched his face as the onion-top domes of Moscow appeared below. He hovered the *Tetra* over the city of his birth, then glanced at his watch. Not much time. The *Tetra* turned ninety degrees and began moving east, fast enough to cover distance, slow enough for Nick to make out landmarks. Gor'kiy—Kazan'—a little north now—there's Sverdlovsk—slow—slow. The jagged teeth of the Ural Mountains poked through the heavy mantle of snow and ice.

The *Tetra* dropped lower and lower as Nick began picking out landmarks—a small town, a narrow road, a wide valley, a round lake, an island and a house. Carefully, he brought the *Tetra* to a halt directly above the island, then not trusting his hands on the joysticks, shifted to the console keyboard. He initiated the hover program and turned the camera directly downward. He carefully entered commands on the keyboard and numbers on the numeric keypad.

Nothing happened.

He repeated the process with new numbers. Nothing again. On the third try, he detected motion. Snow and ice crystals swirled away from the island in all directions. With trembling fingers, Nick entered a new set of numbers. With eyes glued to the screen, he hit ENTER.

Water and ice fought to fill the spot where the island had been. Hurricane winds tried to stop them. The surface of the lake sunk in an ever-widening circle until it reached the shore, then the motion reversed itself and the waves rushed back to meet in a grinding crash that sent water and ice flying skyward. Nick smiled at the unexpected beauty.

"What was that place?" Becca asked from the shadows behind him.

Nick jerked, but quickly regained control. He rose and turned to face her.

"It was the *dacha* of the man who killed my comrades," he answered simply.

Becca walked to him, took his hand in hers and sat in the second chair, gently pulling him down into his.

"No one was there," he explained, but Becca patted his hand reassuringly.

"I know. You wouldn't do that." She waited quietly.

"He invited us there many times—not for our enjoyment, but for his. He thought himself an artist, but he had no skill—not even imagination. He was only an imitator, and not a very good one. He had spent years carefully molding and shaping hundreds of clay figurines to build a miniature army—like the terra cotta warriors of Emperor Qin Shi Huang. To the rest of us, they were ugly misshapen lumps, but to him they were precious and priceless works of art—comrades, friends."

Nick looked at Becca. He appeared to be at peace with himself. His face was relaxed, and his voice was calm when he spoke.

"One day soon he will come. He will discover that his comrades and friends are gone—taken from him forever, as are mine."

EDWARDS

After the NSA chopper pilot strapped Duke in like a help-less child, he took off in a gut-wrenching gyration that quickly settled into an unrelenting shaking. *This is like being inside Jonah's whale when it's panting after a heavy workout.*

Duke clenched his teeth together. Not that it helped block out any of the sound. The incessant pounding of the helicopter blades and the whine of the engine worked their way into the very pores of his body. The headset, which was supposed to provide both noise suppression and com-munication, did neither. The pilot never spoke a word—at least not to Duke.

Two hours went by. They felt like a week. He tried to look for landmarks out the side windows, but clouds blocked the view. Duke actually dozed off for a while. He woke with his shoulder aching from tackling the NSA agent. *Poor bastard. His next assignment will be on the Kwajalein atoll.*

Another hour. *Either this thing flies slower than I thought, or we're going farther than Edwards Air Force Base. When will it end?*

The answer came with no warning. They dropped fast, sending Duke's stomach up around his ears. The fall ended as abruptly as it began with rotor blades smacking the air in loud protest. He slammed down and back in his seat, cer-tain that they must have crashed.

Duke willed his legs not to buckle as he stepped down

on the tarmac. A blast of hot air hit him, laced with the stench of kerosene. He instinctively crouched as he walked until he was well clear of the rotor blades.

Satterfield himself leaned against the SUV. *Just as I remember him—crew cut, ill-fitting suit, sunglasses, and the ubiquitous earpiece. Security written all over him.*

"Mr. Wainright, it's good to see you again. Thank you for coming." Satterfield said nothing further once they got in. Duke turned and started to ask a question, but the other man shook his head, nodding in the direction of the driver.

Duke expected to be taken to a room where he would meet the other members of the think tank. Instead he found himself in a small, cold room with only Satterfield and a technician present.

Satterfield laid some papers on the table. "Standard non-disclosure agreements," he said. "Your security clearance is still current."

Duke scrutinized the papers, but found nothing unusual or suspicious. He signed.

"You'll meet the others in a few minutes. We will have some specific questions to ask in your area of expertise, but first we want to get your candid observations. After that we'll meet and put our heads together.

Candid? Not if I can help it.

"Ignore what you heard on the news," Satterfield told him. "There were no onboard computer failures. We went out where the laser signals came from and found something orbiting. We photographed it from every possible angle, retrieved it, and brought it down. The device was lost with the shuttle, but fortunately the crew carried the film with them when they got off. You know the rest."

Yes, I do. More than you can guess.

"The still shots are laid out on the table over there. Take a look at them and think out loud if you will, please. Part by part and for the unit as a whole, tell us what it is, what it does, what it's made of, and how it works."

He sure hasn't changed. Tell me as little as possible, milk as much out of me as he can.

Duke took his time approaching the table. *Remember, you've supposedly never seen this thing before. Act like it. Man, I wish they'd turn up the heat in here. It's freezing!*

He walked slowly along the table, looking at several rows of pictures, each one from a different angle. *My only ribbon generator with a full roll of ribbon. It'll take weeks to replace it. Hey, the input reel is gone. Wonder what happened. Okay, give them only what they can figure out themselves, and throw them off wherever possible.*

"All right," he began. "The clamshells are thick-walled and hinged. They obviously come together to form a sphere. This would appear to be a latching mechanism opposite the hinge, so I'd guess it was a vacuum chamber that was opened after being placed in orbit. This wheel or disk is too big to fit inside, so it must have been added after the sphere was opened. The wheel is large relative to the rest of the structure. It might be a gyroscope...no, I don't see any supports.

"The boxes on each side of it don't offer many clues. Electronics, more than likely, but I don't see any wires. The threaded fittings on the front of each box—they might be electrical plugs or plumbing. I see no solar panels or other external power source, so maybe there's a battery or fuel cell inside. If so, then there's less room for complexity.

That's about it from the still pictures. Maybe I'll see something else in the video."

"Very good," Satterfield commented. "Tell the operator to stop, go, replay—whatever you need. We can magnify and enhance anything you're particularly interested in."

A piercing screech filled the room just as the technician started the video. He scrambled to mute the volume, but the sound continued for another couple of seconds. "Sorry sir. That was weird," he said to Satterfield. "I don't know where that came from. There's no audio on the tape."

Satterfield made a dismissive gesture. "Proceed."

Duke was astonished to see the open cargo bay of the shuttle less than ten yards away from the ribbon generator. *How did they know where...*He dropped his head as the realization hit him. *Duke, you dumbbell. The clamshell is solid steel—a perfect radar reflector. You may as well have put a flashing light on it!*

He cussed himself through the first minutes of the video, then started paying attention. The view jerked from time to time. Duke assumed the camera had been affixed to the shuttle's retractable arm and maneuvered around the ribbon generator to capture the pictures.

He noticed flashes of light reflecting off the generator and turned to Satterfield. "Is that from the still camera?"

Satterfield nodded. "Right."

"Wait a minute." Duke motioned to the operator. "Go back to that last flash, please. There. Can you zoom in on the area where the light reflects off the wheel?

"Yes, there." He turned to Satterfield. "See that rainbow of colors. Optics is not my specialty, but I'd say the surface of the wheel has diffraction grooves like on a compact disk."

Duke knew he was walking a thin line—notice too much, and he would give away more information than he wanted to. Notice too little, and Satterfield might get suspicious.

"Go ahead. Let's see the rest of it," he instructed.

The video ended, and Duke turned to face Satterfield. "If the boxes on the sides are filled with electronics, then this is a very sophisticated device. There's no solar panel and nothing that looks like an antenna. There are fittings with nothing plugged into them. That and the empty spot here beside the big wheel makes me wonder if you might have grabbed this thing while it was still under construction. We may be trying to make sense out of the first few components of a much more complex structure."

Satterfield's face fell. Duke could tell that he'd heard that idea before and didn't want to hear it again.

"Very well, but for the moment, assume that it *is* complete. What can you tell us about the unit as a whole?"

Duke pressed his lips together and shook his head. "It's not what you want it to be—not what they called the interface window device. The wheel is the only part that has a recognizable plane. If a force goes out perpendicular to that plane, it would rip the whole structure apart. I won't rule out that it is a complete unit, but I need to hear the others' ideas before I can speculate on its function."

Satterfield nodded and rose. "Wait here," he instructed. He returned quickly carrying an easel and flipchart. Two men and a woman filed in behind him.

Only three? Wow! They're keeping this tight.

Satterfield made the introductions.

Roger D'Alessandro—mechanical and structural engineering—was nearsighted, overweight, and angry. He lumbered into the room with a deep scowl, obviously directed at Satterfield.

Bullard Resnick—process engineering—was sunburned and had a two-week beard as if his vacation had been interrupted. Duke nodded. *Probably was.*

Melody Sharpe—materials specialist—was anything but melodious. Her voice was low—not sexy, but bordering on a growl. She was somewhat attractive, but had a jutting chin that ruined the overall effect.

Satterfield introduced Duke as John Wainwright—microelectronics and molecular films.

Duke noted that he gave only names and discipline—no titles or organizational affiliations.

Satterfield set up the flipchart where all could see. Duke saw some of his own observations at the bottom. "Mr. Wainright, the rest of us have a head start on you, so I'll summarize where we are at this point and explain why we brought you in."

I'm all ears.

"Each person, yourself included, made some of the same observations—most notably, that the device may be incomplete. No means of propulsion, no solar panel, no antenna, and a hole beside the wheel. Be that as it may, Mr. Resnick and Ms. Sharpe proposed one scenario in which the device *is* a complete unit. Not, as you observed, the one we had hoped it would be, but possibly related. I'll let them explain it."

Uh oh. This is not good.

The woman picked up one of the still photographs.

"We saw the same thing that you saw—the diffracted light, but I attributed the diffraction to wrapped layers of thin film instead of grooves in the surface of a flat wheel. We analyzed the reflected light with a spectrograph to determine what kind of material the film might be made of. We got something of a surprise. It's recording tape—some kind of polyester film with a plastic binder containing metal oxide particles. The reason we called you in is that the analysis also shows the presence of silicon. We think the surface of the recording tape is coated with a very thin layer of silicon. I'll let Mr. Resnick take it from here."

Oh, man, if they've figured out the ribbon, they're bound to stumble onto the rest.

Resnick picked up another photograph—one that looked straight down the hole beside the wheel. "I think a reel of unprocessed tape is mounted here," he pointed to the empty slot on the photograph. "It's twice as wide as the reel we see, so I propose that the tape is split in half inside the box. Silicon is applied to one or both halves, which are then folded into a sandwich and wound on the output reel. We presume that the two fittings allow the replenishment of raw materials. Our question to you is—how do they get the silicon to adhere to the tape—we haven't had any luck— and of course, why?"

Think, Duke! Think! They've got the process. They've even tried to duplicate it. You've got to throw them off the track! He stroked his face with his hands, thinking hard, but not about what *they* wanted him to think. He took a deep breath.

"The process you described doesn't make sense to me based on what I see. You called the wheel a reel, but there *isn't* a reel. And if this is an output roll of tape, it's not wound on a reel either. Why wouldn't they wind it on a reel? One wrong move and they'd have a tangled mess on their hands. Why would they take that kind of chance? Weight is obviously not an issue. They've got anti-gravity."

"We don't know," Sharpe admitted. "I'll concede that we're missing something with respect to the reels. Help me out here, guys. We didn't find any, so they must not need them. If they don't need any, then they must be confident that the layers will not shift even during handling. What would make them stick together?"

"It's a friggin' Scotch tape dispenser," D'Alessandro sneered. "Come on, Satterfield. You're wasting our time. Face it. The NSA screwed up. You got Jack shit to work with and lost our only operational shuttle in the process."

"Roger, you've made your point repeatedly. Now drop it," Satterfield ordered. "This team is going to pursue every idea—*every* idea—to its final disposition. In case you didn't notice, you inadvertently contributed a good idea. The tape adheres to itself. Let's work with that. Adhesion is one explanation. What else?"

"Magnetism, of course," Resnick answered. "That should have been obvious to us. It's supposedly recording tape, after all."

Think, Duke! You're the resident expert on films. You've gotta convince them it's something else. Anything!

"I'm going to put a team together to work on the magnetism idea," Satterfield said. "I think it offers some interesting possibilities."

No! Duke wanted to scream. *That's the last thing I want—someone experimenting with silicon coatings on magnetized tape.*

"Mr. Wainwright." Satterfield startled Duke out of his panic. "Let's talk about that possibility. Assume for the moment that we are dealing with a roll of magnetic tape with a micro-thin film of silicon. This is your area of expertise. How do they apply the film? What's going on inside the boxes where we can't see?"

Wonderful! Now you put me on the spot. Either I tell you something I don't want you to know, or I arouse suspicion by looking stupid.

"I'm not sure I can answer your question—at least not right away. I'm used to working with semiconductor materials. This is clearly going to require a different kind of process."

"Come join us at Los Alamos. We'll provide you with whatever you need," Satterfield assured. "Facilities, state-of-the-art equipment, people—you name it."

"I appreciate your offer, but I have to ask—are you sure you're not on a wild goose chase? I can think of lots of manufacturing processes that we would like to try under zero-G conditions, but it's too expensive. What if this device is simply an experiment—one of many that they have floating out there? What if it has nothing to do with anti-gravity?"

D'Alessandro shot an I-told-you-so look at Satterfield. He opened his mouth to speak, but Satterfield cut him off.

"Too much is at stake to allow that possibility to stop us. We will continue our research until we have exhausted every lead, every suggestion, and every idea."

"And every dollar," D'Alessandro amended.

"So be it." Satterfield turned to Duke. "We expect budget approval will come in the next few days. I will contact you then."

That's it? It's over? You're letting me go? Relief flowed over Duke like a warm blanket. He wanted to run—to get out of there before they changed their minds, but knew his legs wouldn't allow it. He stood carefully and eased toward the door.

Satterfield accompanied him and seemed in no hurry as they made their way out of the building. He walked hesitantly and finally stopped.

"I don't like digging around in people's private lives," he said, "but one thing has led to another. There seems to be a possible link between you and the signals from space."

Duke felt as if someone had poured ice water down his back. Had he still been walking, he would have stumbled. *How could he know—or even suspect? And if he did, why the think tank ruse?* He shook his head and looked questioningly at Satterfield. "How...?"

Satterfield waved the question away. "Dr. Coleman's car is parked beside your trailer. Your research group is funding her project at Kitt peak, is it not?"

"Oh." Duke's heart resumed beating. *He hasn't really tied me to the signals—only to Becca. I can explain that. I wonder what he meant about 'digging in people's private lives'. Does he think we're having an affair?* A thought occurred to him.

"I'm surprised, Mr. Satterfield. You should already know about my relationship with Dr. Coleman. Remember the imaging chip I developed for project Barn Door?"

Satterfield's head jerked left and right. "What about it?"

"Were you not aware that I developed a much smaller, unclassified version of the chip for Kitt Peak? The terms of agreement I signed authorized me to do so. Dr. Coleman was the astronomer chosen to test it. We worked together off and on for close to a year."

Duke could almost follow Satterfield's thoughts by watching his expression—embarrassment that someone in his own organization had missed such an important detail, frustration that the connection between Duke and Becca tied neither to the signal source, but still some questions. Duke chose not to wait for the questions.

"There's a G-rated explanation for her car at my place, too," he said. "She's sick of being hounded by the news media. It's a good place to hide."

Satterfield pursed his lips and nodded. He didn't look satisfied—didn't look *anything* Duke could identify. His face was a mask. He stepped forward and shook Duke's hand. "I'll be in touch. Don't forget our offer about Los Alamos." He turned and headed toward the building, pulling a cell phone from his pocket as he walked.

The helicopter blades were turning slowly as Duke reached the tarmac.

WARNING

Angie ran towards Duke, but the downwash of the rotor blades nearly knocked her off her feet. She crashed into him and held him.

"Oh, Duke, I've been going crazy waiting for you to get back."

"Angie, I told you not to worry. They haven't connected me to the ribbon generator."

"That was only part of it," she replied. "Come on. Let's get back to the others."

Duke headed for the tunnel, but Angie stopped him and handed him a bottle of whiskey. "Becca said you would want a shot of this as soon as you got back."

"I wonder how she knew how my day went."

"It's not for how *your* day went."

"Uh-oh." Duke looked at the bottle. "Maybe I'd better not. Something tells me I'm going to need a clear head."

"You weren't far off when you expressed concern about the anti-gravity police," Becca explained. "Apparently Hercules doesn't like noisy neighbors. In fact, he doesn't like them so much that he gets rid of them—permanently."

Duke wasn't certain what she was saying, but she continued before he could ask.

"According to the Octals—I named them that because they have a base-eight numbering system—when Hercules detects an anti-gravity beam coming from a new source, he starts a countdown. That's the fifteen-to-zero sequence we've been receiving. It's sent four times. After the last preliminary sequence, he sends a long string of alternating ones and zeroes. I assume you heard the screeching sound about two-thirty this afternoon our time?"

Duke looked startled. "Yes, we did. We thought it came from the audio-visual equipment."

"No. I think that was the Octals telling us what to expect. The four sequences are like a warning countdown to the string of ones and zeroes, which is an anti-gravity field being turned on and off at a high frequency. The sound alone will drive us all crazy, but the long-term effects are devastating. It will displace a large portion of our atmosphere toward the other side of the planet causing colossal storms. On top of that, the pulses will heat the atmosphere like in a microwave oven. The Octals indicated that Hercules cooked two civilizations that way. Looks like we get to be number three."

Duke sat down heavily. "Between the pictures of the ribbon generator and the brainstorming session, the NSA has already figured out most of the An-G technology. I thought that had to be the worst news possible. Now I understand the whiskey bottle."

He rubbed his forehead with his fingertips and sighed. "All right," he said as he hauled himself to his feet. "I haven't had any supper. Come to the kitchen—all of you. You can fill me in while I eat."

Angie held his hand as they descended the spiral stairs. "I'll fix you something," she volunteered as they entered the kitchen.

Duke slumped into a chair. "Where are we in the countdown?"

Becca looked at her watch. "Twenty-two hours and some change."

Duke's expression didn't change. He acted as if he hadn't heard her. His eyes watched Angie moving around in the kitchen. Finally he spoke.

"We've got a thrust disk that's one foot in diameter. We need to build one that's nine thousand miles in diameter to shield the Earth—all in twenty-two hours. Even if I gave An-G technology to every factory in the world, they couldn't generate enough ribbon, and we couldn't get it into orbit in time."

"That's true, but we don't need a shield that big," Becca answered. "The distance is, for all practical purposes, infinite. That means that our beam and their beam will appear as dimensionless point sources. The tightest beam we can generate will fan out bigger than their solar system at that distance, same as theirs does when it reaches us. It will intercept their beam and, if it's strong enough, it will cancel or possibly reverse the force."

"Doesn't that bring us right back to where we were? We need a bigger thrust disk than theirs so we can generate a stronger force. They've undoubtedly got a bigger disk than we do and more experience with the technology. What about the Octals? Can they help us?"

"No. They're just about even with the Hercules system in the Genesis field. What I mean is—a thrust disk aimed at Hercules would be parallel to the Genesis field."

"The sine of zero is zero," Duke summarized.

"Exactly. No force."

"I don't suppose you've discovered any *other* neighbors who could help while I was gone."

"Yes and no. The Octals' cube showed two other systems that use anti-gravity, but they apparently don't communicate with one another. Probably because of the danger of being detected by Hercules. Mind you, I'm guessing about a lot of what they've said."

"How far along are you in developing a vocabulary with them?"

"Better than I expected. Several dozen words or concepts, and some graphics. We've got a pretty good three-dimensional picture of where everyone is in relationship to one another, except for scale. Why? What do you want to say to them?"

"Help!" Duke talked around the food in his mouth. "We can't save ourselves. Maybe if all four worlds blast away at the same time, we can get the bad guys before they get us."

"Three," Becca corrected. "The Octals can't shoot at all, and none of us can 'blast' at anyone. The maximum beam we can throw may spread until it's only a few ounces of force when it reaches Hercules. It depends on how tightly focused it is and how far away we are."

"You're just full of good news, aren't you?" Duke looked at the faces of the people sitting with him. *Angie is more worried about me than herself or the world. Becca is a team player, ready to do whatever I ask, but she's looking to me for direction. Nick—he's clearly waiting for orders from the leader— me again.*

Duke closed his eyes to concentrate and organize his thoughts. He didn't really have any options—only things to do—and the sooner the better. He shoved his chair back from the table.

"Angie, I need you to run to town. Get us some pills that will keep us awake. Most truck stops have them. Read the labels and use your judgment—they have to allow us to remain alert. Becca, ask the Octals to contact the other two An-G sources to see if they will help. Nick, you and I have to dismantle everything in the workshop that's got the smallest scrap of ribbon in it. We'll piece together as big a thrust disk as we can."

Angie started the truck and headed across the parking lot. Duke and Nick had nearly reached the mouth of the workshop tunnel when Angie slammed the truck into reverse and skidded to a stop. She screamed as she ran toward them.

"Duke, the Leap of Faith! The Leap of Faith!"

He looked at her, uncomprehending for a second, then grabbed her by the shoulders and kissed her so hard she nearly fell over backward when he released her.

"Yes!" He turned to Becca and Nick. "There's a ten-foot thrust disk at the bottom of the vertical shaft that I used as an elevator before installing the spiral stairs. We'll attach the disk to the *Tetra*'s framework somehow."

Duke was so excited he didn't stop to think that a ten-foot disk might still be pitifully small. He was just happy to have something constructive to do.

Becca headed up the stairs as Angie kissed Duke and trotted toward the pickup. Duke and Nick disappeared into the workshop.

COUNTDOWN

H-HOUR MINUS 22:

"What can I do to help?"

Duke spun around, startled by Becca's voice.

"I thought you were going to contact the Octals to see if they or the others can help," he said.

"I did. They won't. I'm done."

The news hit Duke like a fist in the gut. The thrust disk from the stairwell seemed huge when he and Nick were manhandling it over to the workshop. Now it looked hopelessly small—an umbrella against an avalanche. "We're on our own," he said in a hushed voice.

He turned to Nick. "Would you bring the *Tetra* down? We don't have much time."

Nick sprinted for the mine entrance.

"Are you going to be okay?" Becca asked.

"I don't guess it makes much difference. Okay or not, it'll be over in a few hours."

Duke took a big breath and let it out slowly. "From Day One this discovery has shown its negative side. When I was a kid, I used to dream about anti-gravity—flying cars, floating cities, near-space as full of traffic as our air space is today. None of that is going to be possible. The nature of the force, human nature, and now alien nature all combine to make the discovery next to useless." He paused—a sad smile on his face. "I'm okay—just disappointed."

H-HOUR MINUS 20:

Angie returned to find the others struggling to prop the *Tetra* in a camera-up position. Both men had removed their shirts, and their bodies were glistening with sweat. Becca's blouse was more wet than dry. Angie hurried to help. They finally stabilized the craft and the four of them stood puffing from the exertion.

"I expected you to be talking longer than this," Angie said to Becca.

"Yeah, me, too. The exchange was brief. They said, 'Push source, source push,' which to me means if they direct a beam at Hercules, then Hercules will direct a beam at them and they will be destroyed, too."

Angie's hand sought Duke's. "I brought food."

"Thanks." Duke squeezed her shoulder. "Let's all take a break."

The four of them sat on the ground, munching fast food as Duke outlined the plan.

"We'll stick the disk to the framework with epoxy. I want to unwind enough of the ribbon from the center to make a peephole for the camera, then I'll attach the ribbon to one of the lasers inside the sphere. It'll be a lot more powerful than the light I used in the stairwell. Becca, do you think if we send a test beam to the Octals, they will provide feedback on the accuracy of our aim and the strength of the beam?"

"Seems like the least they can do under the circumstances," she answered.

H-HOUR MINUS 17:

"I never thought about that happening." Duke examined the cracked epoxy. "It's a good thing we discovered it before we put this in orbit. All right, we're getting tight on time. We need to come up with an alternative way to attach the disk to the *Tetra*—something that won't be affected by the shear forces and by the temperature extremes in space."

The "something" turned out to be simple straps bent around each end of the struts and screwed to the back of the big disk, but it took two hours to finish the task.

H-HOUR MINUS 15:

"I'm going to the trailer," Angie whispered to Duke. "Pit stop."

"Hurry. We're about ready to road test this mess." He busied himself tugging on the jury-rigged structure to check its integrity.

"Duke!" Angie called from the doorway of the trailer. "The message light is blinking."

"Uh oh. This can only be trouble." He trotted across the dusty ground followed by Becca and Nick.

"Wainwright... Satterfield here. We've made some progress on our research, but we need your help again. I hope you're there and get this message. I'm sending a chopper to pick you up at 0500 tomorrow. We're counting on you, Buddy."

"I'm not your buddy!" Duke snarled. "Of course he didn't leave a number." He pushed the recall button on the caller ID.

UNKNOWN NAME.

"All right, there's more than one way to skin a cat." He

picked up the phone and punched *69.

Three ascending tones preceded a female voice with a nasal twang. "Your call cannot be completed as dialed. Please check the number and dial again."

"Fine! Your chopper will just waste a trip out here," he yelled, banging the phone down. "Let's go," he said to the others. "We've got to get the *Tetra* up before it gets light."

The foursome hurried across the lot toward the workshop tunnel. A sound stopped them before they reached the *Tetra*. The crisp cold air carried the thumping heartbeat of a distant helicopter.

"Duke! He'll see the *Tetra!*" Angie screamed.

Duke turned nearly full circle, searching. "The workshop tunnel! It's the only place. Can you back the *Tetra* in there?"

"I won't be able to see where I'm going. You'll have to direct me."

"My cell phone is in the control room. There's no time to get it. Call me on the trailer phone. Go!"

Angie ran for the mine entrance with Becca and Nick at her heels. Duke looked at his watch: 4:51. He hurried to the trailer. He was stretching the phone cord toward the door when the phone rang.

"Ready!" Angie gasped.

"Good. Use the keyboard. Straight up one foot, then start the hover program."

The props stabilizing the *Tetra* fell away as the craft rose. The windows of the trailer began to throb.

"Pitch forward ninety degrees, then go backwards about three meters." Duke could tell that the craft was misaligned with the workshop opening, but he was too far away to judge the distance accurately.

"All right, come to your left about a meter and yaw left twenty degrees."

"He's here," Angie yelled. Duke could hear the hollow echoing from the central shaft coming over the phone.

"We're almost there. Back up another meter."

Suddenly the world exploded with blinding light and deafening sound as the helicopter cleared the mesa top and began settling in the clearing between the trailer and rock wall. Duke shielded his face as dirt, sand, and small rocks pelted the trailer and swirled through the open door.

"I can't see anymore," he shouted over the phone. "I think you still had a couple of meters to go, but don't go any farther than that. I'll be back as soon as I can." He hung up the phone and stepped onto the tiny porch, pulling the door closed behind him. The chopper's whirling blades spun menacingly close.

Duke walked in a crouch to the front of the craft where he could see the pilot clearly. He pointed to himself, then to the pilot, shaking his head in an exaggerated motion.

The pilot held up a gloved finger. It seemed like only a few seconds. The finger pointed repeatedly at the trailer, then the pilot made the unmistakable sign for "telephone" with his thumb and little finger beside his helmet.

The phone was ringing when Duke opened the trailer door.

"Hello.... Yes, I did.... No, I..." Duke rolled his eyes and sat down. The more Satterfield talked, the deeper the scowl on Duke's face became.

"Whoa. Hold it. Stop right there!" Duke interrupted the tirade. "You're wasting your time trying to lay a guilt trip on me. My patriotism is above question—by you or anyone else. As to helping you out before, yes, I did, until I found out what you were up to. I saw the news clips—what happened to the beam weapon—same as you. I also saw the hole in the ground at Edwards. If you want to ignore that message, it's your skin. I want no part of it…. What do you mean?"

The color drained from his face as he listened. "Yes, I get your drift…. Both of us?…Yes…. When?…No, that's not acceptable. You don't need me there for that…. Don't be ridiculous. Where would I go?"

Duke placed the phone in the cradle carefully, then collapsed back on the couch. He hardly noticed the trailer shaking as the helicopter pounded its way skyward. His mind was numb.

"Duke! Duke!"

Angie's screams jarred him out of his funk. He opened the trailer door, and Angie flung herself into his arms, gasping for air. The gasps became sobs, and she cried uncontrollably as Becca and Nick entered the trailer.

"I thought…they took…you away," Angie managed to get out.

Duke held her close until the sobbing subsided, then took her to the couch, where they sat side-by-side, fingers interlocked.

He looked at Becca and Nick. "They figured it out."

"Anti-gravity?" Becca asked.

Duke nodded. "Satterfield couldn't say that over the phone, but he left no question what he was talking about."

Becca studied his face. "There's more," she prompted.

He nodded again. "They can't afford to have any loose

ends floating around. I know too much about what they're working on, and you know that I know."

"Join them, or else," she surmised. "When?"

"Well, I'm sure his plan was to whisk me away this morning, temporarily at least. They're going to do a system test sometime this week. They don't really need me for anything—I think he wants me on a leash. You, too. He gave us until the eighth."

"Then what?" Becca insisted.

"There are four of us, and we have a year's head start. He doesn't know it, but he's not the one calling the shots here."

Duke shrugged. "If we're still here tomorrow, I'll worry about it then. Hercules may cook us first. If not, then Satterfield may blow the planet out from under us. I don't know which scares me more. I'd like for all of us to be in a different galaxy right now."

H-HOUR MINUS 14:

"Angie, it's not your fault. You couldn't see, and neither could I." Duke tried to console Angie while evaluating the damage. One edge of the disk had caught the rock wall as the *Tetra* backed into the tunnel, ripping the screws and straps loose from the backing. "We can put new straps on in a few minutes."

"Yeah, but it will be light by then," she pointed out.

"We'll just have to deal with it."

H-HOUR MINUS 13:

"Stay in our valley and below the rock wall if you can," Duke instructed. "Get the feel of it. The disk is going to make it try to slip sideways instead of going forward, so take it slow at first."

Angie eased the joystick forward. Immediately, the picture on the screen began to slew sideways. "Whoa!" she yelled as she pulled back on the stick. When the craft was stable again, she repeated the maneuver with the same result. "Here, you try," she said to Nick.

His first attempt came dangerously close to crashing into the ground.

"Can you fly it like a helicopter?" Duke asked. "I mean turn the camera sideways and fly with the disk parallel to the line of flight."

Nick tried, but the craft became unstable when the wind caught the disk. "Not good," he said.

"What if you spin it?" Becca suggested. "Like a helicopter—the disk and frame rotate while the camera freewheels pointing forward. It would generate some stability."

"I don't have a program to provide lateral thrust with the craft rotating," Duke told her.

"What about thrust along the axis of rotation?" she asked.

"Hmm. Yeah, it can do that. I don't like the idea of the freewheeling camera, though. I'm afraid the gimbal bearings will get hot and seize up."

"Let the camera spin with the structure. It's only until you get out of the atmosphere. Then you can stop the spin," Becca reasoned.

Duke looked questioningly at the pilots.

Nick nodded, and Angie shrugged.

"All right, bring it back to the workshop." He grabbed his cell phone. "Put on your headset. I'll be down there to watch for problems when you start it spinning."

Duke hurried down the staircase and out the tunnel. The *Tetra* arrived in the open space by the trailer at the same time he did.

"All right, I think it would be best if you turn the camera facing down. That way you can see if the spin starts wobbling. I'm ready when you are."

The craft hovered a few feet off the ground with the bottom of the sphere at Duke's eye level. It began to turn very slowly.

Good. She's being careful. I know we need to hurry, but we can't take chances. As he watched the fragile craft rotate in front of him, he started to shake. The enormity of the situation began to unfurl from the corner of his mind where he had suppressed it. *Tomorrow could be the end of the world.* He looked at his watch. *Today,* he corrected, *and I am responsible.* He felt numb—disconnected from reality.

He heard a voice in the distance. It took a moment for him to realize it was Angie shouting on the cell phone. The *Tetra* was gyrating wildly like a child's top right before it falls over.

Duke forced himself to concentrate on the immediate problem. "Take it up a little ways to give yourself some maneuvering room," he instructed, "then apply a braking torque. The wobble will stop with the rotation. I'm coming up."

Duke hurried up the stairs—*had* to hurry, but feared their efforts would be too little, too late.

"We think it's the movable thrust disk," Angie announced as he came into the control room. "It shifts the center of gravity away from the axis of rotation."

"We can't do without it, and there's no time to relocate it," Duke pointed out. "Any ideas?"

"Aim the thrust disk outward and apply enough thrust to counteract the centrifugal force," Becca suggested.

Duke shook his head. "The angle of the disk would be constantly changing with respect to the Genesis field. We wouldn't be able to maintain a steady force."

He waited for more ideas, but none came. "All right," he said, looking at Angie and Nick. "Forget the rotation. Take it up—as fast as you can, as slowly as you have to. I know it's going to be stressful fighting the sideslip. You two trade off as often as you need to. Becca, can you be ready with a message to the Octals? We'll sweep our beam from side to side and then top to bottom, and they can feed back the intensity at each angle. We need to know where our strongest force is."

H-HOUR MINUS 9:

"Are you sure they understood what we want?" Duke asked.

"Yes. I sent a beam with the small disk, and they gave me feedback from it," Becca answered. "The big disk simply isn't working."

Duke pressed his head between his hands. "It worked when we tested it." He looked helplessly at the others. "Bring it down," he said almost inaudibly.

H-HOUR MINUS 5:

"It must have been the helicopter," Duke said. "There's grit all over the surface, and the ribbon is broken here near the center. We're lucky a rock didn't crack the camera lens."

He worked quickly, but carefully, removing the damaged portion of the ribbon and unwinding a short length from the remaining spiral. When the final connection was completed, he straightened up. "I'll stay down here to see if it works. Align the disk parallel to the Genesis field so there won't be any force generated. I don't trust the filter."

The craft pitched forward slowly until the face of the disk pointed obliquely at the ground. Duke's cell phone rang as the craft stopped turning. "Ready," Angie announced.

"All right, turn the laser on." Nothing happened, but nothing was *supposed* to happen. "So far, so good," Duke said. "Use the keyboard this time. Make it turn only a fraction of a degree."

The turn was imperceptible, but the beam was obviously being generated. A blast of wind scoured the ground where the disk was aimed, and sent dirt and gravel flying.

"Yes!" Duke said, shaking his fist.

H-HOUR MINUS 1:

"That's it?" Duke asked incredulously. "That's all we can deliver?" He looked at the graph Becca had plotted from the Octal's measurements. "We're dead."

"Not so fast," Becca countered. "It's not much, but it's still sixty percent of what Hercules is throwing at us. That beam gets attenuated the same as ours. Plus, Hercules is closer to us than the Octals, so the beam that hits Hercules will be stronger than what they measured. We might have as much as seventy percent."

"Can they cook us with the thirty percent that gets through?" Duke asked.

"Yes, I'm sure they can if they stick with it long enough," she admitted, "but it might buy us enough time to do something."

"I can't imagine what. All right, get locked onto the target as quickly as you can. We've only got a few minutes." He fought to keep despair out of his voice.

Nick slid into the chair at the console, and Becca began directing him while looking at the stars on the screen. "Go to wide angle for a minute, please," she asked. "Good. There's Vega. We need to swing west about twenty-five degrees. Slow, now. Wups, too far. That's Eta Herculis. Tell you what—go ahead and zoom in right there and put the crosshairs on it. We can let the computer do the fine tuning."

She consulted her notebook. "Okay, come north 5.45 degrees, then 3.22 east," she instructed. The star field shifted slowly on the big screen, then stabilized.

"That's where they would be if we could see them," she said. "Now, our maximum beam is a little off center, so we need to come right 0.12 degrees and up 0.31."

Nick typed the commands, but the change was imperceptible on the screen.

"So we're ready?" Duke asked.

"Ready to shoot," Becca confirmed. "I'll send a continuous beam to the Octals using the small disk. That way they'll know when we get hit, because the Hercules beam will cancel it out."

Becca worked to align the smaller thrust disk. She finished at the same time as the countdown stopped. "Could be any time now," she warned.

Duke rolled his head around and tried to stretch out some of the tension in his neck. The long hours were taking their toll. Angie came from somewhere behind him and began massaging his shoulders. *It would be so easy to simply go to sleep and let someone else worry.*

Pain shot through his head with an intensity he had never experienced before. *No! I can't get a migraine now. I've got to be able to turn on the laser when the attack comes.*

H-HOUR

Time stopped. Only pain remained. Duke knew he was supposed to do something urgent. It was nearly impossible to think. *Please! Make it stop!*

Only seconds passed, but they seemed like hours. *Turn on the laser!* The thought finally broke through the pain. His finger shook so badly that he missed the button on the first two tries. Then he hit the key three times before he could remove his hand.

The pain stopped when the An-G beam turned on, but Duke found it difficult to think clearly. His eyes were seeing, but his brain was not interpreting. *Why is the floor fuzzy?* Dust hung suspended above the sandstone floor like wisps of fog over a lake on a cold morning. One quadrant of the big screen flickered, alternating between stars and snow.

Becca moved toward Nick, who had a trickle of blood emerging from one nostril. Angie dabbed her own nose and handed a tissue to Duke, who suddenly realized his sinuses were draining.

The sensation of slow motion gradually dissipated, and Duke's mind began to clear. "Is everyone all right? We may have to get out of here," he cautioned, finally making sense of the dust clouds. "The vibration may have weakened the rock."

"We can't," Becca responded, "unless you've got another control center somewhere else. What if our beam drifts off target? Plus I've got to figure out how much of Hercules' beam is getting through. We need to know how much time we've got left."

"Whatever it is, it's not going to be enough." Duke shook his head. "If we had everything we needed, which we don't, and if we all worked twenty-four by seven, which we can't, it would take a week or more to build a new craft and make enough ribbon to overpower the Hercules beam."

"Does that mean what I think it means?" Becca asked.

Duke nodded. "Satterfield. He might be able to mobilize enough resources to get the job done, but then he'll know about us."

"Damned if we do, and damned if we don't," Becca concluded.

"Yeah," Duke agreed. He stared at the floor, scowling. "See if you can quantify how much of the beam is getting through to us. I'll need to calculate how much ribbon we need."

He turned to Angie. "Are you all right?"

She shook her head carefully. "It's the sound. It's nauseating."

"You mean you can hear it?"

"Yeah. It's way up there—almost beyond my hearing, but it's awful—worse than fingernails on a blackboard. More like cat's claws on glass." She shuddered.

Duke held her, feeling helpless.

Becca pushed her chair away from the table. "Amazing. You stopped all but seventeen percent of their beam," she announced.

"Close only counts in horseshoes and hand grenades,"

Duke answered as he reached for a calculator. He pecked at the keys briefly. "Four feet. We need a disk four feet in diameter. It's so close to being do-able." He looked at Becca plaintively. "I have to ask—how much time do we have?"

She merely shook her head. "Every molecule of our atmosphere is being pushed toward the other side of the planet and vibrating at high frequency. It's happening slowly, but the effect is cumulative. At worst we've got several hours—at best, several days."

Duke leaned over in the chair to pull his wallet from his back pocket. He thumbed through several business cards before finding the right one. "I hope they can route me through to him." With a helpless shrug, he began dialing. Three sets of eyes watched intently as Duke made the most important phone call in world history.

"You have reached the National Security Agency," a voice intoned. "If you know your party's extension —"

Duke punched more numbers. The phone rang several times, stopped, clicked, then began ringing again.

Angie grabbed Duke's shoulder. "It stopped."

How did she know that? he wondered as the phone was answered.

"Satterfield."

Duke took a breath, ready to speak, but suddenly no longer held the phone. Angie did.

"Sorry," she said after pushing the END CALL button. "It stopped," she repeated. Duke frowned, not comprehending. "The sound. The Hercules beam. It stopped."

FINALE

MILKY WAY GALAXY, LOCAL ARM:

    <I sing.>

    <I sense another song. Can there be another…like me? Wonder. A new sensation to perceive. Pleasant. Desirable.>

But short-lived, as the planet below boiled up to engulf the robot in searing hydrogen gas.

HERO

"How is he?" Becca asked as Angie came into the kitchen.

Angie shook her head, buying time to get her voice under control. "Not good. He can't bear the thought of being responsible for the death of an entire civilization."

"Hey, we *all* share that responsibility. Besides, he *saved* this civilization."

"I mentioned that, but it didn't seem to make any difference. He's blaming himself for everything—even the deaths of Nick's friends and you losing your job."

"He didn't make me lose my job, dammit! I told him —" Becca stopped herself, but too late—tears streamed down Angie's cheeks.

"What am I going to do, Becca?" she wailed.

"Take it easy, Honey. We don't need *two* people getting depressed.

Becca came to the dinner table beaming.

"Becca, you've got that look again," Angie said. "The one that says you've discovered another intelligence to talk to."

"Well, yes—several, in fact. They're coming out of hiding now that the Hercules threat is gone. We're going to have more help than you can shake a stick at. However that's not the news I came down to share. Duke, you need to hear this more than anyone else."

Duke looked up, but showed no interest. *Here we go*

again. He knew that they meant well, but he was tired of being polite while they tried to cheer him up. *They don't understand what I've done.*

"You didn't kill anybody," Becca told him. "No one," she stressed.

Now what? Of course I did. Not only everyone, but everything—an entire planet full of living beings, intelligent and otherwise.

"I'm sorry it took so long to confirm, but we simply didn't have the vocabulary until now. On top of that, the Octals didn't know, themselves, until they talked to the neighbors. Here's the scoop." Becca paused to make certain Duke paid attention.

"Hercules was a robotic weapon—a machine that went awry. Its creators taught it how to kill a planet with the intent that the skill be used against their enemies. It worked, but then something went wrong, and it turned on its makers. You killed a *robot,* not a civilization. In fact, you're pretty much the hero of the galaxy right about now."

He heard the words, but took a while to understand their significance. "You mean —"

"I mean it's time for you to get off your duff and start working sixteen hour days like the rest of us," she groused.

"I, uh —" Duke closed his eyes and let out a long sigh. "Thanks, Becca. That's about the best news I've ever heard. I think maybe you stretched things a little, though. If you've only developed a couple dozen word vocabulary, then I doubt that 'hero' is one of the words."

"Okay, Mr. Doubting Thomas, you just haul your ass up to the control room, and I'll show you how easy it is to say 'hero'."

Becca did more hauling than the other three and was out of breath when she sat down at the computer, but she got right to work.

"They sent three pictures," she began. "Before Hercules, during Hercules, and after Hercules. Here's the 'before' picture."

The console displayed a network of lines with various symbols or icons at each node. The display rotated very slowly, making it obvious that it was a three-dimensional network.

"This is where the Octals are," she pointed to one of the nodes, "and this is the Hercules star system. The lines between each node represent anti-gravity communication. Note the lines connecting to the Hercules node.

"Okay, here's picture number two, representing when the robot became active. I'm squeezing them both on the screen so you can see the differences. Here are the Octals and here is the Hercules system, but notice that the original Hercules icon is gone and has been replaced with a new one—presumably the robot. Note also that two other icons are missing. The robot destroyed another star system and then destroyed the civilization that created it.

"The other obvious difference is that no lines of communication exist between any of the nodes. Think what that must have been like. Dozens of highly advanced civilizations using anti-gravity for communication, transportation, power—who knows what else—and suddenly they have to stop. Not so much as a peep. It would be like us getting thrown back into the Stone Age.

"Now here's the 'after' picture. See, Hercules is gone, and a new node has been added over here. That's us. I want you to especially notice that the communication lines are back. Now if that doesn't spell 'hero', then I can't spell."

"I still don't understand what happened," Duke said after everyone had settled down. "Hercules was winning when I tried to call Satterfield. What made it stop?"

"Near as I can tell, it was a combination of luck and math," Becca answered. "Hercules' beam was turning on and off. Ours was on all the time. When his was on, seventeen percent of it got through to us. When his was turned off, we were hitting him with eighty-three percent. That's nearly five times as much, so we were cooking him a whole lot faster than he was cooking us. We're just damned lucky that he didn't figure that out and change his strategy."

"So, one down and one to go, huh?"

"What do you mean?"

"Satterfield. We're way past his deadline. I'm surprised he hasn't called or sent a chopper."

"I think maybe that's not going to happen," Becca said, rather quietly for her.

Duke looked at her questioningly, even hopefully.

"I didn't tell you earlier—figured it could wait. There's a big hole in the ground at Los Alamos. The news didn't give many details, but I think we all know what happened."

The picture was all too clear in Duke's mind. "I missed doing that to myself by only a few minutes. I could have warned them."

He stood up, needing to move—do *something* before depression settled in again.

"This has got to stop. There are too many problems, too many mistakes, and too many people getting killed," he said, shaking his head. "I'm going to do what I should have done a long time ago."

He picked up his cell phone and punched a speed dial number.

"Gramp?...Busy?...Want to be?"

Stinger Stars – Montag Press 2013

A First Contact story with a unique twist—the other intelligent beings are man-made.

Maria de la Cruz discovers that clones created by the head geneticist at M-Gen are showing signs of intelligence. Before she can convince anyone, her boss, son of M-Gen's founder, cuts off one of the creature's appendages in a regeneration experiment. As the animal begins to regenerate its appendage, Maria's stunted arm also begins to grow. She is faced with a dilemma: protect the intelligent animals from cruel exploitation or benefit from their suffering to regain the use of her arm.

Stinger Stars is a captivating tale of mystery, intrigue, romance, and ethos that will engage your mind and warm your heart.